treasure trail

EDITED BY

"Captain" Jack Hart

treasure trail

EROTIC TALES OF PIRATES ON THE HIGH SEAS

This trade paperback original is published by Alyson Books,
P.O. Box 1253, Old Chelsea Station, New York, New York 10113-1251.
Distribution in the United Kingdom
by Turnaround Publisher Services Ltd.
Unit 3, Olympia Trading Estate, Coburg Road, Wood Green,
London N22 6TZ United Kingdom.

First edition: March 2007

07 08 09 00 a 10 9 8 7 6 5 4 3 2 1

ISBN 1-59350-023-8
ISBN-13 978-1-59350-023-8

Library of Congress Cataloging-in-Publication Datais on file.

Book interior by Dan Sause.

CONTENTS

INTRODUCTION

Ahoy, mates.

Sorry, couldn't resist. But as you can see from my new title of "Captain," I've kind of indulged my inner pirate. It's all for a good cause—a hot collection of brand-new erotica, with a theme we can all wrap our legs… uh, minds around.

I've edited a bunch of anthologies for the good folks at Alyson Books, including four volumes in the *My First Time* series, but never did I have such a swashbuckling good time as I did in choosing the tales you are about to read. From the Caribbean to the Atlantic and beyond, it's a near fleet of sleek ships commanded by the most alluring leaders. These pirates are darn fine sexy men who seek not just adventure upon the high seas, want not just the allure of treasure. No, these are passionate, sexy men, with a thirst for men they meet in taverns, men who share their bunks, men who fight alongside them.

It's not all epic, historical tales here; each writer was given free rein over his own writing kingdom to pen his pirate story the way he saw fit. Some stayed tried and true, giving us hearty pirates of the past, while others took the concept and re-imagined their pirates into the modern day. Whatever the setting, whatever the century, you'll want to stow away as our lusty pirates plow away.

See you on board.

—*"Captain" Jack Hart*

JOLLY ROGER

Ryan Field

Though everyone called him Jolly Roger, few truly knew the facts about this title. It wasn't a real name; he'd been christened Roger Julian. Some assumed it referred to his appearance, which wasn't typical of a pirate. Medium height and naturally slender, he was a rare assortment of tawny complexion, blue eyes, and light blond hair. Golden clumps fell to his waist—a thick mane of waves that should have been tied back but often covered half of his face. His legs were slightly bowed, accentuated by black, knee-high boots with a four-inch Cuban heel. Though his features were strong and keen, and his manner as manly as his pirate peers, he never wore anything but white tights and a loose white shirt that stopped at the top of his thighs.

There wasn't a pegged leg and a black patch over his eye, nor was there a parrot on his shoulder—just a wide, sinister grin and one bright, gold tooth. Flying high above his wooden ship was a vivid red flag with a pure white symbol of a heavy sword. At least that's what the long thing resembled at first glance, but when you looked closer it could have been mistaken for a large, curved phallus.

Most men (especially killer pirates) would have overcompensated if they'd had Jolly Roger's fair hair—worn dark clothes and hidden the blond waves with a large hat. They would have taken on the forced expression of a real killer, bragged and boasted about how many women they'd raped and how many ships they'd pillaged. Though he moved with the grace of an elk, and it was impossible to find so much as a dark smudge on his white tights, it was rumored among sailors throughout the high seas that he had the dark soul of a jackal and the ability to conjure devilish cruelties beyond the imagination. (Though other sailors had come to fear him, his only true vice had to do with horny, drunken men... rough, tattooed sailors, to be exact.) So this title, Jolly Roger, was viewed by many as a joke—that he'd laugh and dance while he ripped your eyes out of their sockets and then ate them for dinner, or so they said—and it amused Jolly Roger a great deal.

But the truth to his title was much less demanding than all this. When Jolly wasn't pillaging and adding to his vast fortune, he was jumping into bed with any guy who caught his attention. Though in those days it wasn't openly discussed, it was said that to have had a blow job from Jolly Roger was to have seen the gates of heaven. He somehow knew how to do things to men, things of a sexual nature, that were unique. It was the crew of a British merchant ship that had actually dubbed him Jolly Roger, just after twenty or thirty drunken crew members screwed his brains out. They banged and pounded and plundered his ass from one end of the ship's deck to the other and he kept screaming for more. Back then the English commonly named their stud bulls "Roger," and Roger became generic slang for sexual intercourse, of a rough-and-tumble nature. Sailors in dark pubs who knew the truth often joked that you wouldn't want to leave Jolly Roger alone with your prized stud bull.

Over the years, stories of his insatiable appetite for strong, virile men were either embellished or, in some cases, toned down, but one in particular stood out from the rest: the night he met Captain Jake Hargrove. It was a warm summer night and Jolly's ship, also named the *Jolly Roger*, had been anchored just off the coast of a Caribbean island for a few days when he decided to row to shore for a drink. He knew the pub there very well: a common watering hole for sailors who traveled the high seas on a regular basis. Though Jolly had a large crew of his own (young, well-paid studs, from twenty-one to thirty years old, who were there to run the ship and service his needs, so to speak), he often grew tired of the same faces (and dicks) and sought the company of a rougher, more dangerous crowd. The drunken sailors with missing teeth who hadn't shaved or bathed in weeks, and hadn't been with a woman for months, always satisfied his strapping desires. Because pleasing them, seeing the grateful expressions on their exhausted faces after he'd sucked them dry, was where he gained most of his pleasure. But that summer night, as he entered the pub with the three crew members who were always there to guard him, he had no idea he was about to meet the one man on earth who could match his erotic stamina.

The pub was crowded. Dark, sweaty men were shouting and swearing; the smell of ale and tobacco filled the small room. The only light came from candles, an amber glow that made it all the more sultry. When Jolly Roger entered with handsome young crew members in tow, the room went silent for a brief moment and you could hear the clicking of his high-heeled boots on the cobble stone floor. He didn't just walk into a room—he made an entrance, with an air of arrogance that caused people to stop speaking. Jolly nodded to the stout old bartender, who immediately poured him a tall glass of dark, sweet rum. The men in the pub began to speak again. Some nodded to Jolly; others greeted him with a rough hug, secretly patting his ass as he passed them. As the faithful crew members went off to the side, always watching their captain, Jolly settled the back of his body against the wooden bar, between two dark-haired sailors, men who hadn't shaved in several days. One had a red bandanna around his neck and the other wore two large gold earrings. Jolly couldn't be sure, but he thought the one with the red bandanna had fucked him over a whisky barrel a few years back. He silently laughed; the only way to know for sure was to slip the guy's cock into his mouth. Jolly knew no two dicks tasted the same and he'd never forgotten the taste of a dick he'd already sucked.

The one with the red bandanna asked, "You want to sit, mate?" His voice was deep, with a thick, uneducated English accent.

Jolly smiled, leaned into the man's neck and whispered, "No, mate, I'd rather stand." His smooth cheek brushed against the sailor's rough stubble; he'd just washed his hair in a strong concoction of spices and scents from the Orient. Men who had been at sea for months, he knew, loved this aroma. It was an unspoken way to say, "Feel me up, boys."

While he leaned over to speak, the other man, with the gold earrings, ran the palm of his strong hand up Jolly's thigh and rested it in the middle of Jolly's firm, round ass. The white tights Jolly always wore were so sheer and so tight it felt as though he wasn't wearing pants at all. He could feel the rough calluses on the sailor's hand as it rubbed and squeezed his ass cheeks.

Jolly stood straight, slightly arching his back, and the red-bandanna guy quietly slipped his hand onto Jolly's ass, too. Both men, feeling up one ass cheek at a time. And then, as Jolly had silently predicted, both large hands found the waistband of the tights and they slowly slipped inside to cup his bare ass. He took a large sip of rum, spread his legs wider and rested a knee against each man's thigh. Though the room was dark, and most of the crowd was either too drunk or too stupid to realize there were two guys fingering Jolly Roger's wet hole in public, when Jolly looked straight ahead he noticed an attractive young man was staring directly into his eyes. The man was sitting, with his legs spread wide. His muscular arms were folded across a broad chest, and there was a smirk on his otherwise innocent face. It was Captain John Hargrove, Jolly knew, ten years his junior. He'd seen the young officer in passing several times, and had heard stories of how fearless he could be as a pirate and how enduring he was as a lover. Women, so it was said, were ruined for life after a night with Hargrove's dick.

Taken aback by Hargrove's determined expression, Jolly nodded and looked directly into his eyes, too… dark brown eyes, large and bright with innocence, but clearly ready for trouble. His hair was black, with long waves resting on wide shoulders. He wore a black leather coat with silver buttons and tight black pants that fit snugly against wide, muscular thighs. They were the kind of thighs, Jolly Roger knew, that could fuck and pound for hours without getting tired. The young captain couldn't have been older than twenty-five.

Jolly drank the entire glass of dark rum, with the two men on either side now parting the lips of his hole and inserting their thick, tobacco-stained fingers. As he leaned forward, spreading his legs wider so they could fully enter his ass, the dark young Hargrove leaned forward too, and said, "Let's go outside."

"But I'm having so much fun right now," Jolly said, arching his back. Still locked eye-to-eye with Hargrove, Jolly reached around and rested a hand on the erect cock of the guy with earrings... a rock-solid dick, thick and dirty and ready to be sucked and drained by an expert cocksucker.

Captain Hargrove stood and walked toward Jolly. He was clearly someone important, an officer to fear, because the two men who had been playing with Jolly's ass immediately stopped. Jolly remained silent as Hargrove reached around and quickly pulled Jolly's tights back up to cover his exposed ass.

"You'll have more fun outside, with me," he whispered to Jolly.

"I'm not sure I want to go out right now," Jolly playfully answered, but his eyebrows were knitted together, his expression stern. Oh, he wanted to go out, but he wanted to tease and bait first. He knew this young guy wanted him, but he wanted the young guy to beg for it.

Hargrove smiled, and then leaned toward Jolly's ear. "Get the fuck out now, you fucking bitch, or I'll grab you by the fucking throat and yank you out myself."

Jolly smiled. It was just what he wanted to hear: the rough, hungry voice of a young man with needs. Though no one had ever before been so bold, Jolly loved young men to treat him with force and power. When he himself was younger, the fact that his captain could have taken him out and slit his throat was both frightening and exciting at the same time. But he was now thirty-five years old, and though he could have passed for twenty-five, he found the older he got the more he wanted young men to dominate him.

As the two men started to leave the pub, with the dark captain's hand resting firmly on the small of Jolly's back, Jolly nodded to his crew members that everything was okay and they shouldn't interrupt him. Of course, Jolly knew they would follow at a distance; this was an unspoken rule that was understood by everyone in those days.

It was a warm night, with a half moon. Hargrove led Jolly to a grassy area just at the edge of the beach; private, yet open enough so Jolly's crew members could see that everything was safe. During the walk the young guy had slipped the palm of his hand down Jolly's tights and rested it on Jolly's ass.

"Why don't you slip out of those tights, mate," said Hargrove, slowly sliding the white tights down Jolly's smooth, hairless legs.

They were very easy to slip out of, and Jolly was naked from the waist down in no time at all, wearing only his loose white shirt and the high-heeled boots. The shirt covered his ass and dick just enough so you couldn't see anything but long, soft legs and high-heeled boots. Though Jolly wasn't trying to act feminine, the lines were clearly drawn and he would be the submissive.

"I've been hoping to run into you for a long time," said Hargrove, pulling Jolly up against his hard leather coat, running both palms of his hands up under the white shirt and resting them again on Jolly's killer ass. Hargrove had heard the tales of Jolly's conquests—stories of how Jolly could suck men dry one after the other, of how he could throw his legs in the air while twenty or thirty guys took turns mounting his ass. It was said that Jolly's hole was unique and the lips resembled a woman's pussy; they could clamp a dick on command and cause an orgasm that went beyond the imagination. Hargrove loved to fuck; he loved this more than anything in the world, and he'd been searching for the perfect hole since he was fifteen years old.

"Well, now you have," said Jolly, slowly wrapping his arms around the young captain's neck and burying his face in a wide chest that was covered with a light but wiry fleece. The captain's scent wasn't as painful and unwashed as the other sailors he knew, but it wasn't fresh and clean either. Though the young man was neat in appearance, Jolly suspected he hadn't bathed in a few days.

Hargrove grabbed a chunk of blond hair at the back of Jolly's head and shoved his thick, hot tongue into Jolly's soft mouth. The tongue pounded and circled, tasting of tobacco and booze, spit and young man; Jolly's lips went all the way into Hargrove's mouth and he began to suck the thick tongue as though he were sucking a big dick.

"You taste and smell like some sort of spice," Hargrove whispered, searching for breath. Though Jolly could be dangerous if provoked, he wasn't the typical sailor either, which shocked and excited Hargrove. Jolly had a way of knowing how to treat other men, without coming off as effeminate, or even close to it. His approach was based on a man knowing what another man wanted sexually, and that had little to do with being effeminate. Jolly's excitement came from one thing alone: getting the guy off with a loud, unforgettable explosion.

Jolly slowly slipped the heavy leather coat off Hargrove's shoulders, and then lifted a black gauze shirt over the young man's head. Before the shirt even hit the grass Jolly's soft tongue was licking and circling the young man's right armpit. Dark fur mixing with saliva, a rugged smell of young sweat faintly mixed with rose-scented soap from his last bath. As Jolly licked and sucked the superb armpit Hargrove moaned so loudly the three crew members stepped forward to watch and to be sure their beloved Jolly Roger was safe from harm. Clearly, no one had ever bothered to lick the young captain's sweaty armpits; he had never realized there were so many pleasure points there.

Jolly knew the young man's toes were already curling in his black boots, and he hadn't even touched the cock yet.

But as Jolly ran his hand down the captain's stomach and rested it on his crotch, he discovered a dick so big, pointing upward toward the navel, it was ready to pop out of the young man's waistband. It had been a long time since he'd had a cock that big, and that hard, too. Often the drunken sailors who fucked him were only semi-erect, ready to pass out.

Wasting no time and eager to get sucked off, Hargrove unfastened his black slacks and let them drop to the grass. The lengthy erection slapped against Jolly's smooth waist. Hargrove kicked off his heavy boots and tossed the slacks off to the side. He was now almost naked, but for his dark socks, his 9-inch erection resting in the palm of Jolly's right hand. The crew began to strip out of their clothes, too. They were men who had been hand-selected by Jolly, men who weren't like the rest of the drunken straight sailors; all of them were men who loved and lived for other men.

They knew Jolly loved to be watched, and knew he wouldn't mind if they shot a load while he was getting fucked.

"Let's get you out of that shirt," Hargrove said, yanking the white shirt off Jolly's body so that Jolly would be completely naked as well. As he pulled off the shirt he glanced quickly to the crew members, who were now naked and pulling their own dicks. He smiled, and slapped Jolly's ass three times. "You don't mind that your boys are going to watch me fuck your brains out, bitch?"

"Who says you're going to fuck me?" Jolly joked. "You didn't ask for permission."

"You know it's what I want, and it's what I'm going to get," Hargrove teased, putting the palm of his hand down between Jolly's legs, below his ass, and physically lifting him off the ground.

Jolly just moaned, didn't answer. He was too busy wrapping his arms around Hargrove's shoulders and then wrapping his legs around Hargrove's waist. Few men were strong enough to pick him up like that. But Hargrove didn't flinch; he rested the palms of his hands on the bottom of Jolly's ass and held him without missing a breath. An ass that was naturally smooth, no fuzz or stubble. Slowly his large middle finger found the soft lips of Jolly's hole; the two began to kiss again as he put his finger all the way up Jolly's sweet ass. As the finger circled the soft velvet of Jolly's hole, their tongues circled to the same rhythm.

"Suck my cock," Hargrove whispered to Jolly, pulling the wet finger from the soft hole, rubbing the ass juice all over Jolly's back.

With his arms around Hargrove's neck, Jolly slowly lowered his legs. When he was standing on the ground he removed his arms and prepared to go down on his knees. He preferred to be totally naked, without the boots. But when Jolly began to slip out of the high-heeled boots, Hargrove stopped him and said, "No. Leave them on." He didn't need to utter another word. Jolly had learned that most men really loved his high-heeled boots, begged him to leave them on while they fucked. Some even pressed the soles to their chests and licked the four-inch heels.

Jolly went down on his knees, spreading his legs wide and arching his back. He licked the thin line of black hair that ran from Hargrove's navel to his dick. With his palms placed on the young man's hairy thighs for support, he licked and slurped the taste of young, sweaty male flesh: vinegar and salt... aged cheese and old wine. But still there was a slight hint of rose soap; the young man bathed at least three times a week. While Jolly's palms rubbed against the strong upper legs, his tongue went downward, into a deep, black burl of hair that surrounded Hargrove's massive cock. Down there, in the forest, it just smelled the way young cock should smell... musty and sweet. It tasted like young cock, too. With his lips he gently slid the foreskin back; the cock head was more of an acorn than a mushroom, which Jolly had always preferred. Most men were uncircumcised in those days and Jolly had learned a special technique that drove them wild. While blowing and sucking them off, he'd learned to manipulate the foreskin with his tongue in such a way it that it rubbed against the cock head and doubled the pleasure of getting blown.

"Oh yeah," Hargrove moaned, placing his right hand on the back of Jolly's head.

Jolly's two crew members were now standing right beside them, watching intently as their captain sucked, jerking their own cocks slowly but surely. Jolly had taught them well, how to hold back for as long as possible. Sucking the head of Hargrove's cock, manipulating his foreskin, Jolly looked at them and winked. They smiled, knowing the plan. In a situation like this, Jolly's lover would climax, Jolly would take the entire load down his throat, and then one after the other the crew members would shoot a load down Jolly's throat, too. He not only loved the taste of come, but also truly believed it kept him young and virile. There were times he actually made his entire crew refrain from jerking off for a week so that he could suck them all off, consecutively, often taking in enough come to fill a wineglass—though he never would have actually taken it from a wineglass. Jolly had only one requirement for come: It had to be sucked directly from the cock.

"I'm getting too close," Hargrove moaned, as Jolly sucked, "and I want to fuck that hole."

The cock popped from Jolly's throat and he went flat on his back, down on the wet grass, and lifted his legs in the air. Hargrove went down on his knees, spit a large gob into the palm of his right hand, and lubed his big cock. He leaned forward, guiding his dick toward Jolly's hole with his right hand, and rested his left hand on the grass for support. Jolly spread his legs wider and took the whole 9 inches with one quick thrust. Jolly's hole was unusually positioned, lower than that of most men, making it rather easy for men to fuck him while he was on his back. There were never awkward position problems; the men could simply lean forward, slip it all the way in, and start to fuck and pound. It was one of the reasons why men loved to fuck him so much—there wasn't an awkward move involved. Even the worst lovers, those with no rhythm or talent at all, fucked him as though they were prize studs.

"Bitch, how do you do that?" Hargrove moaned, still fucking. He was referring to the way Jolly could tighten and loosen the lips of his hole. It closely resembled the way lips on a mouth can tighten during a blow job. Not quite a snap—just a light clamp of pressure to jerk the cock off a little.

"Just fuck me harder," Jolly screamed, his legs now resting on Hargrove's shoulders, high-heeled boots bouncing with each thrust.

Hargrove pounded so hard and so fast Jolly had to throw his arms back and brace them against a tree trunk for support. He moaned and screamed and begged for more. The harder Hargrove fucked, the more Jolly wanted. What Hargrove didn't know was that Jolly was always on the verge of orgasm when getting fucked. He didn't have to touch his cock; it came from deep within his body. He had to control it at all times, too.

"I'm gonna blow soon, mate," Hargrove shouted, still fucking as hard as he could.

"No, wait," Jolly said, "in my mouth, please, I want to finish you in my mouth."

Hargrove was stunned. He'd never heard those words uttered before, and it excited him beyond reason, to know that Jolly wanted to swallow his load… that someone was actually begging to swallow his load. So he quickly stopped fucking and pulled his cock out.

Jolly, as though made of elastic, was up and on his knees. He knew there wasn't time to waste. When a man is close to coming you don't tarry. He also knew that so many men just couldn't come like that; they needed to jerk themselves off in the end. And Jolly wanted the entire load down his throat.

He inhaled the entire thing, tasting his own sweet ass juice mixed with Hargrove's ale-flavored spit, and began to suck rapidly. From the base to the head, conscious of when to suck and when to release pressure, his mouth and tongue as accurate and reliable as a warm wet hand, Jolly jerked Hargrove to heart-stopping ecstasy. The strong young sailor's knees began to quiver; Jolly sucked harder and faster as the volcano began to erupt in his mouth.

"Fuck, mate," Hargrove screamed. "Take it all, bitch."

Jolly felt the head begin to swell and, knowing that his young stud was about to blow a full load, he slipped the cock all the way into his mouth (most would have gagged) and began to suck off Hargrove with his tongue. As Hargrove screamed and his entire body reached the best orgasm of his life, Jolly felt the splash of juice hit the back of his throat. A drop of sweat fell from Hargrove's temple and hit Jolly above the left eyelid.

"Ahhh, yeah," said the young man, his legs still quivering.

But Jolly wasn't finished, not by any means. With care he slipped the sensitive dick slowly from his mouth and stopped at the head and began to suck Hargrove dry. There were still a few sweet drops left and Jolly wanted to swallow them all.

But Hargrove was sensitive there, and he literally had to pry Jolly's lips from the exhausted cock.

When the cock was pulled from his mouth, Jolly quickly turned to his right, where his crew member had been watching and jerking off, and inhaled the crew member's 7-inch cock to drain it dry, too. Hargrove, shocked to see that Jolly hadn't had enough dick yet, silently went down on his knees behind Jolly. While Jolly sucked the crew member, Hargrove reached around Jolly's thin waist and began to jerk Jolly's rock-solid cock.

And then, with his other hand, Hargrove shoved three fingers up Jolly's ass and began to finger fuck him.

Though at first Jolly didn't care what Hargrove did (his focus was simply on sucking dick), he was shocked when the young captain began to finger fuck his empty ass. He accommodated by spreading his legs and arching his back; the three fingers were solid and hard and filled his entire hole. His own climax began to well as Hargrove jerked his dick and the young crew member shot another full load down Jolly's throat.

Jolly took it all, moaning and swallowing, now consciously holding back his own climax. It was a full load, filled his mouth, and he had to swallow quickly so none of it would ooze from the corners of his lips. And when he'd finally swallowed, just as he'd done with Hargrove, Jolly finished off the young guy by sucking the head dry; not a drop fell to the grass. The exhausted crew member stepped to the right when Jolly finally released the empty dick. There was one more crew member to suck off, and Jolly wanted it all that night.

"Go, bitch," said Hargrove, when the second crew member stepped up and Jolly began to suck his dick, too. "Suck the boy dry."

This was one of his youngest crew members: twenty-one, with a slim, undeveloped body, short red hair and an 8-inch cock. As Jolly pressed his palms against the young man he slowly rubbed the smooth, hairless skin. Jolly knew the taste of this dick fairly well (every morning for a month Jolly had blown the young man, teaching him how to control blowing a load too soon), but the young man hadn't yet learned to hold back, and Jolly knew he'd blow quickly. So he told Hargrove, who was now gently finger-fucking his hole, "Shove it in mate, hard and fast."

As Jolly sucked the guy off and the young cock began to swell, Hargrove jerked Jolly's dick faster, and then began to ram Jolly's hole with his three fingers. The young red-haired guy began to moan, and as he blew another full load into Jolly's mouth, Jolly climaxed at the same time. Hargrove's fingers were still fucking hard, the lips of Jolly's hole clamping down on them like the jaws of a shark, while he shot his own load all over the wet grass.

Jolly slipped the young meat almost completely from his mouth, but didn't let go right away. His lips were still gently wrapped about the young crew member's cock head, slowly draining the last ounce of juice. He looked up at the young man, while Hargrove now gently fucked his hole with two fingers, and winked. The young man knew this was Jolly's way of saying, "Thank you… thank you for the sweet come, mate…" and he smiled in return.

When Jolly released the drained cock the young red-haired man stepped back to where his other crewmate was standing and they both began to get dressed. The show was over, for the time being, and they knew it was their job to start guarding their captain again. Hargrove pulled his fingers from Jolly's hole and pinched Jolly's right nipple.

But Jolly was taken aback when Hargrove wrapped a strong arm around his waist and whispered, "Don't get dressed yet. I'm not finished with you." The sailors he met were usually dressed and gone by that time. None, ever, had remained even to say as much as "thank you."

"You got what you wanted—so did I," Jolly said, pulling away and rising to his feet. He was casual, unconcerned, not at all ashamed of standing there totally naked except for his high-heeled boots.

Hargrove rose to his feet, placed a rough hand on Jolly's waist and pulled the blond pirate to his body. As the hand slowly lowered to the small of Jolly's back he said, "I still haven't shot a load into that hole yet. And I'm not leaving until I do, bitch."

It hadn't been more than twenty minutes since he'd last climaxed, and yet Jolly could feel the hardness of Hargrove's dick against his pelvis.

"As long as you're up for it," said Jolly.

"As long as you can continue to take it," Hargrove said, slapping Jolly's ass hard.

Then Jolly turned to his crew members, who were exhausted and shocked and couldn't believe the two captains were ready to fuck again so soon, and said, "You guys sit down and get comfortable. We'll be here longer than expected."

THE *DEVIL'S SPEAR*

Curtis C. Comer

I was taken in 1612 on the eve of my eighteenth year, the night the pirates raided our port village and killed my father. Though we had had dealings with pirates before, there was no need in our minds to fear them. Our village, situated on the Barbary Coast, was a sort of supply port to the ships of the French, English, Italians, and the Spanish, military and mercenary alike. My father's business was to exchange goods for gold and precious stones; goods such as flour, eggs, meat, and beer necessary to the mariners on their long sea voyages. Always smaller than my peers, and somewhat effeminate in appearance, with long, curly black hair, I was allowed by my father to help him run his business. Since my dear mother had passed away two years before and was unable to assist him in his business, I seemed the obvious substitute. While other boys my age were sent to the fields and orchards to work, I was busy keeping stock of our inventory and collecting payment from the many foreigners who visited our village. Because I could both read and write, I quickly proved myself an able assistant to my father. I also realized that I had an aptitude for languages, and quickly learned English, French, and Spanish from the sailors and businessmen who frequented our port. I suppose that it was this ability that spared my life the night of the raid.

We had seen their ship appear off shore earlier in the afternoon, and word spread through our village that it was an English pirate ship called the *Devil's Spear*. It wasn't unusual for ships to anchor off shore while they made repairs, so we thought nothing of it. Besides, it was the Corsairs, the North African pirates, who ruled these waters, not the English. And it was a well-known fact among those of us who had dealings with such men that even pirates had their own code of conduct, banning many forms of unruly conduct with the threat of severe punishment. The worst pirates had ever done here was to get too drunk in our taverns and throw around too much of their gold. We supposed that pirates were really there under orders of their government to ambush Spanish ships as they came and went, plundering whatever gold or riches were aboard the ships.

Apparently, though, a series of deaths and misfortune had recently befallen the *Devil's Spear*, causing its crew to resort to desperate measures, and our village paid dearly that night. Buildings were torched, storehouses pillaged and any livestock small enough to catch was ferried away. As I hid on the roof of a building, I watched as every man in the village was killed—run through with swords or shot. Though pirate law forbade the molestation of "prudent women," many of those in our village were raped, along with several young boys. Finally forced to flee from my hiding place because of the intense heat from the fires, I too nearly suffered the same fate, being pushed to the ground by a squat pirate with large, hairy forearms and a barrel chest. Because of my effeminate appearance and the fact that I was wearing only the white, gauzy tunic that I slept in, the pirate mistook me for a girl.

"Where d'you think *you're* going, lovely?" he said with a menacing laugh. He pulled out his shaft and was on me in a flash, reaching under my tunic. When he found my penis the look on his face became menacing, and he shrank back, pointing a pistol at me.

"Don't shoot me, sir!" I blurted in English, shielding my face.

Suddenly, his expression turned from menacing to almost jovial, and he lowered the pistol.

"Bless me soul," he said, revealing a toothless grin. "You speak English!"

I nodded, my heart pounding.

"And French and Spanish," I replied, proudly.

"I think the Cap'n 'll find you quite *useful*," he said, standing to stow away his still hard cock.

He pulled me to my feet and, with the pistol jabbed between my shoulder blades, I was guided to the shore. Happy to have been spared being killed outright with the other men of my village, I was sure that my privileges ended there; I was now a slave, nothing more than the spoils of war. Still wearing only my gauze tunic, I had my arms bound from behind with a coarse rope that scratched my wrists and back. I was unceremoniously placed in a large rowboat that contained a pig, two chickens that clucked pitifully, and crates of stolen loot that I recognized as having come from my father's warehouse. There were four pirates aboard to row, but not one of them spoke as we neared the *Devil's Spear*, its lights reflecting on the black Mediterranean. Only the sounds of their oars plowing the water, the occasional scream of a gull overhead, and the clucking of the chickens heralded my departure. Even the pig seemed too terrified to make a sound.

Tears stung my eyes as I watched my burning village shrink out of sight. Despite the fact that it was a balmy night, I shivered in my flimsy tunic, and the rocking motions of the rowboat on the water made me queasy. I turned to look at the rower nearest me. He was a handsome young man with wild blond hair and a scruffy attempt at a beard that made me guess him to be about my age. I admired the way his arms bulged each time he pulled the oar to him, and was marveling at the size of his calloused fingers when he spoke.

"What are you *lookin'* at, then?" he barked, malice in his voice.

"Leave 'im be, Johnny," said the pirate who had captured me. "The Cap'n I'll want *this* one in one piece."

"Ah, hell, Sweeny," spat Johnny. "Jus' let me 'ave ten minutes wiff me ramrod up his ass!"

Johnny, still rowing, thrust his hips toward me, a large bulge visible through his dirty white trousers.

"*Ten minutes*!" laughed a third pirate, another kid, with short-cropped black hair. "You'd more likely last *one* minute!"

Sweeny and the fourth pirate, an older man with a trim, white beard, shook the boat with laughter.

"He probably could'n even get it out of 'is *trousers* before poppin' the cork!" said Sweeny, wheezing with laughter.

"Fuck off, the *lot* of you!" growled Johnny. "It's not funny that I ain't had me jollies in such a long time!"

The pirates were still laughing at Johnny's expense when we pulled alongside the *Devil's Spear*, the biggest ship I'd ever seen. In the darkness I counted at least seven sails, and a rope netting was lowered down to just above the water to allow us access to the main deck, where men scurried to and fro, passing crates and animals alike down a hatch into the hold. Sweeny, steadying himself as he stood, undid the rope binding my wrists, which felt rope-burned. He pointed the pistol at me and motioned for me to climb up the netting and, as I climbed, I felt a hand grope my buttocks and turned to see Johnny behind me, a grotesque smile on his face.

"Johnny!" barked Sweeny from the boat. "Get yer ass down here an' help Smythe an' Bob unload!"

Johnny begrudgingly complied, lowering himself back into the boat and mumbling to himself as Sweeny joined me on the deck.

"Come on," said Sweeny, pushing me toward a cabin at the back of the ship. As I walked across the deck, the pirates busily loading the hold stopped to stare at me as if I were an apparition, but quickly resumed work with a few choice words from Sweeny. We paused at a door and Sweeny knocked.

"Enter," said a muffled voice inside, and Sweeny opened the door and pushed me into a richly paneled cabin outfitted with a desk, two chairs, and a bed with mosquito netting draped over it. A single oil lamp lit the room and, as we entered, a tall, trim man with dark hair and beard arose from behind the desk. A row of windows behind the desk allowed in a slight breeze that smelled of the sea.

"What in blazes is *this*?" asked the man, standing in front of me. "I thought I made it clear that you were to take no prisoners!"

"But, Cap'n," stuttered Sweeny, "this lad..."

"*Lad?*" asked the captain, cutting Sweeny off. "Throw him overboard!"

"He speaks three or four languages," Sweeny said quickly. "I thought…"

Not taking his eyes off me, the captain held up a hand, which silenced Sweeny.

"Is this *true*, lad?" he asked, raising an eyebrow.

"Yes, sir," I replied, my voice cracking out of fear.

"Aside from English, what *else*?" he asked, his eyes still on me.

"French and Spanish," I said, "and I can *read* them, as well."

The captain turned and walked back to his desk, sitting in the ornately carved chair behind it.

"D'you think we can use 'im, Cap'n?" asked Sweeny, smiling.

"He may indeed come in *very* handy, Sweeny," replied the captain. "You've done very well."

"Thank you, sir," said Sweeny, nearly bowing. "I thought that you might…"

"Take him to Jack," said the captain, interrupting Sweeny yet again. "And tell Jack that I want the boy kept tied up in the hold where he can't escape."

"Yes, sir," said Sweeny, bowing again. "Thank you, sir!"

Without another word, the captain returned his attention to papers on his desk and Sweeny pulled me from the cabin and back out onto the deck. As he guided me across the deck he sang a little song in a broken falsetto, his spirits high from the captain's favorable response.

There once was a fair lass named Regina,
whose skin took on a fine green patina.
And though she rode me harder than most other bitches,
she left a dirty rust spot on my breeches.

Down in the hold Sweeny found the man named Jack. A thin but muscular man with a shaved head, Jack was missing his left eye; there was a knobby mass of scar tissue in its place. Jack was shirtless and sweating with the task of stowing all of the stolen loot in the cramped hold. He looked at me suspiciously as Sweeny pushed me forward, and I noticed that his remaining eye was as blue as the ocean.

"What the hell is *this*?" he asked, wiping sweat from his brow.

"New ship's *interpreter*," replied Sweeny, proudly. "Found 'im *meself*!"

"And what, pray, am *I* supposed to do wiff 'im?" asked Jack, testily.

"Keep an eye on 'im," said Sweeny. "Orders of Cap'n Bowles."

Sweeny turned to leave then stopped, turning back to face Jack.

"Oh, an' Cap'n said to tie him so 'e can't jump ship," said Sweeny, who resumed singing his ditty as he climbed up the ladder out of the hold.

Cursing at his new responsibility, Jack pushed me to the middle of the hold where he produced a pair of shackles, tying my arms behind me to the mainmast of the ship. Letting the mast slide between my back and the shackles, I slowly sank to the floor, peering around the dank hold and listening to the sound of the thundering footsteps above me. The ship creaked and swayed on the sea and, for the second time that night, I felt as if I might be sick. Jack was busily storing crates as they came down the hatch, and I noticed that there was even a makeshift chicken coop, which held the chickens that had shared my ride from the village. The pig was nowhere to be seen, and I shuddered at the thought of what his fate might be.

After about an hour of frenzied activity, the ship fell silent. Donning a white shirt that clung to his sweaty torso, Jack placed a woolen blanket over me, then disappeared up the ladder and onto the deck, dropping the hatch door closed as he went. With the chickens roosting nearby, I fell into an uneasy sleep.

I awoke the next morning to the sound of laughter, and opened my sleepy eyes to the sight of Johnny standing in front of me, his pants around his ankles and a large erection pointing at my face. Bob, the dark-haired boy from the rowboat, was there, too, and was stroking his own stubby cock.

"Stick it in 'is mouth, Johnny," goaded Bob.

Johnny thrust his cock against my face, but I kept my mouth shut, determined only to give in if left no choice. This wasn't the first time I had been molested by men—there were even times I consented willingly—but there was something about Johnny I didn't like, and I refused to grant him pleasure.

"*C'mon*, you know you want it, mate," said Johnny, rubbing his wet prick on the side of my face.

"Give it to 'im up the bum," suggested Bob, still playing with his cock.

Johnny dropped to his knees and grabbed my legs, lifting them up over his shoulders and causing the mast to dig into my shoulder blades. He spit on his hand, rubbing it on his cock, and I could feel his prick pressing against my asshole when a voice caused him to jump.

"What the bloody hell are you *doing*?" called Jack from the foot of the ladder.

"Fuck off, Jack," snapped Johnny. "We was jus' havin' a bit of fun!"

Bob started to button up his breeches, his face red, but Johnny wasn't going to give up, and I could feel his cock force its way inside of me.

Enraged, Jack pulled him off me and threw him across the room where he landed, naked ass in the air, on a pile of straw. Jack strode over to the dazed boy and shoved a rough finger in his ass.

"How 'bout I have a bit o' fun with *you*, matey?" he growled, pushing his finger deeper into Johnny's ass, causing him to jump up, whimpering.

"He's property of the *ship* now," wailed Johnny, "I was just having my share."

"And Captain Bowles doesn't want 'im *harmed*," retorted Jack. "Now get out of here, the both of you, before I tell the Cap'n."

Bob and Johnny scrambled up the ladder and vanished through the hatch, their footsteps echoing in the hold.

"Sorry 'bout that," said Jack, almost tenderly. He leaned over me, pulling down my tunic to cover my exposed lower body. "I'm boatswain, in charge of the crew. They won' bother you again."

Squatting in front of me, his breeches taut over his muscular thighs, he explained the concept of sharing loot on a pirate ship. The captain gets one-and-one-half share, the carpenter, boatswain, and gunner one-and-one-quarter share. The rest is divided evenly among the men. Johnny, he explained, merely regarded me as loot to share among the crew.

"How do *you* see me?" I asked.

He got a peculiar look on his face and was about to speak when the captain's voice sounded from the deck and a brass bell began to ring frantically.

"*All hands on deck! Enemy ship sighted!*"

Jack paused as if he were going to finish his thought, then suddenly turned and climbed the ladder. The sound of running reverberated above me, and I could barely discern the orders being bellowed as cannons were dragged into place. Fear suddenly gripped me as I realized that, were the *Devil's Spear* sunk in battle, I would drown in the hold, shackled to the mast. Desperately, I wriggled my hands, hoping to find some give in the restraints, but gave up, frustrated. Sweat was stinging my eyes when the first salvo from the ship's cannons caused me to start. I heard more booms in the distance and the *Devil's Spear* rocked violently, causing the chickens to wildly flap their wings. The cannons on the deck above roared again and, a second later, a loud, raucous cheer went up from the deck above me. The ship listed to one side, causing some of the smaller crates in the hold to slide across the floor, and pulling my body away from the mast so that the shackles cut into my wrists. When the ship again righted herself there was more scurrying on the deck, followed by the crack of muskets and pistols. I held my breath, praying that I wasn't about to die, when Jack thundered down the ladder into the hold.

"We got 'em, lad!" he exclaimed, his expression exuberant.

He walked behind me and unlocked the shackles, and I sat on the floor rubbing my numb wrists, blinking at the pirate standing before me.

"Jack," I asked, hesitantly. "Is it really necessary to lock me down here?"

Jack blinked his one good eye, no doubt contemplating the reason for my request.

"I'm afraid of drowning down here," I explained.

"Every man's got 'is day to die," he said, harshly. He looked at the shackles in his hands and I could see his expression soften as he tossed them to the floor, exhaling loudly.

"No man should drown like a rat, I reckon," he said, softly. "I'll work it out wi' the Cap'n."

Emerging with Jack from the hold and into the sunlight, I could see that the *Devil's Spear* had pulled alongside a Spanish vessel, its mainmast blown off by a direct hit, and cannon holes in its hull. The dead bodies of her crew littered her deck, and the crew of the *Devil's Spear* was busy looting anything of value. The vessel, the *Contessa del Mar*, turned out to be a good catch; valuable commodities like gold, silk, and spices were being transferred to our hold. Glancing around the deck of the *Devil's Spear*, I noticed that she had taken no visible damage, and winced when I saw the Jolly Roger flapping in the wind and grinning at me grotesquely.

The captain strode toward me, and I feared that I might be reprimanded for being on deck, but he thrust a leather-bound book, tied with a thin leather strap, in my direction. I stared at the book dumbly for a second, admiring the feel of the leather and the small geographical design embossed on its cover.

"It's the captain's log book from the Spanish ship," he explained, sensing my confusion. "I want you to translate it for me."

I looked at Jack, who nodded his consent.

"Do a good job, lad," he said, softly.

The captain gestured me toward his cabin, and a light sea breeze upset my hair as I walked across the deck, the captain in tow. Once inside, the captain pointed me to a chair opposite his desk.

"Well?" he said impatiently, taking his chair behind the desk. "Translate it."

I untied the leather strap and cracked open the book, admiring the parchment paper and the neat handwriting on its pages. The captain listened intently as I read, often asking me to re-read passages. But, when I reached the last entries in the book, where the captain of the *Contessa* recorded that he had left Peru with two other ships bound for Spain, his eyes lit up.

"*Three*?" he asked, rising from his chair and striding to the windows to peer out. "Are you certain?"

Carefully, I re-read the passage aloud to him.

"Then there are two more nearby," he said, mostly to himself.

He turned to face me, his expression one of joy.

"It looks as if taking you on was a good idea," he said, moving behind my chair. I wasn't sure how to respond to this comment, and quietly closed the log book when I felt his hand caressing my hair. I felt myself tense up when his hand moved from my hair down to the nape of my neck and then to my cheek. I instinctively kissed his hand. It was the hand that had caused my father's death, but I wondered whether giving the captain his way might not help my situation. Still holding his hand to my cheek, I looked up into the captain's dark eyes. He squeezed my cheek and smiled, then walked over to the door and bolted it. He pulled his shirt off, revealing a pale, finely formed torso with a patch of black hair in the middle of his chest, then walked over to the bed, which he climbed onto, still wearing his breeches and boots. He patted the spot beside him on the bed, and I shed my tunic, dropping it to the floor beside the chair and walking to the bed naked.

The captain pulled his erect cock out the front of his breeches, and I took it into my mouth as I climbed onto the bed beside him. He moaned, enjoying my services, and played with my curly locks as I sucked, thrusting his hips upward to me. Rolling me over onto my back, he climbed on top, pushing my legs toward my chest. He spat on his hand and smeared the juice onto my ass, then pushed his rod deep inside of me. I groaned at the sensation, and felt my own cock stiffen as the captain fucked me. Holding me by the ankles, he thrust his cock deeper into my ass, his movements quickening. He closed his eyes and exhaled loudly, pumping his seed into my ass as I shot my own geyser onto my stomach.

I quickly dressed, pulling the tunic back on, and left the captain spent on his bed. I found Jack in the hold, stowing that day's take, and I could sense that he suspected what had happened.

"You make the Cap'n happy?" he asked, not making eye contact.

"I didn't know what else to do," I said, surprising myself with my own sincerity.

He turned and impetuously took me into his arms.

"Did he hurt you?" he asked, his breath hot on the top of my head.

Footsteps above us caused him to jump, and he released his embrace on me, becoming all business again.

"All right, lad," he said with a little too much gusto, "if you're to be a mate on this ship, you need to know all about it."

I smiled up at him and he mussed my hair, playfully, before leading me up the ladder and onto the deck. I worked hard to keep my footing as the ship moved through the water, and Jack pointed out the different parts of the ship to me, confusing me with terms like "gaff," "bowsprit," "yard," "jib," and "flying jib."

"There's a rumor," he said, his voice low, "that the Cap'n made a pact with the devil in order to make the ship invincible."

The words sent a chill through me, as I recalled the lack of damage from the earlier battle. Sensing my discomfort, Jack changed the subject and pointed out various crew members. The one called Sweeny was in charge of gunnery; Smythe, the older man with the gray beard from my first night, was the ship's cook; and Johnny was the ship's carpenter.

"He's not well in the head," Jack whispered, "but he's a right good carpenter."

Jack explained the rules of the ship, which covered everything from stealing to smoking tobacco in the hold, and said that punishments could mean being marooned or whipped, depending on the crime.

That evening, I was allowed to dine with the crew and, after a meal of hard tack and bottled beer, one of the men pulled out an accordion and pumped out a melancholy tune which the others recognized. Slowly, they joined in song, led by Sweeny, who sang in the same falsetto that I'd heard him use the night before.

The high seas are rollin',
the brass bells are a-tollin'.
Run the Jolly Roger high,
for tomorrow we all may die.

Feeling a bit sleepy from the beer, I turned to Jack, who was sitting at my side, and asked if it was all right for me to go to the hold to sleep.

"No," he said, matter-of-factly. "You can sleep on the floor in my quarters."

I saw a few eyebrows raised around the table, and Jack turned to the captain, who was seated at the head of the table.

"I think the lad's proved 'is self useful," he said. "I don't think we ought let 'im freeze in the hold."

"I agree," said the captain, waving a hand in my direction. "Show the lad to your quarters, Jack."

"There's room in the crew's quarters," said Johnny, flashing a toothless smile at me. He was quickly silenced by a cold look from Jack, who then wordlessly pushed me through the door and into the corridor. Pausing at the door to his quarters, Jack spoke as he stared at his hand on the latch.

"You don't have to sleep on the floor, if you don' want to," he said, slowly meeting my gaze. "Not to assume anything."

I smiled and touched his rugged face, pausing at the mass of scar tissue where his eye had been.

"Did it hurt?" I asked.

"No," he said, sounding a little put out by my question. "It's a sign of bravery. Besides, loss of an eye earns a pirate one hundred pieces of eight!"

He explained that pirates were rewarded for lost limbs, each body part worth a different sum. Opening the door, he motioned me in with a jerk of his head.

"Off to bed, now," he said. "I'll be back shortly."

Listening to his footsteps retreating down the corridor, I looked around the narrow room, barren of all but a roughly constructed bed covered with dingy sheets and a woolen blanket folded at its foot. Weary from the day, I climbed into the narrow bed and fell into a deep sleep. I awakened early the next day, with Jack's body pressed next to me, his arm draped over me. I felt a stirring inside, but didn't want to move for fear that I would awaken him. I was amazed that I hadn't heard him come in the night before. But he must have been awake, too, because he suddenly spoke, his breath hot on my ear.

"Were you warm enough?" he asked, squeezing me tightly.

I rolled over, so that our faces were nearly touching, and nodded, caressing the bristly face with my hand.

Jack tenderly kissed me on the lips then suddenly sat up, his back to me.

I wrapped my arms around him and kissed his neck. He turned to face me and kissed me again, this time longer.

Then, without another word, he pushed me to the bed and crawled on top of me, lifting off my tunic and kissing my nipples. He emitted a low moan as he pushed his prick into my ass, ecstasy on his beautiful, flawed face. The shoddy bed beneath us creaked with each of his thrusts and, when he finally came, he collapsed on top of me, sweaty and breathless.

"I love you," he whispered, gasping for air.

I squeezed his muscular body, not wanting him to pull out of me, and felt truly happy for the first time since my arrival on the ship.

Captain Bowles eventually gave up on finding the remaining ships and, after trading the stolen loot from the *Contessa* at an Algerian port, announced to the crew his intention of sailing south, toward Peru, obviously tempted by the prospect of more loaded and unsuspecting ships. The *Devil's Spear* drifted south on the sea-lanes for weeks without encountering a single ship, and I continued to share Jack's bed, having fallen horribly in love with the blue-eyed pirate.

After a month on the sea, however, with food running low and whisperings of mutiny among the crew, Jack surprised me one morning with an announcement.

"I been thinkin'," he said, softly, his back to me. "I'm goin' to get you off this ship."

I propped myself up on my arm and touched his bare back.

"I never spent that money what I got for my eye," he continued, "an' this ship ain't no place for a lad like you, so I intend to buy your freedom from the Cap'n."

"What about *you*?" I asked, sitting up in the bed.

"I ain't got nothin' but this," he said, motioning around the small cabin. "But you got a gift for languages and the lot, and don't need a pirate's life."

"Let's *both* leave the ship," I suggested, my heart sinking.

"No," he said, brushing the hair from my face. "Our worlds don' go together. Besides, if I ever get caught I'll be hanged." Without another word, he dressed and left the cabin.

That afternoon, with only hard tack left in the stores for food, the *Devil's Spear* encountered a gale. Huge waves pounded the ship as the crew fought to keep her afloat, and I watched in horror as Johnny was swept from the deck. Fighting to keep my balance, I watched as the mainmast cracked in the middle and crushed the quarterdeck and the captain's quarters.

The large rowboat that had stolen me from my village toppled into the angry sea, spilling Sweeny, Smythe, and Bob. I screamed wildly for Jack over the howling wind, but he was nowhere to be found, and I was pulled from the ship by another large wave. Frantically kicking in the swirling water, I grabbed onto a large section of the mast that was bobbing in the ocean and held on for dear life.

By the time the sea was calm, the first rays of sunlight were breaking through the clouds and I could see, in the distance, a white, sandy beach. Allowing the current to propel me, I rode the ruined mast closer to land, finally letting go when I felt that I was close enough to safely swim. Finally thrown onto the beach by the surf amid broken pieces of the ship, and exhausted from my night in the water, I looked up at a figure running toward me, a figure recognizable to me by the mass of scar tissue where once had been a beautiful blue eye.

PLEASURE AND PAIN ON THE HIGH SEA

Lew Bull

A gentle puff of wind filled the sails of our brigantine as we set sail from the tiny port of Clovelly in Devon, England, heading for the West Indies. I stood on the aft deck and watched the beauty of the shoreline recede, and wondered what lay ahead of me on my first journey. I had only recently been appointed as cabin boy on the *Majestic*, under the leadership of Captain Peter Bloodhound, a large, handsome man with long sun-bleached hair falling onto his muscular shoulders, and dark, brooding eyes. His jaw was set square and pierced through his left ear was a gold ring that was offset by the tanned, weather-beaten skin of his face. He had large hands and arms which must have become developed from strenuous manual labor and fighting over time, and a well-formed chest that resembled the sail of a ship puffed out in the wind.

Captain Pete, as he was affectionately called by his crew, had a reputation for being fair to his crew but being ruthless to his enemy or anyone who caused injustices. Stories abounded of the number of times he had made captives walk the plank into shark-infested waters, but when a crew member needed assistance or care, he was always the first to offer it. However, should a crew member cause trouble, he was dealt with severely and was used as an example to others.

My being chosen to be his cabin boy was as a result of my father having been a crew member alongside Pete many years ago when they were both sailors, and my father had asked Pete if he could offer me a job on his ship. I was proud to serve him, but I was also afraid of the unknown journey on which we were now embarking. We were heading to the West Indies in search of treasure and we could be away from home for up to a year or more.

As we sailed across the Atlantic Ocean, I got to realize that the crew seemed to like me, but I also realized that should be regarded with suspicion. The only crew members with whom I had direct dealings were the cook, named Podgy, a robust man with a hearty laugh, who always found extra helpings of food for me, and the first mate, named Smithers, a lean, gangly man with a scar down the right side of his face. Although this disfigured him, giving him a frightening appearance, he had a gentle temperament and was always looking after me to see that the others did nothing untoward with me. I did, however, learn that his gentle temperament could quite easily be swung to anger if he felt there was an injustice being done.

Throughout our journey, Captain Pete saw to it that I was well cared for and although some of the crew teased me when I went up on deck to get fresh air, because I was still trying to gain my sea legs, they never intimidated or threatened me in any way. Perhaps they knew what Captain Pete might do to them should they upset this young cabin boy.

Amongst my duties was the task of looking after Captain Pete's welfare. Not only did I have to see to the tidying of his cabin and the laying out of clothes for him, but on occasions he asked me to lie next to him on his bed at night. At first I found it a little strange to have this huge man lying next to me, his warm naked body touching my soft skin, but then I grew to like it, as it made me feel safe with him. On many an occasion, I felt his large harpoon rest up against the cheeks of my small ass and gradually harden. It gave me a thrill, yet at the same time frightened me by its size. On occasions like this, he would gently rub up against me until I could feel my own smaller harpoon become stiff and then I would feel a sticky substance fire from his harpoon and cover me, and then he would fall asleep. In the morning we would both rise from his bunk and dress for the day, without a word about the previous night's happenings. As this habit progressed, I noticed how much friendlier Captain Pete became toward me, not that this concerned me in any way.

We had probably been at sea for three weeks when I finally gathered my sea legs. One evening, I was on the quarterdeck, where I shouldn't have been, as that is reserved for officers only, when I suddenly felt a strong arm grip me around the waist. My captor covered my mouth and tucked me under his arm. With my arms and legs flailing, I was carried down below toward the forecastle, where the crew had its quarters. When we reached a dark isolated corner, I was dumped on the wooden floor.

I grunted as my body hit the floor, but before I could rise a huge body fell on top of me, squashing the air from my lungs. I gasped, unable to gather air into my lungs as a mouth covered mine. I could taste and smell the stale rum on the man's breath as his mouth tried to force mine open. All the time I wriggled to free myself from his clutches. In the struggle I could feel something hard pressing against my stomach, and he began to thrust his body against mine. He ripped open my trousers and thrust his hand between my legs, grabbing my now extending harpoon. He started stroking my harpoon vigorously, getting me harder, then suddenly he released his mouth from mine, allowing me to gasp for air, and shot his mouth to the top of my harpoon.

I felt the warm breath on my length and it felt good. Then his mouth slid up and down my harpoon length. I had never in all my life experienced this before, but it was something that I was beginning to like. My gasps changed to groans as his mouth worked frantically up and down. Suddenly there was a commotion and he was flung from my body. In the light from the crew's quarters, I saw Smithers hold one of the crew by the scruff of the neck and then drag him away. Podgy came up to me, still lying on the floor, helped me to my feet, and escorted me to Captain Pete's cabin.

In between sobs, more from shock than anything else, I sat in Captain Pete's cabin thinking about what had just occurred. It was a new experience for me, but deep down within, I had enjoyed what the crewman had done to me—not the manhandling, but the warm mouth wrapped tightly around my harpoon. That evening, Captain Pete never slept in his bed. I had his bed to myself and he sat all night alongside, as though watching over me.

The following day Captain Pete asked me to go down below to the galley and help Podgy with the meal. I thought this strange, as I had never been asked to do this before, but I did as I was commanded. Once I reached the galley, Podgy proceeded to get me busy peeling potatoes.

"Why's Capt'n Pete sent me down here, Podgy?" I asked innocently.

"Never you mind, young man. You just busy yourself with them potatoes."

I did as I was told, but sensed that Podgy knew exactly what was going on up on deck. In between peeling, I heard the occasional cheer from the rest of the crew up on the main deck.

"What are they doing?" I once again queried.

I could see that my persistence was paying off. Podgy opened up and told me.

"It's about what happened to you last night, lad."

"What are they doing?"

"Whipping, boy, whipping!"

"Whipping?" I queried.

"Yes. That man that grabbed you and was doing what he was doing is now getting his punishment."

"Are they beating him?" I asked.

"Probably twenty to thirty lashes with a cat-o'-nine-tails, I would guess," replied Podgy, nonchalantly, "and then maybe the captain might just give him a little extra something."

"What's the extra something, as you put it?" I inquired.

Podgy smiled at me and winked. Was he having fun with me or was there something sinister that he was hiding? It shocked me to think that, because I could imagine the pain the man would be suffering, and I think Podgy could read my thoughts because he added, "You don't touch the captain's property."

"But I'm not his property," I innocently answered.

"On this ship you are, boy, and we all know it."

"What do you mean?"

Podgy stopped what he was doing, put down the wooden spoon he had in his hand, and looked me in the face.

"Boy, the captain has chosen you to be his special friend, if you want to put it that way. You are the only person who shares the captain's bed and therefore no one may have a share of you. Do you understand?" he asked, smiling at me.

Slowly it sank in and I realized my privileged position. Knowing this somehow made me feel safer on Captain Pete's ship. This whipping would be a lesson to others not to touch me and it also brought home to me the fact that by sending me down to the galley, Captain Pete wanted to save me the humiliation of watching the whipping and perhaps the extra something that was taking place up on the deck. However, I felt I had to see what was happening, so I stopped what I was doing in the galley, dropped the knife I was using, and ran as quickly as I could up toward the main deck. Podgy shouted after me to stop, but I ignored his pleas.

As I reached the top of the stairs that led to the main deck, I caught sight of the man's naked body tied to the base of the mainmast, welts across his upper and lower back, and one of the crew members flogging him with the cat-o'-nine-tails. I could hear the "swish" through the air as the rope whip with its nine knotted lashes crashed onto the man's back, followed by a howl from the man and a cheer from the rest of the crew. I didn't emerge from my position onto the main deck, but stayed hidden at the top of the stairs, watching. The man's arms had been fastened around the mainmast as though he was hugging it, and his legs had been spread wide and fastened in position. I sat on the top step and watched.

The man's body glistened in the sunlight from sweat and blood and his naturally white skin had begun to glow red from both the beating and the blood. Somehow I felt for this man. I felt his pain and wondered whether I could have endured such punishment; but seeing this act also made me aware of how precarious life at sea was. After some time, the flogging stopped and I noticed that the crew all turned toward the poop deck where I assumed Captain Pete must have been standing to watch the proceedings. There was silence. I waited in anticipation to see what was about to happen.

Suddenly a cheer rose from the crew and I could see the glee written across the faces of the men. What was happening that I couldn't see? I followed the direction of their gaze and then all fell into place. The giant naked frame of Captain Pete came into view.

Captain Pete's tanned nakedness was there for all to see. I could only see the back view, but from that I could see how muscular he was. His V-shaped back trailed down to a slim waist and a well-rounded, yet firmly formed ass. His legs resembled two tree trunks that might have been used to shape the mainmast of a fine galleon. But why was he naked? The question was soon to be answered. He walked slowly up behind the tired body of the man against the mast and I saw Captain Pete fondling his harpoon, then I saw him bend his knees a little, get closer to the man and then thrust his body forward. This was obviously "the extra" that Podgy had spoken of. Together with the cheers from the crew, I heard the scream of the man on the mast. I watched in awe as Captain Pete's muscular body pounded up against the man's, all the while the man was screaming and the crew was cheering—it was as though the men were encouraging Captain Pete to be even more forceful and brutal. He held onto the man's shoulders and thrust his hips forward and back as I had seen dogs doing it on the mainland back home. I watched with fascination as each muscle in his back, ass and legs strained against the limp body of the man. Finally Captain Pete released a loud gasp and gave one long deep thrust while his body quivered in the bright sunshine. Slowly I watched his body begin to relax and then I saw him begin to move away from the man on the mast.

It was at this point that I caught a glimpse of some of the man's blood from his flogging smeared across Captain Pete's chest, and I fled my hiding place and headed back to the galley. Podgy never said a word to me when I entered the galley, but I'm sure that he could tell from the expression on my face that I had witnessed my first sea punishment.

That evening, Captain Pete called me into his cabin and sat me down across the table from him while he ate his dinner. I immediately thought he had seen me watching the punishment earlier in the day and wanted to reprimand me.

"Lad, I want to apologize for not protecting you better. What happened to you last night must have been painful for you, and for that I am sorry," he said in a gentle voice.

"No, Captain," I intervened. "I really wasn't hurt."

He held up his huge hands to silence me. "It will never happen again, so long as you are on my ship, and if anyone tries to do anything to you which might be harmful, you are to report it to me immediately."

"Yes, sir," came my humble reply.

"Now get your plate of food and join me so that we may eat together."

I did as I was told and after I had a very enjoyable meal with the captain, he went up on deck for a couple of hours. When he returned I had cleared all the plates from his table, tidied up, and was ready to go to my bunk, but he insisted that I spend this night with him. I helped him undress and watched as each piece of clothing revealed more and more of his muscular, tanned body. For the second time in one day he stood naked in front of me. I looked at this sculptured body and had only admiration for it. My eyes followed the contours of his well-formed chest to his flat stomach and downwards toward the long, fat harpoon with its flared head that stood erect and proud.

On seeing this, I couldn't control my actions and fell to my knees, engulfing his swaying harpoon in much the same way that my attacker had done to me. I felt Captain Pete's thrusts into my mouth and soon heard the same sounding groans that had emitted from me the night before, so I knew that he was enjoying what I was doing. After a while, he lifted me gently to my feet and began to undress me.

My naked body lay on his bed, waiting for him to do what he wanted with me. Gently he lowered himself onto the bed next to me so my back was to him, then he put an arm around my waist, pulling me closer to him and whispered in my ear, "I want to harpoon you."

Fear immediately struck a chord with me. I had seen his roughness on the deck with the man and I was afraid that he was about to do the same to me. I tensed and he felt it.

"Relax. I'm not going to hurt you."

The screams of the man on the mainmast echoed through my brain. I had only now seen how big his harpoon was, so I could understand why the man had screamed so much. Was I to be impaled by this weapon? He ran his rough hands over my soft skin in an effort to get me to relax. His hands fondled my chest and stomach, then he ran them over my upper thighs and onto my ass, where my smoothness must have felt good to him because he left them there for some time, letting his fingers explore. I felt a long, thick finger rub up against my entry hole. Somehow, it felt good. I felt a slight penetration of his finger into my hole, but all the while he was gentle and never forced his actions onto me. Slowly his finger entered deeper into me and I began to enjoy its feeling. I gave a soft groan as he slid his finger around inside my hole, but as he began to withdraw it, a strange feeling overcame me—I didn't want it to leave.

I then pushed closer onto him, indicating my willingness to succumb to him, and felt his finger escape and his hardness being guided toward my entry. The enormity of his harpoon made it painful at first, but with a little relaxation, I was able to accommodate him. Slowly and gently Captain Pete sank into the warm confines of my body and at once I felt completely safe. My ass tightened around his throbbing harpoon and his gentle moans fluttered over my neck and ears as he slowly thrust into my depths. It was so unlike what I had seen up on the deck earlier. His gentle thrusts were not in anger, but in love. His chest rested against my back and the hand around my waist moved down to between my legs and clutched onto my harpoon, which he then began to stroke. I found myself enjoying this experience and actually wanting him to go deeper into me. Our groans matched each other's and each thrust from him was met by an equally enjoyable thrust from me. Our combined pleasures became more frantic as we thrust against each other, our breathing becoming more labored until both of us fired our harpoons simultaneously. My sticky liquid covered his hand as he continued to stroke me, while inside of me I felt the jolting throbs of his harpoon as it fired what felt like a twenty-one-gun salute.

I lay in his muscular arms wondering how the same act could be so pleasurable to me yet so painful to the man on the deck, but I still had a great deal to learn on my journey. I closed my eyes, with his body still tightly pressed up against mine, and felt his harpoon continuing to give gentle throbs inside of me until I began to feel both bodies start to relax and drift off to sleep, as the ship continued to rock gently on the open sea.

THE WINDS OF VENGEANCE

P.A. Brown

I don't know exactly when it all went to hell. Maybe I should have just stayed in my cabin that night.

I had been so sure Richard and I were going to get together tonight. He'd been doing some heavy-duty flirting with me for the last two days, ever since we left Bermuda for more southern climes. Tonight he caught me in the stairwell on the way to the upper decks. We played tonsil hockey long enough to leave me with a serious boner that my costume of skintight pantaloons did nothing to conceal. His breath was hot against my throat and I fumbled through his own costume for his cock.

If the couple from the Lido deck hadn't chosen that inopportune moment to stumble, giggling and groping, onto the stairs, who knows how far Richard and I would have gone. Far enough to kill my career on the high seas. The management did not look kindly on their newest activity coordinator getting fucked by a first-class passenger.

But god he was hot. Hot to the touch.

We broke apart, gasping. I still had my fingers wrapped around his throbbing cock. He grinned down at me, his perfectly capped teeth nibbling my earlobe.

"You want it, don't you, Al."

I winced. "Alton," I said. "My name's Alton."

"Whatever." He ground his cock into my hand. "You want this, don't you?"

"Yes!"

"How 'bout we meet up after this shindig? Down on the Coral deck by the lifeboats."

I knew it was wrong, but the thought of his cock up my ass sent all caution sailing off to Davy Jones's locker.

My sword clanked against the stair railing.

"You look ridiculous—you know that, don't you," Richard said.

I thought I looked pretty sexy. I'd picked the pirate costume up in New York before this gig had started. What can I say—I've loved pirates since I was a toddler in my mother's loft in New York. The costume was mostly black and I thought it really showed off my gym-buffed form. Richard's reaction from the first time our eyes met had proved my instincts were still dead on. (Besides, he wasn't one to talk. He'd gone for a rapper look, complete with lots of phony gold bling, and frankly, on him it didn't work.)

That was the unfortunate moment when the Lido deck couple entered the stairwell. Richard jerked away from me.

He put one finger on my lips. "Later," he breathed. "Two o'clock?"

Cool night air slapped my overheated skin. I trotted down the steps, pausing on the promenade deck to stare out at the phosphorescent sea. I spent a couple of hours in my tiny quarters below deck, sipping on beer and wishing the time would pass. Finally it was nearly two and I hurried toward the Coral deck. Richard was by lifeboat number five. We came together in an explosion of lust that had both of us panting in need.

"God, you are so hot," Richard groaned against my mouth. "Get those things off."

I complied, then Richard put his hands up under my armpits. "Climb up there," he said, and indicated the space between the lifeboat and the gunwale.

The position put my raging hard cock right in his face. He gobbled me up and I let go of the railing and gripped the top of his head. I started moaning and rocking into his mouth, my nuts climbing up into their sacs ready to explode. I threw my head back when my orgasm slammed into me with the force of a freight train. There was nothing behind me. My body flipped over the gunwale—I grabbed for railing, but caught only empty air.

My scream was cut off when the sea closed over my head. Darkness rose to meet me.

❀

"Wake up, you lousy dungbie."

I blinked away the fuzziness in response to the odd voice and even odder words. I was lying on some kind of lumpy mattress, naked, barely covered by a thin cotton sheet that didn't smell all that fresh. Beneath me I could hear the creak and murmur of water. I was still at sea, that much was obvious.

"Who—where?" I swallowed, started coughing and had to wait until I stopped to try again. "Where am I?"

The room I was in was dim. I could barely make out the source of the voice. He was a tall man, but slender, his face obscured by shadow. His voice was husky and low. I shivered at the resonance that crept along my nerve endings.

I could just make out the soft gleam of his eyes as he bent over me.

"You be guest to Captain Luca de Cheval of the brigantine *Winds of Vengeance*. Who be you, lad?"

"Uh, Alton," I said shakily. "Alton Winters, of the *Swedish Crown*. Do you know her?" It was all coming back to me. I had fallen overboard. Jesus, Richard must be going crazy. It must have been fun explaining what had happened.

"*Swedish Crown*?" the voice said. "What kind of name be that for a ship?"

I didn't know. I didn't name her. "She's part of the Cunard Line of cruise ships. We were heading for the Bahamas—"

"You be doing business in Charles Town?"

"We were docking in Nassau," I said, having never heard of Charles

Town. "Listen, do you have a cell? Mine's probably at the bottom of the fricking ocean and I really need to call somebody to let them know I'm okay. Or a radio—"

The figure suddenly swung a lantern over my face, briefly blinding me. I shied away from the wash of light, but not before I had seen the man behind it.

He was swarthy, with a close-cropped goatee, a full mouth twisted in a frown, and a pair of cobalt blue eyes that drilled into mine. His dark hair was tied back in a ponytail and hung nearly to his shoulder blades. He wore a loose-fitting tunic top that was opened to the waist, revealing a fur-covered chest and two fat brown nipples over a fine set of pecs I had the sudden insane urge to explore. His legs were encased in skintight leather molded so tightly over the tube of flesh between his legs I could see he was uncut.

I swallowed hard and looked up to meet his eyes.

"You be Rogers's spy?" Luca asked. His grip on the lantern tightened. "If you be the governor's watchman I'll be feeding your cockles to the fishes."

"I'm no spy," I snapped. Not to mention I didn't want my cockles—or anything—fed to the fishes. "And who the hell is Rogers?"

Luca frowned. "He be the Royal Governor of the Grand Bahamas. Surely ye know that—"

"Who are you?" I sat up on the cot, the sheet pooling in my lap. I saw Luca's eyes skim over my bare upper body and I couldn't help but react to the open lust in his eyes. "What the hell is this place?" I looked around and grew even more confused.

I was in some kind of cabin. I could see a patch of pale blue sky through a large curved window that I assumed was in the ship's aft. We were too high up for me to see anything around the ship. The room itself was filled with antiques. Even the bed I had awoken on was a low post bed, probably circa 1700 or thereabouts. Thanks to my mother's obsession with all things older than her I recognized the tambour Hepplewhite secretary covered with papers, journals, a crystal glass carafe full of some kind of golden liquid, and a pewter mug. The secretary practically looked brand new. Mom would have spent hours rhapsodizing over it, then sold my soul for the fifteen thousand she would have needed to buy it. Where the hell had this guy found these treasures? And why would he keep them on board a ship? Sea air was not good for quality antiques. An inkwell with a turkey feather quill pen and a tray of sand sat atop the secretary. No laptop, PDA, or any electronic equipment as far as I could see. I guess the guy really liked to immerse himself in whatever fantasy role he was playing.

"Is this some kind of stupid joke?" I snapped. "'Cause I don't think it's very funny—"

"You're a guest aboard my ship," Luca said. "I'll decide what is funny and what is not. And you are not. Again, be you a spy?"

"No!"

Luca set the lantern down on the floor and reached past my head. He tossed a pair of pants and a tunic, like the one he wore, at me.

"Get dressed. Until you can produce a ransom to buy your way off my ship you'll be my cabin boy. Ye'll do as you're told, too, or I'll be putting you back in the sea where I found you."

"Ransom?" I squeaked. "You're holding me hostage? My family's got no money," I lied.

"Then I guess you'll be having plenty of time to practice your skills as me cabin boy. The last one who had the job took exception to some of my needs and jumped ship at Tortuga. He might have lived to regret his folly if the Bronze John hadn't ended his scurvy-ridden life before I had a chance to do it for him."

"Bronze John?"

"The fever," Luca said, rubbing his handsome face. "Yellow Jack. Have you not seen the curse?"

"Er, no." Hadn't even heard of it. I was getting more and more confused. If this was some kind of elaborate prank—and frankly I couldn't think of anyone with the brains or the resources to pull it off—it had gone on long enough. I said as much.

Luca's face darkened. "Prank? You be calling Captain Luca a prank?"

"Listen, just drop me at your earliest convenience. I'll call home. Mom'll be furious but she'll find some money for you. God knows where my credit cards are—back on the fucking *Crown*, no doubt. I'll make it up to you, I promise—"

I had barely pulled on the cotton pants that were half a size too small when the door to his cabin swung open following the barest knock. Hastily I did up the button fly as two burly, bearded men who looked like they might have shared quarters with a pig or two tromped in, a massive galvanized tub half filled with water between them. Without a word they set the tub down, the thick cords of muscles on their oily-looking arms bulging. They ignored the water that sloshed across the wooden deck and left, but not until their eyes had crawled over me, darkening with gleeful lust. I wasn't the least bit flattered.

Luca shooed them out. He reached for the drawstrings on his tunic. "Ye'll find a sponge aft there. Mind you scrub hard. I've a mind to feel clean tonight."

I found the sponge right where he said it would be. It was a natural sea sponge and felt stiff and prickly in my hand. I turned back to find Luca had shed his clothes and stood beside the tub, the soft glow of the lamp falling over his surprisingly graceful limbs.

The hair on his well-defined chest descended to wrap around the thick tube of uncut flesh dangling between his well-muscled thighs. A pair of fat balls hung on either side and if I'd been feeling braver I might have slipped my fingers between them, stroking their velvet softness. I licked my lips and looked up to meet Luca's gaze.

I took a step forward as he eased himself down into the water. It barely came up to his hips and as I approached him I got the most incredible view of the dark hair on his chest arrowing down into his groin. His cock thickened and lengthened as I stared at it, and my own cock hardened under his intense eyes.

This had a hell of a lot more potential than Richard's little sordid rendezvous. Maybe I was still unconscious and dreaming or I was dead and heaven was a lot sexier than I'd ever heard. Or hell of a lot more fun.

It was either my fantasy or Luca's. Either way I was in.

I dipped the sponge into the water. It wasn't heated and was obviously seawater. I traced the outline of his shoulders, dribbling water down his chest where it glistened and clung to his burnished, sun-browned skin.

"Lean forward," I murmured and he complied. I stroked his strong, muscular back, one hand on his shoulder, the other holding the sponge, tracing his spine and sliding between his buttocks. He shifted in the tub to give me better access. I didn't need any more invitation than that. If this was my fantasy I was taking over.

I dropped the sponge and inserted stiff fingers between his ass cheeks. He caught his breath and stiffened as one digit slid past his sphincter muscle.

"You're a bold one, aren't you, lad?"

I tasted him then, my lips and tongue delving between his shoulder blades and nibbling the flesh behind his ears. He tasted like salt water and warm musky skin.

My hand stole around to his front, sliding through his course pubic hair to close over his rigid pole.

"You ain't seen nothing yet. Stand up."

He did as I asked and I parted the round globes of his ass and peered hungrily at the pink orifice there. With one hand still clutching his cock I used the other to open him up to my mouth. He jerked in my hand when my tongue replaced my finger. He hunched over, exposing himself even more to my ministrations, and I went to work in earnest. I'm not usually a big fan of rimming, but the clean taste of salt and his own personal musk had me hooked. Using my tongue as a miniature cock I plundered his hole until Luca was panting and rocking against my mouth. In my hand his cock grew even more immense and I knew he was close to blowing his load.

I half rose from the crouch I was in and spun him around. His hands came down on my head and silently urged me on. I licked my lips at the treasure before me. His fat mushroom-shaped cock head glistened with precome and was so engorged with blood it poked out of his foreskin. His nuts were drawn up tight against his scrotum. I traced the pulsing veins that climbed his thick column of flesh with my tongue, then used my lips to tease the head all the way out. Luca's fingers twined through my thick hair. He was no longer silent as he rocked forward, demanding I swallow him.

I obliged.

I opened the back of my throat, suppressing the gag reflex. I tasted the rich, salty essence of him while I twirled my tongue around his bulbous cock head. I wrapped one hand around the base of his cock and slid my other hand behind his nuts, teasing the supersensitive flesh there. He was rocking now, his breath coming in sharp explosions. His cock pulsed and I felt the first blast of hot come hit the back of my throat. Five, six times he shuddered until finally he sagged and I thought he might tumble into my arms. I hastily stood and grabbed his shoulders. He stared down at me unblinking. He was still struggling to get his breath back.

"I pluck a ragged, half-dead man out of the sea and ye turn out to be a sea sprite."

I traced the outline of his chest, stroking one of his nipples into a turgid little button. I couldn't resist. I leaned down and tugged at it with my teeth. "Not a sea sprite. Just a very hungry man." I pressed my mouth against his chest, inhaling his intoxicating smell. "God, you taste good."

He traced the outline of my jaw. "More like a lad. How old be ye, boy?"

Slightly indignant I drew back and stared up at his face, looming over mine, wondering just how old he was to think I was so young. "I'm twenty-two."

"You'll be a handy man with a blade, then. But you have the skin of a girl."

Now, that was going too far. I opened my mouth to reply when his hand closed over my still raging hard-on. He unbuttoned my fly and drew it out, stroking me gently.

"But this be no girl's toy," he said huskily. "This be a fine pug—"

Suddenly there was a commotion outside. A harsh claxon began tolling. I could feel it through the soles of my bare feet.

Luca's face lit up in a feral grin. "Ah, our target be in sight." He stepped out of the tub and began scrubbing himself dry with a cloth. He stepped back into his tight leathers and pulled his tunic over his head without bothering to tie the strings. Finally he pulled on a pair of cuffed leather boots. Once dressed he grabbed my tunic off the bed and tossed it at me.

"You can join me on deck for this. Ye may find it interesting."

He guided me to the door, his hand on my back as he pushed the heavy wooden door open. He bent down and murmured for my ears only, "A warning: Never come on deck without me. My crew are a loyal lot, but one as sweet as yourself would soon find himself at the receiving end of more cocks than I think even your sweet dungbie could handle and I'd hate to have to kill the ones who forced themselves on ye. It be bad for morale."

I stared at him as we passed through the door. Then I was too overwhelmed to consider his words further.

Back when I actually was still a "lad," my mother took me to Boston to see the tall ships. I remember being overcome at the sight of all those wooden vessels with their tall masts and snowy white sails. I think that's when I developed such a love for the sea and the ships that sailed on it. When I'd joined the cruise line and been assigned to the *Crown* it was more than a dream come true.

I was vaguely aware of Luca leading me. I was more conscious of all the men who swarmed the orlop and poop decks, unloading the rigging and doing God knows what to prepare the ship. Luca's ship, *Winds of Vengeance*, as far as I could tell from some pretty extensive reading, was a two-masted, square-sailed brigantine. Her sails weren't quite as white as I remember as I would have expected and even from down here I could see they'd been extensively repaired. The crew scrambled through the rigging with an aplomb I found unnerving. They were so surefooted, in an environment where a fall would almost surely be fatal.

A stiff breeze carried the odor of tar and rank, unwashed bodies. Under it I could smell the sea and death.

Vengeance was about 150 tons and could be armed with up to 10 cannons. Designed for speed and war, it was considered an ideal pirate ship. A *captain's* pirate ship. I turned to stare at Luca, who had taken his place at the big ornately carved wooden wheel, which he handled with a delicate touch that was almost sensual.

"Who are you?" I whispered. I guess I still thought he'd admit to being some weird jillionaire who got a hard-on playing pirate and had gone to the ultimate extreme. He couldn't be a real pirate, though, could he? On a ship like this he'd be caught in about two seconds by the Coast Guard and the Navy. So who the fuck was he?

"I be Captain Luca de Cheval and this be the finest ship on the seas and we are about to lay by some booty."

I heard cries of, "Swing the lead, swing it by," followed by, "Land ho. Thar she be, Captain."

"There *what* be?" I strained but couldn't see anything off port or starboard. A fine mist lay on the horizon. Luca pointed at it.

"Bermuda," Luca said. Then he pointed to port, where I could barely make out a sail on the horizon. "And there be our target."

I blanched. "You're going to attack it?"

A shout went up. I looked up and felt lightheaded as I saw two flags unfurling over the foremast. The first one was almost comical, it was so clichéd—the white skull and crossbones of the Jolly Roger—and the second was a blood-red flag with a pair of crossed blades.

"What are those for?" I whispered.

"Warning. If they fight, they die. Their choice."

"You can't kill those people!"

"And I won't, if they do not resist me."

We were moving fast now; I could feel the slap of the ship's bow riding the stiff waves. The distant ship was close enough now to make out her sails. A schooner. Her sails went up and it was obvious she was trying to run. A cheer went up on deck and I didn't get it at first.

Luca was happy to explain it. "She's heading into the reefs. They don't call her Devil Island for nothing."

I remember that was in our indoctrination—Bermuda was home to more than 500 wrecks, the result of a unique ring of reefs that made it one of the deadliest stretches of ocean in the world. Luca was driving the schooner into the shallows, where she would surely be caught.

And that's exactly what happened. The schooner suddenly grounded, shuddering to an abrupt stop, her masts and sails trembling violently as she began to settle over on her keel.

Vengeance cut her speed and we eased toward the trapped schooner. I cautiously moved toward the port side gunwale. I could see the stony reefs below the choppy waves and the occasional fish dart through my field of vision. The schooner was off our port bow, close enough to see the name emblazoned on her bow: *Dona Marie*. Spanish or Portuguese.

The activity over my head increased as the sails were reefed and the *Vengeance* coasted to a gentle stop only a few hundred feet from the trapped schooner.

Someone came up behind me. I could tell it was Luca because of his delicious smell. He put his hand on the back of my neck.

"Ye might be wise to return to the cabin," he said.

"Why—"

Something small but moving very fast whicked past my ear and slammed into the mainmast behind me. Belatedly I realized we were being shot at. Several people stood along the schooner's gunwale holding what looked to my disbelieving eyes like muskets.

Luca hurried me toward the cabin, shutting the door with a stern, "Stay in here until I come get you."

The sun slid below the horizon and all around me the sounds of battle raged. The boom of cannon, pounding feet and shouting voices drove me to retreat to the farthest corner of the cabin. I elected to sit at his Hepplewhite. I poured a double shot of the golden liquid and tasted the sharp bite of whiskey. I found a flint and figured out how to light the hurricane lamp. Leaning back in the chair I closed my eyes, trying to block the sounds from outside. I wasn't very successful and the whiskey didn't help.

Luca didn't return until long after dark had fallen. I glanced at him from where I sat at his desk but didn't speak. I realized I was in a prickly situation here. Even if I still had no idea where *here* was, I knew only too well that I was totally at Luca's mercy and I was beginning to wonder if he had any.

He tossed something on the desk in front of me. I picked it up without enthusiasm, knowing it was booty from that poor ship.

"Ye'll be happy to know we left the crew alive. They'll make their way ashore and be the latest residents of yon bonnie island." He indicated the package. "Ye seem to be the scholarly type. This might amuse you."

I glanced at it. It was a newspaper wrapped in oilskin. I read the masthead: *HE London Evening Post*. Then I glanced at the date.

Sunday, August 21, 1720.

The words blurred and my head spun. I met Luca's puzzled gaze.

"I don't understand."

"Understand what?"

I stabbed at the dateline. "This is a hoax. I was born in fucking 1985. The twentieth century. Not the eighteenth."

Suddenly Luca started laughing. He threw his head back and roared.

"You are a strange one, Alton Winters."

I spun around in the chair. "Where did you find me? Exactly."

"Six hundred and twenty nautical miles south southeast of Summer Islands."

"Was I dressed? Where are my clothes?"

Luca looked sly. "You were as buck naked as a babe."

I went off the side of the *Crown* in the year 2007. Now I was supposed to believe I was almost 300 years in the past. Yeah, right.

Luca slid his hands around my neck, slipping under the open collar of my tunic top. Hot fingers kneaded my cold skin. I shivered.

"Cold?" Luca asked.

"What are you going to do to me?"

Luca pulled me out of the chair and pulled my hips against his. His erection pressed into my belly. "I am going to fuck you until the sun comes over the yardarm. Then I may sleep fora while before I fuck ye again."

I couldn't help it—my cock jumped at his words. He unbuttoned my fly and shoved my pants down around my knees. My cock leapt out into his hand and I groaned.

Luca leaned down, his open mouth inches from mine. "Does that sound good to you?"

"Tell me how I got here," I whispered. "Tell me how I can get home."

"I can't do that," Luca said. He pressed him mouth over mine, his tongue slipping past my teeth. He tasted of rum. A celebratory nosh with the crew after a successful plunder? "I can take you back to where I found you adrift. Mayhap that will tell you something?"

"God, I hope so—"

His mouth laid a trail of fire down my chest. I kicked my legs free and Luca stripped the tunic off, tossing it on the chair behind me. His clothes joined mine and he spun me around, pressing against my back. His rough, calloused hand closed over my cock and he nuzzled my throat as he began to stroke me hard.

It didn't take me long to come to the brink. I moaned and slammed into a gut-wrenching orgasm. Luca scooped my come up and smeared it between my ass cheeks. One stiff finger pushed past my sphincter muscle, then a second. A heartbeat later I felt the head of his precome-covered cock replace his fingers. Pain lanced through me, then faded as a new heat invaded my gut. Luca's rough fingers tightened on my hips as he rocked against me, working himself up my dark channel. Finally he came to rest, his thick, coarse pubic hair snug against my ass.

I grabbed the back of the chair I had recently vacated and spread my legs to take him deeper. His teeth worried the back of my neck, muttering hot words against my damp skin.

At first he fucked me with even, measured strokes, sliding in and out, pausing at the upswing to let me savor how full he made me feel.

"Ye like that?" he moaned. "You like the feel of Luca up your chute? God, ye are a tight one."

Slow and easy didn't last long. He began pistoning into me until we were both grunting. Each stroke pummeled me and his grip tightened on my hips. I could feel his cock swelling deep in my bowels. He called out my name as he slammed into me one last time. Hot come blasted out of his cock, hitting the walls of my fuck hole. An incredible sensation for someone who'd never barebacked in his life.

I sagged over the chair; only his arms around me kept me from tumbling to the deck. He startled me then by scooping me up in his arms and carrying me over to the bed. I was even more shocked when he gently traced the outline of my chin and mouth and murmured, "I do not know what we will find when we return to where I rescued you. Mayhap you will indeed discover a way to go home." He left only to come back seconds later with a damp cloth which he used to clean both of us off. Finally he stretched out on the bed, our hips and shoulders touching. "Or mayhap you will grow accustomed to my world."

I thought of everything that had happened since I'd fallen overboard. Part of me hoped I'd be able to go home—my friends and family were there, hell, my whole life—but another part wanted to stay here a while. I was falling for a pirate captain. A real live pirate. Imagine that.

I framed his face and twined my legs around his, pressing my hardening cock against his hip.

"Mayhap I will."

MATELOTAGE

By Erastes

Napier opened his eyes and rolled over, his mouth sour and dry, his head sore from the previous evening's revels. A warm wind was blowing off the coast of Hispaniola and Napier could tell from the stars that the ship was swinging around on her anchor; it was that that had woken him. He smiled grimly; they would sail with the new wind at dawn. His blood stirred at the thought of the open sea and the anticipation of the chase.

The captain's cabin was unlit, but the moon, waxing strongly, shone onto Reuben's curved spine and pale buttocks that were always a joy to wake to, whatever the hour. Reuben's skin gleamed in the heat. He had kicked off the sheets in the night, and Napier's eyes feasted on the contrast between his brown back, marked with the hazards of a sailor's life, and the rounded temptation of his alabaster arse.

Like this, Napier thought, as he reached forward to slide his fingers into the warm crevasse, *when he's face down and I don't have to see his lying face, I can almost believe he's worth keeping. I should never have claimed him.*

☸

But he had, and regretted it almost every moment since. Reuben Pyke had bewitched the captain, some of the crew believed, with his easy grace and his honey-eyed careless smile. He'd sauntered on board one drunken night, made his mark in the ship's register, and from the moment Paul Napier had laid eyes on the newcomer's pretty face and tight striped trousers, his blood turned to burning rum, and his loins to a sea on fire. Napier knew from that first moment how it would end: that he had to have him, had to claim him as a captain's prize, had to pin Reuben Pyke beneath him and make him his own.

It was a smooth boarding. Reuben had fallen into bed with the captain with the same dangerous ease that he spitted an enemy or slit a throat, and for a while Napier had been content. Reuben was a willing fuck, a pleasurable whorish fuck, doing more in a night than Napier had experienced in a lifetime, but it came with a price: The crew grew sullen as Reuben began to display to them that, as the captain's lover, he considered himself better than them. He began to wheedle and hint to Napier that he should have a greater share of the ship's haul and when this was rejected out of hand, he disembarked at Cayonne and went missing for two nights.

Napier fumed and raged and drank; the crew stayed out of his way, knowing of his tempers, which were deadly in their fury. He rampaged below decks, setting off cannon and angering other captains whose ships were moored in the bay. Finally sobering, he sent a gang into Cayonne to bring Reuben back under a charge of desertion, and he was dragged aboard, bruised and bound. Napier lashed him himself, not trusting another man with the Cat.

Shortly after that it was rumored throughout the ship that Napier was drawing up a Deed of Matelotage, the binding sailor's contract by which a man cleaves to another on board, closer than blood brothers, closer than wives. The only things that stopped the crew from mutinying were their fierce loyalty to Napier and the night of liberty he gave them in Cayonne, where they drained the town dry.

I should have hanged him, Napier thought, reaching for the a crystal bottle by the bed. Reuben stirred, as Napier slid oil-slicked fingers into his cleft and deep into his willing little hole. *If this wasn't so sweet, I'd hang him today, instead of leaving him behind.* As Reuben woke, groaning in pleasure, Napier shifted, placed himself on top, propped up with braced arms, and slid home, sweet and easy like a ramrod into the barrel of a gun. Reuben began to buck under him, grunting with every thrust, rubbing himself against the bed linen.

"*Merde*, Paul. Did you not fill me to the gunwales last night?" Reuben's voice was muffled against the pillow, but Napier took no notice. His hips snapped forward and back, his body slapping against Reuben's creamy arse, till he felt his balls strangle and his seed spiral upward. He grunted in pleasure as powder sparks went off behind his eyes.

He rested a moment, letting his tongue taste the charcoal and sulfur of Reuben's skin, and fell asleep again, his cock still buried in his mate.

☸

The sky was pink with the promise of a dawn squall when Napier next woke, his skin stuck damply to Reuben's. He felt groggy and warm, and his cock, still lodged in Reuben's arse, was twitching with interest and begging for another voyage of delight, but other than a couple of half-hearted thrusts he decided against it. It would be harder to do what he had to do if he fucked Reuben in the light of the day. He pulled out and away, sat on the edge of the bed, and pulled on his clothes, gaudy scarlet and gold.

"Get dressed," he ordered, as he dragged his boots from under the bed. His voice was the one he used on the quarterdeck and for the first time since their relationship began, Reuben looked up at Napier with worried eyes, clouded with what looked like suspicion and guilt. Napier gritted his teeth and reached into his sea chest. He pulled out a silken scarf tied in a knot, which rattled as he lifted it. Without a word, he left Reuben behind and marched onto the deck, leaving the cabin door unlocked.

☸

The crew had been complaining about petty pilfering for a while and the grumble had become too hard for Napier to ignore, as the accusations were aimed at Reuben. He'd given the matter to his quartermaster to investigate. The quartermaster, a one-eyed rogue called Brundall, had been at sea with Napier for fifteen years. His interrogation of the crew had found that so many thefts had taken place that Reuben was just about the only man who had not lost some trinket or bauble or some small share of the ship's haul.

"'E was the last man on board, Cap'n," Brundall had reported back, "an' the men don' trust 'im, even with...your...your..."

"Partiality?"

"Not a word I would have used, Cap'n." Instead of replying, Napier had frowned. "'Ave you not lost anythin' yourself, sir?" Brundall continued. "Or Pyke 'imself? Would not look so bad, if 'e 'ad. On the other 'and, if *you 'ad* lost somethin'...with your cabin bein' locked, an' all..." Brundall's eyes were eager. There was no doubt as to his meaning.

Turning on his heel, Napier had marched to his cabin and searched it thoroughly. On a surface inspection it seemed that nothing was touched; his pistols, silver and ebony, were lying snug in their velvet-lined case. His precious collection of pocket watches, each wrapped in an oiled piece of satin, were all accounted for, all safe. But his grandfather's ring was gone from his trinket box. It was of Welsh gold, unmistakably pink, set with an alexandrite stone which turned green in daylight, purple by candlelight.

With a stony face he had walked back out to Brundall.

☸

Out in the dawn, the horizon was scarlet and gold.

"Foul weather coming," Brundall said, as Napier hauled himself up to the quarterdeck. On the leeward side there was a small island, its white sands and palm-fringed beaches clearly visible from the deck.

"Best we get this done before the squall hits, then." Napier said as the bosun joined them. "Bring him out. There's punishment for thieves."

The bosun went pale, and dared to speak. "But Cap'n..."

Napier turned on him, his black eyes burning with anger. "Well? What would you have me do? The man *stole*. Stole from the crew, from the ship.

Would you have me favor him? Pardon him—just because I fuck him?" He was grimly satisfied when the bosun dropped his eyes, turned away, and spat into the ocean. He actions said it all.

Napier stared across the ship's deck, keeping himself under control. He didn't watch as two sailors dragged Reuben, naked and shouting, out onto the deck.

The young man's voice became gradually more panic-stricken as he realized that Napier was serious. "Napier... Paul... *Captain*... come on… a jest is a jest... but this is..."

The men were baying with laughter, but Napier stood firm and looked as cold as he felt inside.

"I told you to get dressed, Pyke," he said, as Reuben was manhandled onto the ship's rail. He wobbled, and turned his handsome face up to Napier, who remained wordless at his appeal.

Brundall had his eyes fixed on his captain, his sword an inch away from the young man's arse.

"Reuben Pyke," Napier said, his voice carrying easily to the watching sailors below. For those who knew him well, it held a trace of bitterness. "You have been found guilty of stealing from this ship's crew." He reached behind him and lifted the bundle wrapped in the silken shawl, throwing it down onto the deck. It rolled open, spilling petty treasures: pipes and scrimshaw, ribbons and hoops. "Do you have anything to say in your defense?"

"Ain't my stuff," Reuben said.

"No, it's really not," Napier said, his lip curling. He'd expected Reuben to lie. A couple of sailors were sorting through the trinkets with muttered oaths and most of the crew was now advancing toward where Reuben perched on the rail. "Give him what he's owed," Napier shouted, stopping the men in their tracks, "and get rid of him."

He turned, and descended the steps, followed by the bosun and Brundall. He didn't look around as he heard a scream and a splash.

The bosun ventured a further comment. "Do you think he'll make it?"

Napier looked into the sea. Reuben was swimming as fast as he could toward the island. "If he doesn't attract the sharks, I'd say he has a fair chance."

"Not much chance of that, Cap'n," Brundall said, showing him the end of his cutlass. "I'm afraid I may have pinked him a little."

Anger surged through Napier at that. Bad enough to maroon a man, but you gave him a chance. It wasn't like Brundall not to play to the Code. His voice cut through the shouts of the men, silencing them immediately. "Throw a barrel after him," Napier said, "with the things he's entitled to—in case he makes it." He looked at Brundall for a moment, as the quartermaster gave orders for a bottle of water, trousers, and a pistol to be packed in a barrel, and he paused for thought. Marooning a shipmate was one of the worst punishments a captain could bestow on a comrade—worse than certain death—and despite their dislike of Reuben, even some of the crew members looked unhappy as they watched the young man swim to shore. Napier's eyes narrowed. So why did Brundall look so happy about it?

"Weigh anchor, Cap'n?" Brundall asked. The ropes were singing above them as the wind freshened. "Good huntin' wind."

Napier shook his head. "We'll lay over a day more," he said, and saw a look of discontent pass over his quartermaster's face.

That evening, Napier drank with his bosun and quartermaster in their small cabin, seemingly celebrating the good riddance of a thief and troublemaker. Napier's own stomach was lined with a layer of the chef's goose grease and he was still relatively sober when the swarthy dogs passed out, face down onto the mess table, dead drunk to the world.

Then he searched their cabin as thoroughly as he had searched his own. It took a while but eventually, finding a loose nail at the head of Brundall's bunk, he discovered a cheap wooden casket behind one of the wall panels. With the butt of his pistol he smashed it open and was not completely surprised to find the more valuable of the items that had gone missing from the crew, items that everyone had assumed Reuben had fenced on the mainland. And there, gleaming softly in the candlelight with its rose-gold band and purple stone, was his grandfather's ring.

Anger rose up in him like a tsunami, vicious, deadly, and unstoppable. He drew his cutlass to slay Brundall where he lay. Then he stopped and smiled, and if anyone had seen Captain Napier smile that night, they would have been more afraid of him than if he were charging them with both pistols firing.

He lowered the boat and rowed to the island. The night was well advanced. For the first time since this sorry business began, he allowed himself to feel concern about Reuben. From the moment he'd seen the blood on Brundall's blade, he'd known that Reuben was more to him than he'd ever allowed himself to think. There might be no contract between them, but Napier knew he was bonded to Reuben as surely as if there was. If he'd used the pistol he'd been given and had killed himself, like so many marooned sailors, Napier vowed he would keelhaul Brundall himself and say no words over his corpse but send him to Davy Jones naked and alone.

It was a very small island and it didn't take long to find Reuben. He was sitting by the broken barrel, his face pointing away from the direction of the ship, his arms resting on his knees, the pistol in his hand. When Napier spotted him, all his doubts fell away; Brundall and the rest of them go hang, he thought. He'd have Reuben and no other, and Davy Jones take the next man who dared voice dissent. Reuben looked up as Napier approached, then leapt to his feet and raised his pistol. With deliberate slowness, Napier raised his hands.

"Nay, lad. Soft now."

Reuben's hands were shaking. "God's blood, Paul. I should kill you for what you did."

"You should. You can. I don't even have a blade, let alone a pistol." Gently he pulled aside his coat to show he was unarmed.

"What?" Reuben's face registered his confusion and shock.

"It was Brundall," Napier said, slowly. "Brundall did this to you."

"The lily-livered, whoring son of a diseased wharf—"

"Yes. Precisely that. Now—are you going to shoot me or am I forgiven? Are we going to punish the bastard together?"

Reuben dropped the pistol and in two steps he was in Napier's arms. Napier groaned, and pushed Reuben to the sand, rough and eager. It took mere seconds to divest Reuben of the thin trousers he had on and Napier was wrapping calloused hands around Reuben's cock, wanting to touch all of him at once, wanting to brand his handprints on him to say, this is mine. *This is mine.* Reuben rolled over, straddling him around the waist, and kissed him hard; stubble bit against stubble, teeth clashed, tongues dueled. Reuben slid down, pushed open Napier's shirt, and unlaced the captain's trousers with practiced skill.

With no one to see, no one to hear on the lonely beach, Napier shouted in delight as Reuben swallowed his cock to the root. No whore in Hispaniola could do the things that Reuben could do with his tongue and fingers. After the initial swallow, Reuben pulled away and began to tease, soft delicate kisses starting from Napier's hips, his fingers drifting up and down anywhere but to the waving flagpole of a cock. Napier arched his back, his fingers seeking purchase helplessly in the sand, like a butterfly pinned to a board. Reuben teased him mercilessly, never staying in one place, never giving any hint of where he'd kiss next, or how hard the next kiss or lick might be. By the time he'd sucked Napier's balls into his mouth, one at a time, Napier lost his control.

"I swear," he cried, "I'll tie you to the mast. Thrash you within an inch of your life." Reuben continued his torture, and Napier grew more desperate. "Everything," he gasped, "every pearl I own, every treasure of the deep...just never—ever—stop."

Napier heard a deep chuckle as Reuben, seemingly taking pity on his poor desperate captain, shifted up and, inch by red-hot inch, he swallowed Napier's cock. To Napier it felt like heaven, the cool wetness extinguishing the heat and desperation, but lighting its own fire as Reuben's tongue began its black magic. It lashed around the shaft of Napier's cock like a loose hawser, whilst eager fingers massaged and pulled on his balls with just the right amount of pleasure and pain. Reuben sucked and lapped, his tongue teasing the slit, his teeth grazing the crown in every subtle way he knew, until Napier knew that he'd expend himself if the boy didn't stop.

With savage reluctance he put his hand on Reuben's head and pulled it up and away. The lust would stay, he had no doubt of that, but there were more important things, like getting back to the ship. He had been too long away as it was. If Brundall woke and found his captain gone, they'd both be stuck on this narrow spit forever.

"Later," he said, his voice thick with want. He pulled Reuben to him and kissed him hard. "I'll not let you off my ship again," he growled.

"What'll the crew say?"

"They'll do the telling when they hear the truth. I'll let them deal with Brundall. I'm sure they'll be inventive as to a punishment for a man who not only stole, but blamed a shipmate and allowed an innocent man to be marooned."

They rowed swiftly and quietly back to the ship, and Napier felt complete. His ship. His mate. Reuben would make a good quartermaster. He fastened the jolly boat to the ladder and clambered up and over the side, pausing to pull Reuben up after him. The deck was deserted save for a watchman who knew better than to show any surprise at his captain's sudden appearance with a naked Pyke in tow.

In three short sentences, Napier let him have the truth of the matter. With a face like thunder, the sailor strode away. Sounds of an accordion and singing filtered up from the hold, and the two men stood and listened as the music stopped and angry voices broke out. Reuben moved ahead as if to go toward the crew's quarters, but Napier caught him roughly by the arm.

"Where do you think you're going?" His voice was a dangerous purr. He drew Reuben to him, gratified to see his eyes widen in surprise. Napier grinned, like a shark approaching prey.

"I thought you'd want to see what happens."

"I will," Napier said. "They'll finish him tomorrow with me as witness. What they do to him tonight is their business. The bosun can cope. They don't need the new quartermaster getting in the way, especially when he's got duties with the captain to attend to."

Napier put his arms around Reuben. He slid his hands down to cup his arse and dug his fingers into the hard muscled cheeks. "You belong here," he said huskily. He turned Reuben around, pushing him over a barrel, then unlaced himself and slid his cock into the delicious crease, finding his target. "And I belong here." With a shove, he pushed home.

As Matelotage ceremonies went, it was short, but just as effective as any other.

THE PIRATE'S SWORD

Neil Plakcy

By the end of the five-month voyage from Boston to Owyhee, I was desperate. I questioned everything, from my decision to become a missionary to the heathens of the Pacific, to my faith in God and the Bible.

Life at the Crawford School had been so much simpler. After my parents died, my uncle, a prominent merchant in Boston, paid for my tuition at the Protestant academy, with the idea that I would one day become a preacher. I was smart and well spoken, and I cut a fine figure in my black frock coat. My uncle believed the pulpit was the place for me.

Ethan Davis was two years ahead of me at Crawford, and I idolized him. He was blond, well muscled, and dashing. Six of us boys lived in a common dormitory, and often I would lie in bed a moment longer than the others, to watch Ethan rise from his sheets wearing only a pair of white linen undershorts.

I did not understand why my body reacted as it did to the sight of Ethan's rippling biceps, his flat stomach, and the outline of his erect penis, the sign of a bladder desperate to be emptied in the outhouse behind the dormitory. I was not supposed to feel that way about another boy.

And yet I had none of these feelings on Sundays, the one day when we Crawford boys were exposed to young women. During the long church services I saw the other boys exchanging glances with girls, who lowered their eyes, eyelashes fluttering like the wings of tiny birds. My eyes only wanted to feast on Ethan, resplendent in a dark coat, crisp white shirt, black bow tie, and black woolen pants that seemed molded to his buttocks.

I was despondent when Ethan graduated and left the Crawford School. My last two years at school were hell, as I tortured myself with worry that I was not good enough or strong enough to become a minister. Then, just before graduation, Ethan returned, with a demure young woman by his side, to announce a mission to preach the Lord's word to the heathens of Owyhee.

As a man, Ethan was even more handsome than he had been as a boy. His frock coat seemed to fit him more snugly, and there was something of the dandy about the way the collar of his white shirt stood up so stiffly. Ethan took the pulpit after the homily, and I thought he was looking straight at me when he announced the need for young men to join this effort.

"The men and women of the islands worship pagan gods," Ethan declaimed. "They spend their days in slothful indolence, often clothed in nothing more than a simple breechcloth."

I couldn't help remembering those mornings when I'd stared at Ethan clad just as simply, and I felt a stiffening in my loins that reminded me just how weak and sinful I was. "There will be a meeting this evening for those who are interested," Ethan announced. "My fiancée Rebecca and I will be discussing the ways of the heathens and how we may reach them."

Of course I attended the meeting, and boldly signed my name to the paperwork Ethan offered. My impure desires made me unfit to live and preach among God-fearing people; among the heathens, I could at last feel confident enough. I imagined working side by side with Ethan, perhaps sharing a common shower as we had at the Crawford School, where I'd occasionally seen him freshly scrubbed, his body glistening with droplets of water.

Once, even, I'd caught him leaving the shower with his towel wrapped around his head, exposing the entire length of his fair, blond body. I'd forced myself to look away after a moment, but that memory had stayed with me.

The next few weeks were a flurry of activity. I joined Ethan and Rebecca as they traveled the countryside, recruiting missionaries and soliciting funds. A week before we were to depart, we returned to Boston. As I stepped out of the horse-drawn carriage in front of my uncle's house, Rebecca said to me, "I have good news for you, Jonah. Tonight, we have arranged for you to meet a woman who is also interested in missionary work. Her name is Hannah."

"I'm sure I will be pleased to speak with her," I said.

Ethan laughed. "You will be pleased to do more than speak with her once you are married."

"Married?" I asked.

"Of course," Rebecca said. "You did read the agreement, didn't you, Jonah? All missionaries must be married before departing for Owyhee. We must provide good examples for the heathens."

"And you wouldn't want to be tempted by the native women," Ethan said, smiling roguishly.

I suffered fresh despair that evening as I waited to meet my appointed bride. Was this really the path God had chosen for me? But by the time I returned to the church that evening, I was determined. God had brought me a calling, and if he brought a wife to go along with that calling then I was not to complain.

Hannah Simpson was a tall, plain-featured woman of thirty years, nearly ten years older than myself, but she was a woman of great faith and determination. I was sure marrying her was the right decision. The following Sunday, the day before our ship was to depart, we were married, with my aunt and uncle in attendance.

That night, at the festivities following the wedding, which coincided with those celebrating our departure for Owyhee, I tasted rum for the first time. Not realizing its powerful effects, I drank perhaps a little too much, and so passed my wedding night in a drunken stupor. Hannah's virginity remained untouched.

The next morning I was suffering mightily from the effects of drink the night before, and Hannah had to take my arm and guide me into the ship.

There was little privacy there; the four missionary couples shared a single room, and we all learned to avert our eyes when another needed to use the chamber pot in the corner.

Three weeks into the voyage, Hannah took sick. Her sturdy body seemed ill-equipped for long confinement, and she began to shake and shiver as a fever wracked her system. Within another week, she was dead, and I was a bachelor once more, never having enjoyed the marriage bed a single time.

The temperature warmed as we neared the islands of Owyhee. We were bound for the whaling port of Lahaina. From there, we were to be dispersed throughout the islands, though with Hannah's death I imagined I would remain at Lahaina with Ethan and Rebecca, to help them.

It was not to be. The night before we docked at Lahaina, Ethan took me aside. "Though I'm sure Hannah's death has been a blow to you, you must carry on," he said.

"The Lord would wish it," I said.

We were so close I could feel the heat rising from his body. He had abandoned the custom of wearing his frock coat, at least amongst ourselves, and had opened the collar on his white shirt. At his neck I could see a triangle of fair skin, and I longed to have him take me in his arms and hold me. I fantasized about working side by side with him in the islands, our shirts off in the heat.

"Rebecca and I have decided that you should go to the island of Oahu, as planned," he said. "The natives there are in desperate need of our help. We cannot forsake them."

"If it is the Lord's will," I said.

When he left me to return to the cabin, I stared out at the sea. The sun was rising over the waves and a salty breeze swept across my face. But I could take no pleasure in it, knowing that the wind filling the sails only brought me closer to parting from Ethan. How would I survive, alone in a heathen land?

We docked at Lahaina the next day. Within a week, Ethan had found passage for me on a small ship that moved between the islands. He divided the stock of Bibles, food, and clothing among the four missionary groups and then accompanied me to the dock. "Goodbye, my friend," he said. "I hope we will meet again."

"I hope so, too, Ethan," I said.

And then he embraced me.

In that touch was the fulfillment of all my dreams. Ethan's lean, strong body pressed against mine, touching at a dozen points. I smelled the lime and bay rum of his shaving lotion, felt the heat of his breath. His chest pressed against mine, as my hands found the curve of his shoulder blades. For the briefest of seconds, in passing, his cheek brushed against mine.

And then it was over, giving me a memory that would have to take the place of his physical presence in my life. My heart heavy, I climbed aboard the small ship, and waved to Ethan on shore as the anchor was lifted and the sails unfurled.

"We should have an easy voyage," the captain said to me, as I made my way to the tiny cabin below. "As long as we don't run across any pirates."

"Pirates?" I asked in alarm. "Surely there are none in these waters?"

"There was a Frenchman some years ago," he said. "Hippolyte de Bouchard. He sailed off to California, but there have been rumors that some of his men remained in these waters. They have a secret lair on one of the outer islands, and they plunder any ships that happen to pass near them."

"I hope our course shall not take us into their grasp," I said. "I will ask the Lord to give us safe passage."

However, my prayers were not answered. A storm arose that night which battered our tiny ship and threw us off course. Several of the sailors were lost in the storm, leaving only the captain and a single mate struggling to keep us afloat. Both sails were gone and we were at the mercy of the tides. All I could do was pray; I had no skill and little strength.

I was on deck when another ship appeared on the horizon. "God has provided," I said. "We are saved."

The captain raised a spyglass to his eye and surveyed the horizon. "Not God but the Devil," he said. "Yonder's a pirate vessel. See the guns on her bulwarks? The black flag with the skull and crossbones?" He dropped the spyglass and his face was grim. "The rumors must be true."

We had no defenses. The captain sent me below, hoping to negotiate with the pirates, and I know not what happened to him or the mate. I heard the blast of a cannon, several gunshots, and a great deal of yelling. Finally two rough and ragged pirates found me in the tiny cabin. Unshaven, shaggy-haired, wearing simple undershirts and short pants, they seemed the very embodiment of evil.

I brandished my Bible at them, calling on the Lord to save me, but he was occupied elsewhere. I struggled against their grasp and was hit on the head. The last thing I remember was being grabbed and carried out, just another of their spoils.

When I awoke, I found myself in a narrow bed in a cabin not much larger than the one on the ship that had foundered. I was groggy, and the feeling reminded me of my wedding night. I could tell we were moving at a fast clip, and through a porthole I saw that the sun had set.

The door to the cabin opened and a man entered, carrying a stub of a candle. In the brief, flickering light I could see he was shirtless, the muscles of his chest and arms rippling as his body swayed slightly with the motion of the ship. "You are awake," he said. "Good."

He wore a pair of cotton trousers that reached just below his knees, cinched with a great leather belt. "Who are you?" I asked, sitting up in the bed, though the motion made my head ache. "I demand to be returned to my ship."

"There is no ship anymore," he said. "And you are in no position to make demands."

"I'll have you know," I said, attempting to stand, "that—"

The pirate pushed me back roughly to the bed. The imprint of his hand on my chest was warm, and my flesh burned where he'd touched me. He moved over to the bed and towered over me. "What is your name?" he asked.

"Jonah," I said. "Jonah Harkness. Of Boston, Massachusetts."

"I am Roger Coverly," he said. "I am the captain of this ship and its crew. Where were you bound?"

"To Oahu," I said. "I am bringing the word of the Lord to the heathens there."

He laughed. "You are well off course, Jonah Harkness."

I couldn't help staring at his body in fascination. He was a bit stouter than Ethan, his body much more a man's. His arms were stronger, more well muscled. I could see his ribs delineated against his chest, and a light dusting of fine black hair led from just under his neck down to his belt buckle. As my eyes dropped lower I saw his penis clearly outlined against the cotton of his pants.

"Do you like what you see?" the pirate captain asked.

Embarrassed at being caught, I stuttered, saying nothing much. And then, to my astonishment, he unbuckled his belt and his pants dropped to the floor of the cabin. He was wearing nothing underneath, so he stood before me as naked as the day God made him.

I remembered the brief moment years before when I had seen Ethan come out of the shower. The pirate captain's body was even more perfect than Ethan's had been, and as I watched, his penis grew and swelled, sticking out from his body like a sword.

Deep in my woolen pants I felt my own penis do the same. But I was frozen, unable to move.

"Touch it," Coverly said. "You wish to, don't you?"

I did. As if in a dream, I reached up to his penis with my hand and cupped it. The pirate's whole body swayed, and he sighed. "In your mouth," he said.

I looked up at him. I was so naïve in the ways of physical activity. "Take me in your mouth," he said. He put a hand to the back of my head and pulled me forward.

I opened my lips willingly and tasted the skin of another man for the first time. My whole body quivered with tension.

Roger Coverly moved my head back and forth at first, until I got the idea, taking his stiff penis in and out, trying to get as much of it in my mouth, and down my throat, as possible.

My own hands moved around to his buttocks, as if of their own accord.

They were smooth and firm, covered with a fine dust of hair like his chest, and I found myself pressing and squeezing them as my mouth assailed his penis.

Suddenly, Roger Coverly cried out, "Thar she blows!" and a river of hot fluid flowed out of his penis and into my throat.

He stepped back, releasing our connection, and with his right hand caressed my cheek. There was a bitter, salty taste in my mouth, but I forgot all about it when he leaned down to kiss me. His lips were rough and chapped, and they pressed against my own with great force.

His tongue, as strong and pointed as his penis, probed my mouth as he joined me on the bed, kneeling before me, my legs outstretched on either side of him. We kissed and kissed, and he began undoing the buttons of my shirt.

I was extraordinarily conscious of everything around me. The tang of salt air coming through the porthole, the rough muslin sheets beneath me, the slippery sheen of sweat that rose off Roger Coverly's body and mine as we kissed and embraced. Soon my shirt had been shucked off and our chests touched, just the way I'd longed for my chest to meet with Ethan's.

But Roger Coverly was so much more a man than Ethan had been, and he was there in my arms, where Ethan had only been a fantasy. Roger's hands stumbled awkwardly as he tried to open my pants, and in my fever I pushed him away and undid the clasps myself, pulling them open and exposing my own penis to the air and to the glance, and touch, of another man for the first time.

As he continued to plunder my mouth with his tongue, Roger grasped my tender penis in his rough, work-hardened hand and began stroking me. I felt my whole body give itself up to him and could not imagine any higher plane of pleasure.

Then he lowered his head to my groin and took my penis in his mouth.

What had I known of pleasure before that night? Nothing. A casual glance, the feeling of my own hand when the temptation to sin overwhelmed me. It was as if the high seas themselves were roiling inside me, and Roger Coverly was the pirate captain who ruled them. My whole body twitched and shivered, and I felt low moans escaping from my mouth, sounds I'd never made or heard another human being make.

A fountain burst out of the head of my penis, and Roger Coverly swallowed it, then raised his head to kiss me again. I tasted that same sour tang on his lips as we shared our bodily fluids.

Roger sat back from me and laughed. "You're a fine fellow, Jonah Harkness," he said. "You have the fine nature of an educated man, but the physical appetites of a lusty youth." He stretched. "And now we must satisfy our other appetites. You wait here."

He pulled on his pants and strode out the door. I sat back on the bed, still naked, and considered what had just happened. In the space of a few minutes, I felt that the closed doors of my inner self had been flung open, exposing my heart and soul to the demons of lust and desire.

And I'd loved every minute of it. I finally understood the hypocrisy of trying to preach the Lord's gospel when my own desires ran so counter to that which I had been taught. And yet, I remembered how many times I had read of the union of souls in the good book. Surely that was what Roger Coverly and I had experienced. How could that be a sin?

Roger was back a few minutes later bearing a tray filled with the exotic fruits I had learned grew rampant in the islands. Taking a short sword from his belt, he whacked off the spiky head of a pineapple, then with quick strokes he sliced it into rounds, then halves. It was both brawny and oddly domestic behavior, and when he handed me a rich, juicy wedge, I saw the pleasure dancing in his eyes.

Roger shucked his pants again, and the two of us explored each other's bodies as we shared bread and berries and other fruits whose names I had not yet learned. Roger delighted in placing bits of fruit over my body and then removing them with his tongue and teeth, making me feel like my flesh was being served up for his consumption.

As we ate, we spoke, of our lives and our desires. The sense of communion between us grew with every moment, until I realized, without a doubt, that I had found my true soul mate in this handsome, rapacious pirate. He unleashed appetites I had long suppressed, both physical and emotional.

Just as we were finishing, there was a rough knock on the cabin door. "Cap'n, we're coming to shore," a male voice called.

"On my way," Roger said. He stood up and pulled his trousers up over his softened penis. "You stay here," he said. "But you might want to dress yourself again." He smiled. "After all, you are a man of the cloth."

The ship's movement ceased, and I heard many loud noises. First the ship banging against a dock, ropes being thrown, an anchor splashing into the sea. Then the voices of men and women, speaking both English and a foreign tongue I took to be the native one. There was much rejoicing, and the sound of many items being tossed from the ship to the shore.

The noises were dying down outside when Roger Coverly reappeared at the cabin door. I'd dressed myself by then and stood waiting to meet him. "Is this Oahu?" I asked.

"No, as I said, you were well off course by the time we found you. This is our own little island. The natives call it Miliki."

"Will I be able to get a ship here, for Oahu?"

Roger Coverly shook his head. "We don't have regular trade here," he said. "This is a pirate island."

He took my hand. "Come, let me show you my home. You'll see, Miliki is paradise on earth."

The sun had risen as the ship was docking, and looking up I saw a blue, cloudless sky. By the time we came to the deck of the ship, most of the people I'd heard had dispersed, though we saw the occasional giggling young native woman, topless, sometimes holding hands with one of the pirates as she led him off to one of the small cabins.

From the central square, by the dock, we climbed a narrow path, surrounded by lush foliage. There was a sweet, floral scent on the air, and the sun dappled through the treetops. Brilliant green and yellow parrots cheeped and cawed, occasionally swooping just above our heads.

As Roger led me up the dirt path, under soaring coconut trees, children peeked out from between the underbrush, staring at the new arrival. He grabbed one of them by the scruff of the neck. Brown as a coconut, wearing only a loincloth, the boy could not have been more than ten, and something about his features showed the mix of white and native.

"Kimo, fetch Mr. Jonah some clothes," he said. "Something of your dad's will do, a pair of short pants and a shirt for evenings."

"Yes, Captain Roger," the boy said, and scampered away.

Very soon, we came to a small clearing. At the far side stood a wooden platform raised up off the ground, with two steps leading to it. A roof thatched of palm fronds protected the floor from the rain. As we crossed the clearing I saw a low table with mats on the floor around it, and a screen framed in wood, covered with a bright floral pattern, which seemed to shelter the sleeping area.

Roger Coverly took my hand as we climbed onto the platform and led me around behind the screen, to a large wooden bed, American in style, with a mattress and box spring. Big fluffy pillows sat at the head, and the whole was covered in a colorful quilt. I had learned in Lahaina that the missionaries encouraged the Hawaiian women to make these with the remnants of cloth left over after sewing together their muumuus.

"My one indulgence," Roger said. "A comfortable bed." He looked at me slyly. "I like to spend a lot of time there."

I didn't know what to do—but Roger did. Much more gently than he had done the night before, Roger began unbuttoning my shirt. When he finished I let it drop from my shoulders. "You are a beautiful man," he said, between kisses. "Back in Boston you covered up all your beauty in wool and cotton. Here we revel in the beautiful way the Lord made us."

My back arched as he lowered his lips to first one nipple, then the other. I had never imagined my body could feel the way Roger made it feel, as if every square inch of skin burned with a thousand candles. My penis was so stiff that it hurt as it pressed against my woolen pants.

"We are pirates," he said, when he raised his head. "I make no apology for that. We live here in nature, and we take what we need to stay alive." He smiled sardonically. "The sea provides whatever the land does not."

He kissed my lips. I didn't care if Roger Coverly broke every one of the

Ten Commandments as long as I could live with him and feel his touch. This, surely, was God's plan in bringing me to these islands, so that I could meet this man, who could make me feel this way.

I struggled with my pants, eager to drop them away. "You have so much life in you, Jonah," Roger said, as they fell to the floor. I unbuttoned my shorts as well, as he undid his own belt, and soon the two of us were naked together, the gentle wind floating under the thatched roof and caressing our bodies.

Roger led me to the bed and directed me to lie down on my chest. A moment later, his head was at my buttocks, his tongue licking me eagerly. Even more new sensations! I felt myself opening to him like a flower in the sunshine. "This is oil of the coconut," he said, bringing his fingers to my nose. The coconut was sweet but pungent, and he began massaging my back with the oil, and then my buttocks.

And then he took a single finger, coated in the oil, and used it to penetrate me. "Do you like that, Jonah?" he asked, his breath hot on my back. "Your body tells me you do."

I writhed beneath his touch, sensations coursing through me from parts of my body I had never considered before. When he'd opened me sufficiently, he coated his penis with the oil and then entered me.

At first it was painful, and I cried out. "Hold, Jonah," Roger said, caressing my shoulders as he lay his body over mine. And gradually I grew accustomed to the invasion, and wanted more of him inside me, wanted him moving in me, and I bucked my hips and he shook his loins and we moved together in a loving rhythm. He panted and gasped and then cried out, "Thar she blows!" once again as his penis erupted inside me.

The gentle breeze moved the aroma of the coconut over us as Roger turned me on my side and then lay facing me.

"I have sailed the high seas looking for a man like you, Jonah," Roger whispered to me as we cuddled together, our ankles overlapping. "I've taken men in fire and loved men in warmth, but I never met a man who responded to me with the same passion I felt, until you."

"I never knew such passion was possible," I said. I told him about

Ethan, how I'd longed just to touch him, and how deeply I'd felt our final embrace. "But that was nothing compared to what I've felt with you," I said. "My whole body is alive."

"And what of your mission?" he asked. "Do you still want to go to Oahu and spread the word of the Lord?"

"I want to stay here with you and spread your legs," I said.

"Life is not all pleasure and coconut oil," Roger said. "I am a pirate, you know. I live by plundering the wealth of others."

"Then it's a pirate's life for me," I said. "Now that I have found you, I will not be parted from you."

"You'll have to learn to sail, and wield a sword," Roger said.

"And I will," I said. "Starting with this sword here." I took my penis in my hand, and then Roger took it in his .

We practiced swordsmanship for many years together.

THE PRIZE

Jay Starre

A stiff wind off the southwest tip of Jamaica blew the two ships across the same path. It was a Capricious Fate that pushed the hurricane-damaged and isolated Spanish galleon into the merciless hands of English buccaneers. That island-scented breeze also tossed the two young men together, English pirate and Spanish nobleman. Jonathan and Carlos would find themselves bound together by the fickle Luck of the sea, but it was up to them to make what they could of that stormy sea's offered fortune.

❁

The once-stately galleon rose and fell over heavy swells, its masts broken, its crew exhausted as they struggled to repair the damage from the storm that had separated it from its fellows. On the Spanish Main, even the Spanish did not sail unescorted, lest they risk falling into the hands of pirates.

It was all too easy for Captain Daniels to swoop down and capture the limping prey. The sleek English pirate ship sent a cannon volley across the bow of the careening Spanish vessel. Surrender was swift, and under glittering blue Caribbean skies, a treasure trove of Peruvian gold was captured and transferred to the *Dancing Dolly*.

"Set the Spanish bastards adrift in boats and burn the fucking galleon.

We can't safely crew it to shore, so it's no bloody use to us as a prize."

Captain Daniels barked out his orders as the disheartened Spanish crew was herded toward small boats that looked like they'd be death traps on those swelling seas. But Capricious Fate intervened for the second time that morning as first mate Jonathan Diggs stepped forward and made his plea.

"Begging your pardon, Cap'n, but why don't we just le-leave them their ship. It's not too far to Hispaniola, and th-they'll probably make it there. We've got their bloody gold; that's all we w-want."

A tall redhead, Jonathan was usually soft-spoken, perhaps because he stuttered so much, but he was respected aboard ship. In fact, he was more than respected. He was the sweetest bit of bum-meat any of the lusty pirates had ever tasted, when offered the rare chance for a lovely suckle on the redhead's luscious cock or ass. Captain Daniels himself was not immune to Jonathan's alluring qualities.

"As you say, Jonathan my boy," Daniels growled. He fumed at the contradiction to his orders, in front of the men and all, and he looked around under dark, cruel brows for something to vent his anger on.

The pirate's awful gaze fell on the huddled Spanish crew. Recent battle-lust easily transformed into sexual lust. He'd pluck out one of the hapless Spaniards for a bit of nasty fun. His smile fooled no one as he quickly scanned the pickings, and most of the men cringed away from that frightful grin.

Not so one of them. Of medium height and stocky build, he hadn't called attention to himself previously. But now, his demeanour isolated him. Standing erect, with sturdy legs in torn breeches spread wide apart, his tattered blouse was obviously of better cut than a regular seaman's. His manner alone—head up, eyes open and, although not challenging, not looking away—marked him as different. But it was his body as well, not exactly fat but muscular and fleshy from good living. No arduous hours swabbing decks for this man.

Silken black curls grazed the nape of his neck. Amber eyes under pencil-thin brows, wide cheeks, a generous mouth, a smallish nose, and a dimple in the chin made him look very young, while a slim goatee traced his chin line and challenged that immaturity.

"That one. He's mine. The rest of you bloody buggers can keep your fucking ship and the hell with you!"

It was done. Rough pirate hands seized the Spaniard. He didn't resist, but his muscular arms and thighs tensed and his full lips tightened. He would prove no whimpering coward, those who watched could see.

Captain Daniels felt a stiff prick throb under his breeches. He would open that tight mouth shortly, with the dripping head of his cock! His mood returned to its previous state of treasure-intoxicated joy, until his first mate's stuttering voice once more smashed that happy equilibrium.

"Sir, no!" Jonathan's shout rang out above the hubbub of greedy pirates about their lucrative business of transferring gold. A sudden hush followed as eyes swung to the pair, captain and first mate.

"Sir, I claim the m-man as my prize. I forgo my share of the g-g-gold instead."

Outrageous! Captain Daniels was on the verge of stepping forward and backhanding his insolent first mate. But the crew watched, and Captain Daniels was a wily leader. Buccaneers were fickle in their allegiances.

The pirate captain grinned. "Take him, and be damned with you, Johnny! I'll take your bloody fucking gold in his stead and be glad." Then Captain Daniels stepped in close, his hot breath hissing in Jonathan's face. "And I'll expect your willing hole, mouth or sphincter, for my prick later, since you've robbed the hungry pole of its prize this morning!"

Jonathan nodded and smiled. His soft green eyes didn't falter as they stared back into Daniels's dark orbs. The Captain was cruel, but could be counted on to keep his word. The Spaniard belonged to Jonathan and for some insane reason that morning, that was all that mattered.

Jonathan sidestepped his burly captain and moved quickly to take charge of his prize. For a moment, he wondered what had come over him to challenge Daniels in that way, and for what? But then his calloused hand wrapped around his captive's firm forearm and their eyes met for the first time. Jonathan felt the breath of fate, as warm and immediate as the stench of Captain Daniels's cruel breath only recently inhaled.

"Come. I'm Jonathan. First m-mate of the *Dancing Dolly*. I won't be h-hurting you none, man. Just d-d-do what I tell you. Can you s-speak English?"

"*Sí*," a husky voice replied. Jonathan felt a small tremor in his spine at the sound of that voice, and his prick nudged its way upward in his breeches. The Spaniard was handsome, and brave, too.

Jonathan had his own cabin, one of the four aboard the English pirate vessel. Cramped, with a real bed, and barely any floor space but a commodious cupboard for his belongings, the room was tidy and clean.

"I'm locking you in. It's f-for your own bloody good, man. There's water in the tub and soap if you want to take a b-bath. *Comprendes*?"

Jonathan and the Spaniard stood close in the small room. Eyes like molten gold gazed into Jonathan's sea-green orbs. The Spaniard nodded, glancing at the round copper tub sloshing in the corner. Jonathan himself had been about to bathe when they'd spotted the Spanish galleon. The water was clean, although only lukewarm.

"I'll be back. What's y-y-your name?"

"Carlos Ernesto Rodriguez y Morales. *Gracias, señor*."

Jonathan tore himself away, realizing his fingers were still clamped over the Spaniard's muscular forearm.

He locked the door behind him and strode into the maelstrom of a reveling pirate ship enjoying its good fortune. For the next hour he managed to force the crew, many of them already drunk, to steer the heavily loaded vessel away from their abandoned prey and into calmer seas along the nearby coast of Jamaica. They would be relatively safe in the quiet waters while the crew got down to inevitable business of a drunken orgy.

Fortunately Captain Daniels himself was the first to take to the rum. He was safely in his own cabin slaking his lust within the upended bottom of a dark-skinned former slave turned pirate. The young Solomon's black butt cheeks spread wide would capture Daniels's pirate prick and attention for the remainder of the day and night, hopefully.

Jonathan picked his way through grappling pirates locked in sexual contest. Slurping lips roamed up and down turgid pricks in some cases, while naked white arses rode fat purple cocks as other pirates pleased each other. In couplings, or sometimes more, with three or four randy pirates taking turns, they thrust pricks into their companions' sweet orifices. All this randy lust transpired in broad daylight on the deck itself under the cloudless afternoon sky.

The sights and sounds of pirates in lust, the smell of spit and spunk, tar and canvas and hemp rope, the heavy stench of salt air now redolent with a tropical shoreline's heady smells, combined together in Jonathan's nostrils. His senses reeled by the time he reached his locked cabin. He hesitated at the door, uncertain as to what he would find, or even what he himself intended.

The Spaniard was obviously a nobleman. Realistically, Jonathan could earn a lucrative ransom and thus offer the man his freedom once that ransom was paid. His intentions were not evil toward the unfortunate Spaniard, not really. Yet Jonathan's prick, a lengthy pole of throbbing desire, had its own selfish agenda.

He wanted to fuck that comely young Spaniard. Fuck him in the mouth, and the ass, and in the mouth again. And in the ass again. He had never wanted to fuck anyone so much. But he also had never desired an unwilling sexual conquest. And why would this Carlos be willing to have sex with a pirate like Jonathan?

The redheaded first mate unlocked the door, undecided and trembling, slid inside and then locked the door behind him before he turned to look for his captive.

Jonathan gasped aloud. Carlos Ernesto Rodriguez y Morales was naked. Entirely naked.

And he was sprawled out on Jonathan's narrow bunk in the most provocative position possible—on his belly, with his thighs spread apart, his ass crack exposed and his full ball sac and swollen prick laid back between his parted legs on the bed. Gaze soft, his half-shut golden eyes peered boldly up into Jonathan's, while a lush mouth slightly open revealed straight white teeth.

Jonathan's own eyes roamed greedily over the expanse of naked flesh. Powerful arms with bulging biceps folded under a smooth chest. Broad shoulders and a back packed with muscle descended toward a waist that was not feminine slim, but manly fit.

Below that waist, ass cheeks swelled into twin mounds of amber-smooth perfection. Parted in a beckoning spread, the deep valley between those cheeks hid a hole Jonathan yearned to explore. Lower still, thick thighs and powerful calves ended in elegant bare feet.

"I'll t-take a bath, Carlos," Jonathan blurted out. His instinct was to leap on the prone Spaniard and slake his own burning lust, but something stronger urged caution.

Jonathan stripped, with those golden eyes watching his every move. Scabbard and sword hit the floor with a jangling thump. Garish crimson blouse floated up from his upraised arms; heavy, blood-spattered navy-blue breeches slithered down his lean thighs. His prick, swollen into a lengthy fuck-sword, was unashamed as it thrust out from his naked hips.

Jonathan wondered what Carlos thought of him, his looks and naked body. He had been told he was handsome, with his mop of thick red hair and freckle-tanned complexion. His features were bold but regular, a small goatee of reddish-auburn emphasizing a strong chin. Twin gold rings dangled from his ears and a heavy silver chain from his neck, reminding one he was a pirate after all. His was all lean muscle traced with scars from years of violent buccaneering, even though he was almost as young as this Spaniard, who looked so smooth and unmarred by life's travails.

He trembled under Carlos's gaze and one of his hands accidentally grazed his own lurching pole as he stepped into the small copper tub. Jonathan gasped aloud as he noted his prone captive's response to that inadvertent stroke.

Carlos was watching Jonathan's every move from those lidded, golden eyes. When that hand rubbed against Jonathan's lengthy prick and the drooling pole had jerked like a living thing, Carlos let out a deep sigh, rolling his hips at the same time to lift and spread them farther apart.

Jonathan's throat constricted in reaction to that sensual roll. His cock twitched and dribbled precome. His entire body shook as he crouched down and began to bathe in the lukewarm bath water. It was a nasty delight to be washing in the water that his captive had only recently bathed in. That same water that slid down his own naked body had run down Carlos's naked form, into the heated crevices, over the belly and down into the crotch, the asscrack.

Carlos lifted his head and watched even more intently. His thighs opened up and his ass cheeks clenched and then relaxed. Jonathan could see the Spaniard's cock, lying against the bed covers down between his spread legs. The hood slid back as that fat snake swelled and lengthened, revealing a pink head and a slippery slit.

Jonathan had never enjoyed a more sensual, exciting bath. While he soaped up, paying careful attention to lathering his raging hard-on, Carlos watched and waited. As Jonathan's calloused hand stroked his own soapy boner, Carlos began to emit low moans, roll his luscious hips more wantonly, and spread his thighs farther apart.

The bath ended abruptly when Carlos offered the ultimate tease. Sliding one of his muscular arms downwards across his back and then into his own parted crack, he buried an elegant hand in that deep valley, probing and poking.

Jonathan grunted aloud at that lewd display. He reared up out of the bath and dripping wet, lunged for the bed. Carlos, who had been staring intently with mouth half-open, suddenly smiled, a golden flash of delight that sent a shiver of pleasure through Jonathan's lean and vigorous limbs.

"I have to h-have that arse!" he gasped out as he settled down on the edge of the bed, wet and naked and sporting a raging pink boner.

"*No problema*," a husky whisper promised. Accented English followed: "I am your prize."

Jonathan sat on the bed sideways, facing toward that amazing arse now within reach. His own lean thigh, smooth and white, pressed against the thicker amber flesh of Carlos's leg. Staring closely, Jonathan realized the Spaniard was mostly smooth too, but that a soft down of dark hair coated the naked flesh along the swell of ass mounds and into the deep crack between—where Carlos's own hand rooted in lusty abandon.

Jonathan yearned to explore that hidden valley. He wanted that ass, and that hole! It was his prize, after all, and Carlos was not objecting, far from it. Jonathan still hesitated, a natural caution holding him back. What did he want? Just a hole, a beautiful hole no doubt, but just a hole?

His thoughts were scattered to the winds by the Spaniard's next move. Carlos lifted and heaved his hips, his magnificent ass opening farther, while the fingers of his rooting hand splayed. Long fingers spread open the butt valley, revealing and displaying a puckered pink hole.

That hole quivered, pouted and clamped, slightly swollen to prove a finger had just been teasing it. Jonathan's eyes were locked on that tempting offering. A pair of fingers, tanned and calloused, rubbed over that smooth orifice.

Those fingers were his own! Jonathan had reached out without thinking, caution abandoned. He was touching that silken hole, feeling the heated flesh, the twitching sphincter, the half-gulping need of the little anal mouth as it pressed back against his exploring fingertips.

"*Sí, sí, ohhhhhhhh,*" Carlos moaned, lifting his hips and rolling them as he rubbed his own butthole against those blunt fingertips.

It was in that first intimate touch that Jonathan sensed the willingness of his lusty young prize. At times, his sex partners had been merely craving release, and Jonathan was only a convenient body to aid in that release. Rarely had a craving been this strong and this obvious. Jonathan believed, rightly or wrongly, that this craving was for him, for Jonathan alone.

The young pirate's fingers traced the outline of that gulping hole, teasing it open, stroking the sensitive lips and exposed inner flesh. He gazed in awe at the way it tightened like a vice, then pouted outward to clutch at his fingertips. The heaving ass mounds, so full and sexy, thrust up from the bed against his hand, begging for Jonathan's touch. The redheaded pirate's other hand came out to knead and fondle that smooth pair of butt globes, delighting in the roll and heave of hot muscle.

Carlos's hand moved to clutch at Jonathan's rearing dick, pulling it down and against a satin ass cheek. Those elegant fingers stroked and pumped cock while pressing it against heaving ass, creating a nasty image of hard, dripping prick ready to spear pouting, pink hole at any moment of their choosing.

Jonathan spit down into the spread crack, his saliva landing right on target. The slippery goo dribbled into the gulping anal maw and the pirate followed it with his fingertips. Two blunt digits slid between the pursed butt lips, spit easing the way into a clamping inferno of quivering guts.

"*SÍ! DIOS!*" Carlos grunted out as that pair of fingertips wormed their way inside him.

Jonathan heard his own guttural moan. He smiled, all at once in no hurry, wishing only that the moment would never end, the gentle rocking of the ship never cease, the slanting evening sunlight streaming through the small porthole remain the same forever. That hole, opening to his insinuating fingers, would open to him forever too, welcoming him inside and never letting him go.

Jonathan fingered the hole, gently but with insistent pressure. He twisted the pair of fingers in circles, stretching the sphincter to Carlos's moans. He pressed inward so the knuckles rubbed the tender rim, spitting down on the hole to add gooey lubricant. He frigged in and out, a smacking slurp loud in the room's stillness. Carlos heaved and rolled, fucking his own ass over those probing fingers, taking them in, spitting them out, his hole growing more slack by the minute.

When Jonathan added a third finger, Carlos's hand on the pirate's cock squeezed fiercely, which only added to their mutual excitement. Jonathan's prick drooled against a heaving amber butt cheek, stiff and long, while his three fingers slithered deep inside the Spaniard's oozing hole, twisting on their way inside, meeting slack acceptance and throbbing heat.

Jonathan gazed down at that nasty sight. Three of his rough, calloused fingers were buried between swollen, pink ass lips. The Spanish nobleman's beautiful butt quivered and humped, fucking itself on that hand with groaning need. Carlos's cock, pressed downward on the bed, rubbed and pumped against the rough woolen blankets. Jonathan's cock was trapped in Carlos's fingers, oozing precome in a constant drizzle against the mound of Carlos's writhing ass.

Jonathan was going to fuck that hole soon enough. But for now, he reveled in the slow probing, the knuckle rubbing, the twisting and withdrawal that had Carlos whimpering and grunting.

One more thing to do first, he thought with a nasty grin. Pulling out his three spit-lubed fingers, Jonathan bent over and buried his face between those heaving mounds. The hole, swollen into a gaping pit, welcomed the warm stab of tongue, sucking it inside. Jonathan slurped and smacked as he ate ass with a need more powerful than any hunger for either silver or gold.

He spread that ass with both calloused palms, rubbed his goateed chin against satin ass mounds, probed hole with his darting tongue, and sucked wet ass lips open and outwards with his hungry mouth. Carlos crooned out a constant encouragement in garbled Spanish, his thighs wide apart and his cock humping the woolen blanket beneath.

Jonathan abandoned that nether mouth with a reluctant smack of his lips. He mounted the sprawled-out Spaniard. Feeling his own naked limbs slide over the smooth flesh beneath him, he reveled in the sensual touch of belly against butt, arms against sides, knees against thighs, calves shoving calves wide apart. He planted his hands on either side of Carlos's broad back, pinning the Spaniard's arms at his chest. His raging boner slithered between the satin butt mounds, rubbing up against a spit-soaked sphincter.

"I'm going to f-f-f-fuck your sweet Spaniard arse," he hissed.

"*Por favor, sí,*" Carlos replied in a husky whisper.

Jonathan aimed his prick head at the wet centre of Carlos's crack. The anus was stretched and hungry, but Carlos was so excited he clamped and snapped his sphincter against the drooling cock head. Jonathan merely rubbed up and down and back and forth along the snapping butt lips, teasing and soothing at the same time. He was going to fuck, and there was no need to rush it.

Carlos was in more of rush, his need almost desperation. For a moment, Jonathan sensed that desperation, realizing the awful position his captive was in. A prize to a pirate, his future uncertain.

That thought slid away as the sensual delight of the hole opening to his prick took over. As he thrust, Carlos pushed back, hole lips gaped apart, and gooey prick head slipped inside. Jonathan, feeling that quivering anal mouth throb around his cock, lost control and shoved with all his might.

He impaled the Spanish nobleman with his pirate fuck-sword, to the root.

"*Dios!*"

"Bloody h-h-hell!"

Torrid anus encircled Jonathan's prick. Smooth ass heaved up to push against his belly and balls. The young pirate now had what he wanted, hole possessed. His prize had given that sweet slot up, surrendered his most intimate treasure. Jonathan fucked ass.

The redhead slammed his cock in and out, driving the hapless Spaniard all over the bed. A raging heat burned upwards from the battering head of his prick, through the pummelling shank, into his belly and heaving chest and pounding heart. Right into his heart. Never, never, had he fucked so savagely, yet with such rare emotion at the same time.

Carlos reveled in the rough pounding, his asshole rubbed and massaged and worked into a gooey pit of passion. His own prick slammed down into the bed beneath them, forced against the rough woolen blanket, battered by their slamming bodies.

Jonathan fucked with all his might, and felt Carlos responding with equal ferocity, driving upwards with his hips to impale himself on lengthy pirate prick, twisting and writhing and massaging his own guts with that relentless pole driving into him.

Carlos surrendered his load quickly. Incessant pummelling of his sensitive anal ring and aching prostate combined with the mashing of his prick against rough wool and drove him to savage orgasm. His body lurched, his thighs tossed even farther apart. His asshole sucked in prick and his own prick spewed out semen.

Jonathan continued pounding ass, reveling in the flopping orgasm beneath him, and then the slack, welcoming hole in its aftermath. Carlos had not had enough, not by far. His asshole craved that cock, even more now that his own prick's need had been satiated. Now he was only hole, hole for his pirate captor.

Sweat soaked them both in the closeness of the room. Sunlight coming in from the porthole winked out and twilight replaced it. Jonathan's own orgasm was held at bay by an unshakable desire not to let this moment end. He wanted to fuck his prize forever. Never let the young Spanish nobleman go.

Jonathan rolled Carlos over onto his back, gazing down in his handsome face as he lifted the heavy smooth thighs and pushed back the knees. His prick slammed back inside the pouting, fucked asshole as Carlos let out a grunted whoosh of breath.

They kissed. Mouths opened and tongues dueled, sloppy, greedy. Carlos was a pair of wet pits for Jonathan's pleasure. The sweat-soaked pirate thrust with his hips violently forward, deep-drilling into the hole with growing ferocity. His lengthy, glistening pink prick exited completely, quivered against the smooth butt crack for a brief moment, then slammed balls-deep to both their grunts.

Orgasm came, inevitably, sadly. Jonathan sucked in Carlos's tongue as his prick again exited the steamy hole and then squirted. Sticky, reeking come splatted the Spaniard's upended butt crack and pouting hole.

They continued kissing while Jonathan's body writhed in orgasmic rapture. The kiss lasted until eventually both their bodies subsided into an exhausted slackness.

The moment their kiss ended, they began to talk, Carlos in halting, heavily accented English, Jonathan in stuttering shy pauses. It was night, and they could barely see each other in the dim light from the porthole, a full moon on the sea outside offering that pale illumination.

Carlos told of his plantation on the Spanish island of Puerto Rico. He explained he had been headed to Spain for a year of university. Jonathan admitted he had been a pirate since he was twelve, more than ten years, since Queen Bess had given the English ships her permission to ravage the Spanish in their Caribbean stronghold.

They fondled each other as they spoke. Jonathan stroked Carlos's smooth, lush chest and pert nipples. He slid a hand back down between Carlos's warm thighs and into his deep ass valley, teasing the just-fucked hole with dipping fingertips. Carlos ran elegant hands all over Jonathan's lean limbs, rubbing a stiff prick and cupping full balls.

It was several hours later they both stopped talking and realized the ship had gone deathly silent. The drunken orgy around them had come to its inevitable conclusion. Most of the crew was unconscious. It would have been the first mate's task to make certain someone was on lookout, someone was watching the anchor, the wheel.

Hands stopped roaming at the same moment. Voices halted. Their heads were close, Carlos's dark curls nestled in the crook of Jonathan's lean shoulder.

"It is time, Señor Jonathan."

The pirate understood. With a shaky intake of breath he rose, reluctantly abandoning warm arms and thighs. He lit a candle, its feeble light flickering and swaying in the gentle rock of the ship. All at once he felt fear. Fear that he was about to lose something vitally important.

But he dressed anyway, as did the Spaniard nobleman. Together, they slipped out into the corridor and up to the deck. A fat full moon cast eerie light over a deck in shambles. Pirates had fallen where they stood, dead drunk.

Carlos climbed stealthily into the small boat and Jonathan lowered it from above, gazing down as the Spaniard gazed up. When the boat made a quiet splash onto the surface of the sea, their gazes were locked.

Carlos waved him down, moonlight illuminating his smile, his soft curls. Jonathan hesitated. How could he take such a risk? He would lose either way, his life as a freebooting pirate, or this new thing, a body and a man suddenly more important to him than anything else in life.

He stared down at Carlos. He felt as if he would die if he never saw that smile again, or caressed that body, plunged his cock into that hot, willing ass. Jonathan trembled violently, but then he all at once grinned.

He was a pirate, after all! He took risks. He loved adventure. With an agile leap, he bounded off the deck of the *Dancing Dolly* and down into the waiting boat and Carlos's welcoming arms.

As they rowed silently toward shore, Carlos whispered to his new pirate lover. "Did you steal some gold?"

Jonathan's mouth dropped open. He hadn't even thought of it! What kind of a pirate was he?

Carlos laughed quietly, reading that look for what it meant. "*No problema.* I took some from a sleeping pirate. We will buy you a ship with it. *Sí?*"

Jonathan laughed too, but couldn't care less about the gold. He didn't look back. He had his prize.

CODE OF CONDUCT

William Holden

I realized later that I would have fared better if I had let him kill me. I had the chance then to join my mother and father at last, after years of living alone on the streets in a small village near Bridgetown on the isle of Barbados. But when the time came and I was faced with death, I chose to live. It was the year of our Lord 1749. Thinking back and knowing what might now become of me, I wished I had let him fire his flintlock upon me—but instead I did the unthinkable. I reached out and caressed Captain Blair's leg.

I'm not sure why I did it. I had never acted upon my desire for men. But there he stood before me, alone in a dark, desolate alley with his men bellowing in the distance as they pillaged . His pistol was aimed and ready to extinguish my life. There was no fear inside of me at that moment, only a longing to be with another man before my life ended. The muscles in his leg tightened at the first touch from me, yet he didn't pull away. His legs were stout and strong with coarse, black hair covering them. I moved my hand further down to his ankles, and then his feet. They were dirty and calloused yet the feel of them drew me closer.

I cautiously sat up from my makeshift bed of old linens. Captain Blair kept the pistol in hand, but moved it away from me. My hand moved back up his leg until I reached the hem of his knee breeches. They were thin and worn looking. I could tell by the movement underneath the cotton that he was intrigued. I moved my hand away from his leg, and placed it over his breeches. I felt him rise to my touch. He backed away quickly. His pistol once again aimed directly at me.

"Why do such a foolish thing, boy?" His rough voice echoed through the small street. "Don't you know many of men have been hanged for such an act?

I sat speechless. My body trembled with fear and desire. "I am sorry, sir. I fancied that…that perhaps I could be of service to you, if you would only spare my life."

"You are a bold one, aren't ya. How old are you, boy?"

"I am nineteen, sir." My body jumped as a cannon fired in the distance. The darkened sky exploded in a blaze of orange and red.

"Yes, mighty young you are to be living such a life." He pointed the pistol at my makeshift home. "What is your name, boy?"

"Adam, sir." I watched him look me over, as if questioning my abilities. I was not as strong as most men in the village. The lack of a trade kept me low on coins for food and proper nutrition.

"Adam, is it?" He placed the pistol in his belt and walked toward me. "The name of the first man, but not a very manly name. What makes you think I or my men would have any use for someone like you? Have you got any skills?"

"No, sir, but I am good with my hands." I looked up at him as he towered above me. His natural parts dangled behind his thin breeches. "I'm sure I could be of use to you somehow."

"Your accent is unusual for these parts." He looked at me questioningly. "Perhaps I could use a young lad as yourself. It's been a long time since I've had the proper company."

My heart beat like a drum in my chest as I watched him unbutton the front flap of his breeches. My hand trembled as I brought it up and entered the flap. I could feel the heat of his body as my fingers lay upon his prick. It was thick and damp. I felt him lengthen in my grasp as I pulled it out of his garment. It hung heavily in front of me, its base covered in a mass of tight curly hair. I was amazed at how different it looked than my own. I brought my face closer to it. The acrid musk of his sweat turned my stomach at first, but after a few moments the scent became intoxicating. My lips trembled. I licked them to remove the dryness, as I opened my mouth to take him in. The feel and taste of him was like nothing I could have expected. The soft, almost silky skin filled my mouth with such pleasures I became dizzy. As I took more of him in, I wondered if all pricks were like this. Would mine feel and taste the same way?

He continued to grow inside my mouth. His length became more than I could take. He pushed into me. I gagged and had to withdraw.

"Boy, you need to do better than that if you expect to please me."

"I am sorry, sir." I looked up at him as I moved my hand up and down the length of him. He moaned with pleasure. "You are just so big and I lack experience." I took a deep breath to calm my spirits then wrapped my lips around him again. He stopped me.

"As I can see." He laughed. "Stand up and remove your garments. There's yet another way you can service me."

I stood up at his request and began to unbutton my blouse. The heat of the night air nuzzled my skin as I removed the cloth. I unbuttoned my trousers and stepped out of them. His eyes widened as he stared at my nakedness. My hard prick was damp with excitement. Its lack of heft caused it to stick out in front of me. I touched myself as I have done many times, but found it somehow more exciting this time.

"Turn around and get down on your hands and knees, boy." His voice was more forceful than before. I was nervous at the thought of what he intended to do with his prick, yet somehow thrilled. I did as he asked. I felt him lower himself behind me. His thickness lay heavily against the small opening I was offering to him. He spat in his hand then rubbed it over my arse. I felt its large head push against me. He grabbed my hips for leverage and entered me. Pain ripped through my body like nothing I could have imagined. I gasped and yet I said nothing. I held my breath against his thrusts, fighting back the urge to pull away. The pain began to lessen. My prick became hard once more as pleasure swept through my body. I became light headed at the feeling of him inside of me, his prick pushing longer and harder into me. The sounds of our action echoed around us. My prick began to swell. I touched it and began frigging myself. The pleasure continued to build inside of me through every crevice of my sweating body. His prick thickened again inside of me as he continued to use my arse. My hand quickened upon my prick as I felt the rush of his hot semen unload into me. He thrust himself into me one last time to release again. In a rush of burning heat I spent in a spasm of pleasure.

He laid his body down on top of me; our bodies were worn and exhausted. Suddenly a voice bellowed behind us.

"Captain, what have you done?" The tone was one of disgust. "You've buggered this young lad!"

I felt Captain Blair remove himself from me as he stood to confront this man. He quickly tucked his shrinking prick back into his breeches. The two faced each other. Without a word Captain Blair pulled his flintlock and shot the man. The other fell to the ground. His life poured out before me.

"Rory was a worthless soul, a no-good powder monkey and an untrustworthy man," Captain Blair exclaimed as he turned to me. "No person shall bear witness to our acts and live to tell about it. You boy, get off the ground. You shall take Rory's place upon my ship, the *Libertine*."

Three months after that night, the smell of death and the picture of Rory's lifeless body lying in front of me still haunted my sleep. He lost his life because of me, and now I feared more would die for what I had done or what I might become.

☸

Most of the crew had already boarded the *Libertine*, drunk with ale and their victory. Everything about them was unkempt, including their manners. They stared at me, mistrust in their glazed eyes. One of the men approached us. He was tall, with broad shoulders. His long black hair hung below the kerchief tied around his head. He studied me before speaking to the captain.

"Why bring this lad to our ship, Captain?" He spoke with an accent different from the captain's. "And where is Rory? He was supposed to fetch you from the village."

"Alas, Gregor," the captain replied, as he tightened his grip upon my arm. "This boy has found himself in a bit of trouble tonight. He has taken upon himself to do away with Rory."

My heart sunk inside my chest as I heard the captain tell the untruthful tale of my crimes against the crew.

"Then he shall hang for his actions!" Gregor shouted, echoed by the others. Cheers and curses rang through the air as the rest of the crew gave their approval.

"He shall not hang tonight," the captain shouted.

"Ah, it is not up to you, Captain. According to the Code of Conduct, as quartermaster I can call a vote by the crew to determine this boy's fate."

"I know the Code, Gregor." His voice carried an edge to it I had not previously heard. "A vote you shall have, but not before I have my say." His grip loosened on my arm. He looked down at me. His eyes were ablaze with desire. "It is true that this boy, who calls himself Adam, has taken Rory's life. But we still have more trouble ahead of us. We sail for the Dutch Antilles and we need proper weapons and powder. Without Rory, we shall lack shot when we defend ourselves against the Dutch army. Adam here shall take Rory's place aboard the *Libertine*, making us powder and cleaning our weapons. If he proves useless or untrustworthy then we shall hang him, but not until we have succeeded in reaching our destination."

I watched as the crew talked among themselves, deciding my fate. I looked up at Captain Blair, wanting to speak, to ask why he told such a lie. He must have seen the question in my eyes.

He turned to me and whispered, "Boy, if you say anything against me, you shall live to regret it. No one must know of what we did or we shall both hang. You pledged your service to me back there in the village, and you will keep your promise." He glanced back toward his crew, who were still debating my future, then turned to me again. His breath, hot and sour from spirits, battered my face. "You are a mighty fine young boy. You serviced me well and for that I have spared your life. You will not doubt me, or my actions. You shall do what I say, when I say, without murmur and without fail. Do you understand me?"

"Yes, sir."

"And what interests might the two of you have to be discussing?" Gregor's voice came from behind the captain. He walked over to me. His eyes watched every move I made. He turned to the captain. "You were wise in your actions to bring this boy on board. The crew and I will not overrule you."

"As I thought," the captain grumbled as he walked away. "Take him to his quarters. He shall begin his training in the morning."

"Yes, Captain." Gregor grabbed my arm and led me away. When we reached the lower deck he stopped and turned to me. I felt as if he read my body, looking for its lies. His face was rough and dirty, masking what was left of his strikingly handsome youth. He was unlike the others in that he had no beard or whiskers upon his face except for the day's growth. "The captain has never allowed an islander on our ship before. You have no skills or trade, so why does he bring you? What are you hiding?"

"Nothing, sir." My voice trembled, but not from fear. It was desire that shook my voice—a strange, overpowering desire for Gregor.

"We shall see about that." He moved in closer as he spoke, surrounding me with his musky scent. "A word of warning to you. Captain Blair is a cruel and hateful man. If you are to survive, you must know that he cannot be trusted. Do as he says, but know that he always speaks from his own greed."

"Thank you, sir." I took another breath of him in. Something stirred inside of me. I felt myself thicken in my breeches. "I'm here to do what is asked of me. Captain Blair spared my life and for that I owe him my service."

"You are a young and foolish boy, then." He rested his hand on my shoulder. "Your sleeping quarters are through that door." He turned me around and pressed his body against my back, his face rested next to mine. "I'd advise you to rest—your training will start in the morning." We both stood there in silence. I felt his body rise up and down against mine with every breath he took. I didn't understand the closeness Gregor afforded me, but welcomed it all the same. I left him standing there and entered my small quarters. The wooden planks creaked in the distance as I heard Gregor turn and leave.

I lay there in the darkened room touching myself, the lingering scent of Gregor in my nose. I became hard almost immediately. From behind the closed door I heard footsteps approaching. My heart quickened with hopes of Gregor returning. The door opened as Captain Blair walked in.

He stood looking at me without saying a word as he undid his breeches. His heavy prick fell out of the thin material. He stroked it. I watched as it lengthened in his hand. My desire for another man overcame me. The captain repulsed me with his filth and demeanor, yet I couldn't risk his finding that out.

"What are you waiting for, boy?" He whispered. "Get over here on your knees."

"I thought perhaps you might prefer to remove all of your garments and lay with me?"

The look on his face startled me. "Remember your place, boy. You do not question me." He stepped toward my cot. His prick swayed with the movement. "I am not like you. You have the filthy desire for men, for the unnatural act. You are nothing more to me than a vessel for my lust. My whore."

He pulled me roughly around to stand over me, a leg to each side of my body. He grabbed the back of my head and pulled me closer to him. My desire overcame my repulsion. I eagerly opened my mouth to receive the soft silkiness of his prick. It was already moist with his need, the flavor of which made my hunger grow. I reached inside his breeches and began caressing his large, hairy bollocks. I felt him lengthen in my mouth and prepared myself so as not to gag. The large tip pushed against my throat. I took a deep breath to relax, letting the full length of him inside.

"Now, that's better," the captain moaned. "You learn quickly."

I felt his movements quicken against my face. His curly bush became damp with my spit and his moisture. He continued to pierce my mouth. I moved my hand between my legs and touched my own swelling need. I too was wet with desire. I moved my hand up and down the length of it, feeling more of my excitement expel from it.

The captain's prick suddenly began to feel hot within me. I could feel the pulse of his blood running through the thick veins of his prick, which now filled my mouth. His body began to tremble, then to shake. He grunted and groaned like an animal in heat. I could feel his raw unmet needs building inside of him. He grabbed my head with both hands and thrust himself into me. My mouth became flooded with his thick, bitter liquid. I swallowed the first of it as it exploded into my throat. The feeling and taste of a man's semen was like nothing I could have expected. My hunger for more grew as another jolt of him washed into my mouth. I continued to suck his prick, trying to devour every drop. His movements slowed. Then without warning he pushed me off him. I fell against the cot. I lay there with my swelling prick in my hand and the taste of him still on my tongue. I began to frig myself in front of him, hoping he might touch me instead. He stared at me with disgust. I could feel my release getting closer. My body damp with sweat lay trembling on the bed. A moan escaped my lips as he turned to leave. The familiar pleasure swept through me as he closed the door behind him. I showered my body with my own hot liquid as the thought of Gregor returned.

☸

That was how my life began aboard the *Libertine*. Every night Captain Blair returned to my room to satisfy his needs, and each time he became more heartless and cruel. I thought about resisting but knew I couldn't. So I reconciled myself to allowing his use of my body, in hopes that some day someone else would in turn allow me the privilege of his body. That night came within a week of the *Libertine* reaching the Dutch isles. It placed me one step closer to the place from which I could never return.

A storm swept up off the North Sea. Many of the hands were drunk on ale when we realized we had to ride it out. I had retired early to my cabin in hopes of easing my sickness from the ship's rolling and turning. I had closed my eyes to rest my body when I heard footsteps approaching. My heart sank with the knowledge that Captain Blair was making his nightly visit, earlier than usual. I readied myself for his use as the door opened. Gregor walked in and closed it quietly behind him.

I raised myself off the cot on my elbows. He sat next to me. This was a closeness I didn't know from the captain. I looked at Gregor, bewildered, when he rested his hand gently on my leg.

"Ah, don't look surprised, Adam." He spoke softly. "You and I are very much alike."

"I don't know...."

He stopped me. "Don't play the fool with me. I've known from the first your hunger for other men. I saw it in your eyes when you first looked at me as you came aboard." He moved his hand farther up my leg. "I know about the captain's visits to your quarters. And I know how hateful that man can be. Remember that it was I who warned you about him."

"Yes, but...I would have fared better without the warning."

"Do you get pleasure from him?"

"No, I do not. But my desire continues to gnaw at me...and I have no other choice."

"You show yourself young and foolish once again. Every man has his choices. He must learn to make them—and to live with what they bring. Do you desire more than what our lovely captain offers?"

I didn't know how to give an answer. I feared yet another trick, then I felt his eager eyes devouring my body.

"As I said, we are very much alike. I too desire the company of other men. I am not like the captain who abuses them for his lust." He then leaned toward me. "It was the captain that murdered Rory, was it not?"

"Yes."

"Rory was the captain's whore before you came along, and now I'm afraid that you will end up as Rory did once the captain tires of you. I could have saved Rory by telling him the things I knew, but I feared he was too loyal to the captain."

His finger caressed my cheek and followed the outline of my jaw. His touch was gentle. My body quivered with some new feeling. I looked into his eyes and brought myself closer to him. I leaned in and laid my lips upon his. They were soft and warm with a heat that poured into my body. He did not pull away; he kissed me back. As we pressed our lips deeper into each other, I felt his mouth open up. I wasn't sure what he meant, but I followed his lead and opened mine. Suddenly his tongue was inside my mouth, running along my teeth and tongue. I could taste the spirits he had drunk earlier. My body quivered again and I felt his arm move to brace me. Suddenly my mind returned to the captain and I broke our kiss.

"The captain...he can't find us like this. I expect him at any moment."

"Do not fret. I made sure that he consumed more spirits than he should. He sleeps drunkenly and cannot bother us, at least not tonight."

Gregor stood up and began to strip off his garments. I watched with new and raw desire as he unveiled his body. His chest was large and covered in a blanket of soft fur. My eyes were carried downward as I followed the trail of hair that led into his trousers. He unbuttoned them and let them fall to the ground. He stood before me, showing me for the first time the nakedness of a man's body in all its glory.

He lay down beside me and began to unbutton the undergarment I was wearing. His large fingers touched and caressed my body with each release of the buttons. He kissed me again. His hand moved down to touch my swelling prick. I thought I would surely die from the sweet pleasure of it.

His mouth left mine to touch my neck and to my chest. I raised my hands up to my head to keep the room from spinning. I felt his tongue graze across my erect tit. Lightning shot through my body as the tongue moved over my armpit. His teeth bit into the soft, tender flesh below the mass of hair as his fingers ran up and down my swollen prick.

"Be with me always." Gregor's words startled me. "And I will give you the world." He looked into my eyes as he wrapped his hand around my prick and began to pump it.

"But how?" I questioned through a moan. I felt moisture come to my tip.

"I've never spoken these words to anyone and never thought it right to do so. But you have changed me." He paused. "I believe I have fallen in love with you, Adam." He kissed me lightly as he squeezed my prick. "Just say yes, and we can be together. I will pledge to you my life and my body."

The motion of his hand against my prick, combined with the words he'd spoken, was more than I could take. My body shivered as the first spurt of seed shot out. He laughed at the spasms of pleasure coursing through me. He brought out of my prick nineteen years of longing. He leaned down and licked a goodly amount of the milky seed off my stomach and shared it with me.

I wanted to stay there with his naked body next to mine. But he rose to dress. He then handed me his dagger. I took it without hesitation, knowing what I would have to do if we were to be together. He leaned down and kissed me again before leaving my quarters.

I lay quietly in my cot, his dagger close at hand beneath the thin cotton sheet. I must have fallen asleep from the pleasure of our encounter, for I awoke with Captain Blair standing over me.

"I've had a bit too much to drink, boy, and have awoken with a stronger urge than usual. You should expect several long sessions tonight." He unbuttoned his breeches as usual and pulled out his swelling member. I did not make any gesture toward beginning my nightly service of him. I could see the anger in his face as he noticed my neglect.

"Boy, I should not have to tell you how this is to go. Get on your knees!" His words were slurred from the spirits as he shouted.

"I will not service you tonight, Blair, nor any night hereafter." I had never called him by his name. My familiar use of it enraged him. His face became red. His hands shook as he towered over me. He reached for my throat and began to choke me. In that moment, I retrieved the dagger from beneath and plunged it into his chest. It felt good to handle a dagger again. The moment dragged and then he knew what I had done. His hands loosened from around my neck. I took hold of his face and held it firmly. I wanted to be sure I was the last thing he saw before being cast into hell.

I sat there with the captain's lifeless body on top of me. I began to recount for myself the events of this journey. It was not supposed to have been like this. I was not supposed to have fallen in love with the enemy. My parents had been tried and hung for treason against the Dutch army and my orders had been clear. If I was to reclaim the family name, I was to get aboard the *Libertine* at all costs and infiltrate the crew. I was to disarm their weapons so that when the time came to attack they were defenseless against the Dutch soldiers. But I had caused the death of a young man, and I had taken a life of my own. Who was I? I wasn't sure I could go back—knowing how I was about to deceive Gregor and cause his death.

Time was running out. It was the last night before the attack was to begin. I was to meet the colonel at the hull of the ship, leave the *Libertine* and its unsuspecting crew behind, collect the coins that was promised to me, and go on with my solitary life with the family name restored.

I thought of Gregor in his quarters. I could still feel his body next to mine. My mind tried to convince me that I could not trust him and that I would be better off going back to my old life—but my heart told me differently. There was only one thing I could do.

I stepped over the captain's body; my hands were covered in his blood. I walked up on the empty deck. The colonel was waiting in his boat as planned. He looked at my appearance.

"Adam. Are you hurt?"

"It is not my blood, but the blood of the captain. The *Libertine* will be yours come morning. Now, wait here—I must fetch a few items before we depart." I didn't give him time to question me. I walked back down and knocked on Gregor's door before entering.

"Gregor, get up. We must leave the *Libertine* now."

"Adam, what are you saying?"

"I have no time to explain. Do you love me as you said you do?"

"Yes, of course. I am not the type of man to express those words without meaning."

"Then you must trust me. If we are here come morning our lives will be over. The Dutch army plans to attack at sunrise."

"Then we shall fight back and triumph over them."

"If you fight you will not triumph. I was trained in weapons by the Dutch army; the weapons I made for the crew are useless. We will not be able to defeat them in battle. The colonel of the Dutch army is waiting for me at the hull. We can overtake him and leave this ship and the others behind. You have to know that the crew will not accept us. Our only chance is to leave, but we must do it now."

My secrets now revealed, I waited. He looked at me questioningly but stood up quickly and dressed. We packed several pouches with water and supplies that we could find around his quarters. As we approached the meeting place, I motioned for Gregor to stand back. I climbed down the rope and into the colonel's boat. I looked him in the eyes. I could tell he saw someone different looking at him. I plunged the dagger into the colonel's chest in the same manner as I'd done with the captain, making it a quick and relatively painless death. I pushed the lifeless body overboard. Gregor jumped into the boat. He kissed me and held me in his arms.

"Thank you, for trusting in me when no one else has." He looked at me and smiled as he took the wheel of the ship in hand. I watched him maneuver the ship as we set out to sea. I never once looked back at what I left behind, for what matters is what we have ahead of us.

DRAGON SHIP

By Armand

Our captain is a Valkyrie, a female Viking. She has flaming red hair that dances in the wind as we row our drakkar, or dragon ship, to the next raid. Her name is Rán, like the goddess of the sea, and she is every bit as tempestuous as her namesake, who captures drowned men in her nets and drags them to her underwater abode. Rán's family was murdered by a band of Jutes, who took her hostage at the tender age of 13. After escaping her captors, she returned to her homeland of Norway, commissioned the drakkar, and raised a crew.

Because my older brother would inherit the family land, I knew that I would need to leave home to find fortune and glory elsewhere. Also, like many Vikings, adventure and wanderlust coursed through my veins, and I could not be contained by my small village in Denmark. For these reasons, I gladly joined the Valkyrie Rán and her crew to sail the ocean in search of booty and plunder. Upon my selection, our first mission was to the verdant island of Britannia, which had been colonized by the Jutes, Frisians, Angles, and Saxons. The Valkyrie wanted to exact revenge on the barbaric Jutes while filling her coffer.

As I stood that first morning as a Viking pirate, looking out at the open ocean, a husky voice inquired, "You are Erik?"

"Yes," I responded as I turned to face the man.

"I am Axel," he said, as he clapped me on the shoulder.

The pirate standing before me was the embodiment of Viking beauty and masculinity. His blond hair would surely rival that of the goddess Sif, and I never before beheld such blue eyes, like the iridescent heart of an iceberg in the sun. Though I had never been intimate with another man, I silently prayed to Freya, goddess of sex and war, to make him my companion.

"I can help you with your sea chest," he offered. "You can sit beside me."

Axel was speaking of the wooden chest that all Viking pirates possess that holds personal belongings and serves as a seat aboard the ship. Resting on the ground beside me, my sea chest was engraved with an image of the tree of life and two fierce wolves.

"Thank you," I finally responded.

"How long have you been a pirate?"

"This is my first voyage outside of the fjords of Scandinavia, but I have sailed all of my life on my father's boats."

"Ha. This is no ordinary longboat that our mistress sails. It is a drakkar beyond the likes of anything you have ever seen. Look yonder and you will know what I mean."

In the distance on the water was a huge longboat that held thirty pairs of rowers. The sail was being stretched, and I could see the red-striped woolen fabric dancing with each gust of wind. On the prow was a golden dragon, warning all in the ship's path to be wary. Along the sides of the hull, each Viking pirate had hung his shield, creating a colorful band of religious and animal images. The sight of this awesome dragon ship amazed and intimidated me. Several members of the crew were already aboard, and I could see that each man was as stout and hardy as Axel.

"Come, my friend," my companion said as he threw a massive arm about my shoulder. "I'll introduce you to the other oarsmen. They're a wild bunch, but I'm sure you'll take a liking to them."

He smiled and I think my Viking heart beat double time.

"So is Rán the only female?" I asked.

"She is. And thank the gods, for she is a fiery one. I daresay the lads are afraid of her."

I gave him a look of incredulity.

"It's true. When we go on raids, she stands at the bow of the ship with her hair flowing behind her like flames in the wind. She screams and beats her broadsword against her shield as if she were completely mad, like a Beserker."

I knew of these Beserkers, though I had never met one. They were bands of Vikings who went to battle drunk or intoxicated on mushrooms, wearing bearskins or nothing at all. They whooped and wailed and jumped about in such a frenzy that the enemy thought them quite crazy. Rumor had it that they felt no pain, making them a formidable and daunting foe.

"And does she have no man, no husband?" I continued.

Axel laughed as if I had made a joke.

"She has all of us."

"Oh. So she chooses from among the crew?"

Axel laughed again and kissed me on the cheek in the way that a drunken man might do. It was a simple gesture that implied nothing but excited me nonetheless.

"Come to the ship, Erik, and I'll introduce you to the others. Do not worry about Rán, for she will be your protector. She chose you for a reason."

That afternoon, I met many young, strong pirates who had decided to throw their lot in with this wild woman with flaming red hair. They were introduced in sets of two, men who rowed side by side. Valdemar and Gregor; Regin and Karl; Thorvald and Jorgen; and many others.

That night I slept in a tent with Axel, and when he curled up next to me, seemingly in a state of unconsciousness, I felt his erect penis against my leg. Though I wanted so badly to explore his body, I used restraint and somehow fell asleep with his sweet breath tickling my neck.

Next morning, Axel took me to the hot springs to bathe before our journey across the choppy sea to the island of Britannia. Without hesitation he stripped off his woolen trousers and leather tunic and stood before me naked and proud.

"Do you need help, my friend?" he asked.

"No, no. I am fine."

Though I was concerned that my body might betray my sexual interests, I steeled my resolve and tore off my boots, tunic, and trousers. My penis was not entirely flaccid, and I feared that it would grow as solid as the giant spar of the drakkar.

Axel was not so flaccid himself, and his organ was thick and impressive. He was sinewy and muscular, with a dusting of hair over his chest and stomach. Each leg was like a tree trunk, and his buttocks were round as gourds. All he needed was a magical hammer and iron gloves to convince me that he was Thor, god of thunder.

"You have a nice, strong Viking body," he said with a broad smile.

"As do you, Axel."

"Let us bathe."

We stepped into the steaming water and sunk to our waists.

I felt the hot bubbles swirling beneath me, and I became giddy with pleasure. Axel came close behind me and rubbed my shoulders and back. I closed my eyes and secretly imagined his lips upon my mouth. When he reached around me to squeeze my chest, I felt his breath on my ear and his erect penis against my leg.

"Relax, Erik," he cooed huskily. "We will be together on this journey. I will take care of all of your needs and protect you from harm. Every night and every day, I will be there to warm you when you are cold, to comfort you when you are lonely, to excite you when you are bored. You and I are going to row side by side, fight side by side, sleep side by side. Do you want me, Erik?"

"Yes," I said excitedly.

"Then it will be as the gods intended."

He continued to rub my shoulders and chest and I was seduced by the bubbles surrounding my body and his voice in my ear. Suddenly, without any warning, my body spasmed, and I ejected my seed into the roiling water. I'm certain that Axel did the same.

Before we left the hot springs, he kissed me on the cheek and gave me a hug like a great bear, and I knew that I would follow this man anywhere.

❁

The journey into the Atlantic and down the channel was quicker than I imagined. We rowed part of the time, but more than not we reserved our strength while the winds carried us toward the Thames River. Often when I looked upon my crewmates, I noticed surprising, tender exchanges between them: Thorvald holding Jorgen's hand. Valdemar kissing Gregor straight on the lips. Once I even caught Regin with his hand in Karl's trousers. And the men slept so close that they became like one large beast. Though such behavior among men was foreign to me, it somehow seemed so natural, as if it were ordained by the gods.

I didn't really know what to make of this, but I presumed that their intimacy could be attributed to a requisite bond among shipmates. Such trust and closeness would be invaluable while on long and perilous journeys at sea. So I gave into temptation and slept with my head on Axel's chest, and it was in those peaceful moments, pressed close to Axel, that I began to realize what had been missing from my life.

On the first day that our drakkar entered the Thames River, we encountered an enemy ship of Angles and Jutes. Excitement overtook my shipmates, and I was swept up in the wave of emotions. The innate Viking prowess in me took over and I leapt into action.

Like any good Norse pirate ship, we were armed with axes, bows and arrows, spears and shortened broadswords. Half the men remained at the oars while the other half rushed to quash the barbaric enemy.

Our good captain Rán rubbed the golden dragon on the prow and spoke to it lovingly. Then she took up her spear and shield and began rousing us with her shouts. The entire time she beat her spear upon her shield and swung her wild flaming hair, and I thought she looked like a true Valkyrie, the divine maidens who choose worthy dead from battlefields and escort them to Valhalla.

Our sail was down so that our drakkar was entirely controlled by the oarsmen, who adeptly navigated us close to the enemy ship. I watched Axel rush to the side of the hull, ready for action.

"Watch for their arrows," my friend yelled to me. "Grab your shield. Stay behind me if you like."

Stay behind! What kind of Viking did he take me for? There was no way I would wait in the background and watch the fighting unfold. I could not have my new comrades and my mistress see me cowering like a scared rabbit. No, they would see me as a strong wolf, so I took my place at the hull beside my faithful companion.

Just then, an arrow struck the shield of our rapacious captain, but she ignored the hit and commanded us to fight, to take out the enemy shipmen and to steal their booty. Once we were alongside the Briton ship, the fighting commenced in earnest.

A spear from our ship sailed over my shoulder, striking a Jute and killing him instantly. Axel repeatedly smashed his axe into the shield of an enemy as the boats careened in a deadly embrace. Just then I saw a Briton pull the spear from his shipmate and hurl it in our direction. Deftly, I rocked onto my left foot and caught the spear in mid-flight. Then I flung it back, killing the one who had intended to use it against us.

Axel saw my actions, as did our captain, and I could see the approbation in their faces. Axel pulled another Briton from his boat, tossed him into the water, and then jumped aboard the enemy ship; I immediately followed. The Valkyrie hurled an axe with deadly aim, killing the Briton captain. With our broadswords and axes, we had taken the enemy vessel within minutes. We stripped the remaining pirates, tossed them over the edge, and watched them swim for shore.

It was a glorious day and a savory victory.

That night, we carried the drakkar onto the banks of the Thames and righted it between the trees. Then Rán walked among the men, lauding our bravery and fearlessness. She tended lovingly, almost maternally, to the wounded and then set about planning a feast.

After gorging ourselves on roast fowl, mead and stolen cheese, the men began to separate into distinct pairs. Some pairs returned to the ship while others stayed on the banks, but all began to touch in ways that I had not witnessed before. Libidinal, intimate, feral ways.

The pirates began to kiss each other squarely, passionately on the lips, as if the goddess Freya had placed a spell on them. They embraced in great bear hugs, ran their tongues over sensitive skin, and groped freely. One by one, each Viking began to undress his companion.

Soon they were all naked and engorged in an orgiastic state of pleasure.

It was a sight unlike any I had ever beheld, and I was confused but excited by the events before me. Then I noted our mistress wandering through the writhing couples, softly cooing to each as if she was encouraging them. I was struck by how pleased the Valkyrie was by the behavior of her men. Clearly this was not the first time that this scene had unfolded.

Then I felt two hands about my waist.

"You fought bravely today," Axel said.

"As did you," I answered. "You were like the great god of thunder, Thor, attacking the evil serpent that encircles the world."

My friend moved his mouth close to my ear as his hand ran over my abdomen and toward my nether region.

"Axel, what is happening here?" I asked.

"Do you not want this?"

"I want it very much, my warrior. But do you?"

He chuckled softly, kissed my neck, and responded, "Feel how much I want it, my dear Erik," as he pressed his erect manliness into my hip.

Next, his hand was on my penis and I was drunk, not from the mead, but from his manly touch.

"Are we all under some spell?" I asked.

"No, my love. We are an entire ship of male lovers."

"And our Valkyrie is aware of this?"

"Of course. It is by her choice. Look how she enjoys our pleasure."

Rán was still roaming among the couples like she was wandering in her garden. As Thorvald knelt before Jorgen she leaned in to watch closely as the former took the latter's penis in his mouth. Then she gently caressed Thorvald's hair as his head began to undulate, bringing Jorgen great pleasure.

My own penis was like a great oak staff; fluid leaked from its shaft, and I wished for Axel's mouth to be upon it, like Thorvald's was upon Jorgen's.

As Axel undressed me slowly, almost painfully so, I watched the men touch each other in splendor. Regin and Karl were laying head to foot so that each could use his mouth to stimulate the other's organ, and I could not believe their skill at pleasing another man in this way. Next to them, Gregor was stroking Valdemar's cock and licking his testicles as if they were ripe, juicy berries.

Suddenly, Axel moved in front of me, and I saw his naked body again in all its glory. His penis was as hard as mine and he walked closer until they touched.

He confessed, "I've wanted to do this with you since I first saw you in Denmark on the banks of the great ocean."

"But I have never done this with a man."

"You will be fine, my love."

"I trust you will show me the way."

And then he leaned forward, pressed his lips to mine and kissed me deeply in a way that no other lover before had ever done. As his tongue moved into my mouth, I could not help but reach down and grab his thick organ in my hand. By his moans, I could tell that he was enjoying my touch immensely.

Though I did not want his lips to separate from mine, I was thrilled when he knelt and began teasing my cock with his tongue. This was wholly unlike the simple pleasure I had experienced with women. Looking down as my friend licked and kissed my member, I began to understand the true meaning of ecstasy. Soon Axel had wrapped his warm, wet mouth around my swollen organ, and I rubbed my fingers through his golden locks.

I felt a hand on my shoulder and looked over to find the Valkyrie standing there. She smiled and rubbed her hand tenderly down my back. Then she touched Axel on the shoulder, and he stopped his pleasurable touch and stood to face me.

"Will you give yourself to this great Viking?" she asked, of whom I was not certain.

"Yes, my lady," Axel answered as he turned to show off his backside.

Then he backed into my body and rubbed his buttocks over my erect penis. It was so shockingly erotic that I nearly lost my seed.

"And you?" she asked of me.

"Yes, my lady," I responded breathily.

Rán smiled at us, pleased by our passion, and then moved on to the next couple.

"Erik, will you use your mouth on me like I did for you?" my companion pleaded.

"Of course."

I was excited by the prospect and I fell immediately to the ground and kissed the head of his shaft, tasting a salty, manly brine. As I slipped my lips over his thick organ, I felt saliva flowing into my mouth, making it easier to work his penis over my tongue and down my throat. Axel's body shivered and he moaned loudly. All around me were the sounds of pleasure, but I was focused on my lover. His hands on my cheeks were tender and encouraging, and I was overcome with the sensation of pleasing another man in this way. I knew that I never wanted to stop.

But Axel pulled his organ from my mouth to delay his ejaculation. Then he pulled me up and kissed me deeply. Instinctively, I wrapped my hands around his body and felt his muscular buttocks. Our cocks were pinned between our bodies and we rubbed them together in a fever. The entire time I pulled at his backside as if I were trying to get to a treasure.

"Let me show you what to do," he said and then he turned me roughly so I could gaze upon the other men.

One man was bent over the side of the ship as his lover was driving his shaft into him from behind. Though I had heard stories, I had never witnessed such an act. Both men seemed to be experiencing intense pleasure. When I surveyed the tableau, I saw that each couple had given themselves over to this type of sex. Some were on their backs; some were standing in a bent position. Valdemar was actually lying over his sea chest as Gregor lunged into him roughly. My concern for Valdemar instantly abated when I heard him beg Gregor for more. Karl was pulling out of Regin, and I thought that they were already spent, but they were merely changing positions as Karl knelt on the ground in a dog's position and accepted Regin from behind.

Axel pushed my shoulders and I bent at the waist. He pulled apart my buttocks and used his tongue to tease me more. The sensation was magical and I could now begin to understand the pleasure that my crewmates were feeling. After his demonstration was over, Axel took me to the ship and leaned over the side clutching at his shield.

"Please, Erik, put yourself inside of me, so that we can become one," he begged.

"Axel, I don't want to hurt you."

"Trust me, my friend. You are big, but I can take it. We will both enjoy this. Start by kissing me there and then slip a finger inside to feel how warm I am."

I obeyed because I wanted to experience everything with this beautiful warrior, so I knelt behind him, pulled apart his round cheeks and gently ran my tongue up and down his backside. He let out a moan, and I knew that I was doing it right. Before long, I was using my tongue like a battering ram to probe at his pink hole. Then I remembered what he had said about my finger, so I wet one and delicately worked it inside the warmth of his backside.

The pressure of his muscle around my finger excited me more, and I could not wait to replace it with my penis.

"I want to fuck you, Axel," I exclaimed boldly.

"That's what I've been dreaming of, Erik. Let me get you wet."

So he spit upon my penis and rubbed his saliva over it eagerly. He kissed me one last time and then resumed his position bent over the ship's hull. Excitedly, I rubbed my erect member between his cheeks until I felt it against his tight muscle. Then I leaned forward as if I were trying to invade his backside. At first, I worried that he would not let me in, but suddenly I breached his tight ring and felt an immense pressure around the head of my cock. He groaned, and I worried that I had hurt him, so I froze in place. Then I felt him wiggling backwards as his rear engulfed my staff.

"Are you well, Axel?"

"Yes, my love. It feels good. I hope one day we can switch places, so you will know how good this feels."

"It feels wonderful," I agreed.

"I am giving myself to you, Erik, my brave Viking."

My organ was buried all the way inside of my lover, and it felt even better than his lips. I watched my cock slip partially out of his body, and I marveled at how he was accommodating my thick member. When I pushed back inside, I felt us move forward as one entity. I began to work my organ in and out of him like a steady wave.

"Fuck me, Erik," he pleaded as he looked back over his shoulder.

"It feels so warm and so pleasurable."

"Show me what a strong Viking you are."

Goaded by his words, I began to rock in and out of him at a faster pace, and I pressed my member harder into his body until even the boat rocked on its dry bed.

"Yes, my love," he cried. "That's it."

"You like it?"

Then I reached under him and found his tumescent shaft.

"Yes. Fuck me, Erik."

And so I continued to rock my body into him as I stroked his penis. In the distance I could see the other pairs doing much the same in various positions, and the Valkyrie continued to walk among us enjoying the sights.

Then I said it, without thought, induced by the passion: "I love you, Axel."

I worried that I had misspoken and wanted to take back the words, though I felt them truly.

His response was a loud groan and then he said, "I love you, too, Erik. I want to do this with you every day."

"Yes, my love."

"You are going to make me spill my seed."

"Yes," I moaned.

"Yes. Fuck me, Erik."

Then I felt a spasm that ran through my entire body, stronger than any I had ever known. I was thrusting into him as my seed was filling up his insides. Just then, his organ shot warm fluid onto the ship and my hand, and I was pleased that I had brought him to climax.

Reluctantly, I pulled my softening member from his backside, and he turned to face me.

A voice in the distance yelled, "Yes, Erik!" It was Karl who was still being mounted from behind. "You are one of us now." Then he stood partially erect and shot his seed onto the ground before him as Regin continued to assail him from behind.

"Welcome to our crew," Valdemar called out, holding his legs aloft. "Fuck me, Gregor. I spill my seed for you." With that, his organ began to shoot semen onto his stomach without even being touched.

Axel kissed me, and I felt a swoon unbecoming of a Viking pirate.

"So you really love me?" he asked.

I smiled broadly and kissed him again before responding, "As Odin loves Frigg."

"Good. Now we are lovers aboard the drakkar."

In our post-coital bliss, we bathed in the water of the Thames and dried each other tenderly. As we prepared our pallet, the Valkyrie came to me.

"You are a good addition to our crew, Erik" she said. "I knew that I was not wrong."

"Thank you for inviting me on this adventure."

"It was Axel who chose you," she divulged.

"Really! Then I owe him much more than I thought."

"And so do you wish to remain a pirate on the drakkar?"

"It would please me greatly."

"Good, because Axel needs a lover like you."

Axel kissed me on the cheek and I could feel his muscular chest pressing into my back, and I felt my penis stirring again.

"A ship of male lovers," I said matter-of-factly. "I've never heard of such, Viking or otherwise."

"No?" she answers. "A great Greek philosopher named Plato once wrote that an army of lovers would be invincible. That is what I needed to punish these enemies and to make my profit—an invincible army of male lovers."

"Ahh. Well then, I'm glad to be at your service and beside my lover."

BEARDED

Shane Allison

You're sitting quiet at the ass end of the bar all blond and bearded, dressed to the teeth in black, nursing on a Bud. It's a weeknight so the place isn't crowded. Just the usual suspects, the same tattooed bartenders who won't give me a second glance past the cheap booze they serve and the five-dollar-a-glass tips I give. It's Smokey tonight. The same tired DJ spinning the same trifling techno. This is where I come on Thursdays 'cause the beer's cheap. Tomorrow night I will lay my hat elsewhere. Stonewall, The Monster, who knows. Aren't too many guys to choose from. Some have already hooked up with their one-night stands for tonight. Men necking in pitch-dark corners, dicks being felt up in tight breeches. The Latino go-go boy waves his dick like a Cuban flag in the faces of tipsy drunkards who don't know their limit. You and I are the only two left, the only guys here sober, lonely. No one to keep us company. I've been sipping on this Corona for half an hour now. Steve, the cutest bartender in here, is onto me. He reminds me that I gotta drink my fill or leave. Things are tough all over since this place was bomb-rushed by the cops last week 'cause some asshole lied about drugs being sold out of its doors.

Everyone ignores you. Creeped out I guess by that patch over your eye, the prosthetic limb with a hook for a hand, but it doesn't bother me. I've seen worse. I smile at you beneath the searchlights, under the gleam of dimly lit candles. Drink the last swig of beer left at the bottom of the bottle and take a chance. *What the hell*, I always say. Worst thing that could happen is you could tell me to fuck off.

"What's up?" I ask you how it's going as you tap your cold bottle of condensation. I pull up a stool. I watch your bearded lips move, make contact with the eye I can see, but I can't make out your words due to the boisterous mixture of horrible music being spun.

"What's that?"

I lean into you for an earful.

"Pretty good," you holler.

I ask how you like the music and you tell me it's okay, that it's the same shit, but it's better than nothing. We introduce ourselves, exchange names like phone numbers written on beer coasters. I shake your hand. Can't keep my eyes off your prosthetic tragedy, that hook. Think of what you would do with it if a guy were to get in your face. I want to know what you're hiding behind that patch, but we just met and I don't want to seem rude. It's too soon to tell you that I'm into guys like you. Started in high school when the cutest boy in school had no legs or gag reflex.

"So what are you drinking?" you ask.

I want something stronger this time, something that's gonna put hair on my balls.

"Gin and tonic." It's the only drink I know. You wave Steve down. He makes his way over to where we are. He's got machine guns for arms.

"What can I getcha, baby?" I love it when they call you baby. Steve sounds tougher than leather.

"Gin and tonic for him and another ale for me."

Ale? Who talks like that around here? I like it. Steve sits your longneck on the bar and pops the tab off the top.

"Your G and T's comin' right up, baby," says Steve.

"So you're just hanging out tonight?"

Steve returns with my drink. We lift them and make a toast.

"I don't live far from here," you explain in your British accent. "Just thought I would come in for a drink." You go on about stopping in after work, during happy hour. You're new to me. This is the first I've seen you.

I mean, hell, I would remember a guy with an eye patch, with a hook for a hand. I sip from my glass of hard liquor.

"So what do you do?" I ask.

You tell me you're in sales and don't go into much detail other than the fact that you've been doing it for eighteen years. When I tell you that I'm a writer, you ask the obvious:

"Have I read anything of yours?" Tell you that I'm mostly into poems. You find it impressive that I've published. Tell me that you would love to read some of my works sometime, like you're so sure that we'll see each other again after the booze and small talk. The bar reeks of liquor and lust. All I want to do is run my fingers through your ratty, blond hair, feel your bearded lips against mine as we kiss. I barely know your name and all I want to do is fuck, cower into one of these corners and fondle your dick. Let the drunkards and muscle-bound bouncers watch us make out under this disco ball. The fog of smoke burns my eyes. Things are starting to wind down.

"You wanna get out of here?" you ask.

We finish our drinks and step out into this metropolitan night of summer.

"G'night," says one of the brutish bouncers.

The moon is blood orange. We stroll like lovers along these Lower West Side streets, admiring the window displays of the gay boutiques. One store has the "Queer as Fuck" shirt I want. You point to the boots you want, the ones that look like something a swashbuckling pirate would wear.

"I know a great piano bar where a friend of mine works. They have good martinis." You might have pianos on the brain, but I've got penises. Electric sexual shocks surge through me, centering at my dick. I'm a little nervous to hold your hand as you take mine into yours. Being from the South, I'm not used to this. We are approaching the bar. "Rose's Piano Bar," the sign reads. You tell me that we made it in time to see the midnight show. The bar is small, but quaint. You ask the host to sit us as close as possible to the stage and lights. You see your friend and wave her over. You two hug and kiss. You introduce us. She's pretty with good teeth. I'm surprised that you remember my name. I feel like such the boyfriend sitting next to you. An older woman who favors Ethel Merman tells us of the drink specials. "We also have dirty martinis for three bucks," she explains. You order for us. I feel like such a hick. I've had New York dreams since I was sixteen. Didn't think I would ever get out of Tallahassee. I used to live vicariously through the characters from "Sex and the City" before I moved up here to go to grad school.

The drinks set my throat on fire. It wasn't the top shelf stuff, the good shit. We chew the fat about the events that brought us here to the Big Apple, and all I want to do is head to your place to fuck. My dick twitches under the table. Your friend sings one Judy Garland tune after another, but she's no Judy Garland.

This thuggish boy buys us drinks. Says he's from Queens.

"They're on me," he says, looking like he doesn't have a pot to piss in. Dude doesn't know us from Adam. Ethel Merman kicks him and his homeboys out for not paying for our drinks. We are so shit-faced tonight. You are big and warm against me. We stay until closing, stumbling out of the bar with liquor in our heads. I'm seeing double, two of you instead of one. I tuck my arm under yours to keep my balance. The thug and his friends are walking a block up from where we are. We stand at the crosswalk, waiting to cross, hoping they won't notice us.

I wonder if we will ever get to your apartment. We are two drunken-ass lushes stumbling up the set of stairs. The hall smells like pork dumplings from the Chinese restaurant below us. Your place is a piece of kitchen with beat-up appliances, two bedrooms, and a single bath. You didn't say anything about a roommate. Place is filled with clothes, electronics and other goods, all with the tags still on.

"Don't worry about my roommate; he's out of town for the weekend." You pull me close and kiss me. Your beard of gold feels coarse against my face. Your tongue tastes like the martinis from Rose's. We make our way into your bedroom where there are more stolen treasures, with Macy's and Nordstrom tags hanging from sleeves and collars of baby clothes, dresses, and leather coats. There are radios stacked in corners, cell phones and iPods strewn across bedside tables and desks.

We peel off each other's clothes, kick ourselves out of jeans and shoes, until we're naked. My foot hits one of the boxes that have "Sanyo" inscribed on the side.

"Careful, mate," you warn.

"What is all this stuff?" I ask.

You look at me with emergence in your eyes—as if I have done something there's no turning back from.

"Can I ask you a ques…a question?" I say, in my state of intoxication. "What happened to your arm?"

We tumble onto your bed of tousled sheets, the covers snaking themselves around us.

"Bloody freak accident when I used to work as an engineer on cruise ships," you explain, with your hand down into my pants, pulling at my hard-on.

"And what about your eye?"

When I start to pull at your patch, you force my arm down to my side and hold me there, leaving only your hook free to explore. It feels cold as you use it to pull at the elastic of my underwear, tugging my Hanes down past my ass and thighs, off my ankles. Your bed feels like a plank against my back. You part my legs, shoving your cruddy finger in me.

"You're bloody tight, mate," you tell me. My fingers clinch the covers. I stare at the ceiling fan that swirls slowly above us. I can hear the commotion of cars and people from your cracked, Bleecker Street apartment window. I watch you in my drunken haze; you lick me from your fingers. You tell me how ripe I taste. Caress the prosthetic, tongue-tickle the cold hook that is pressed against my drunken lips. Your head of rustled hair is but a blur of yellow as I feel your wet lips around my dick. Your beard grazes within the inner realm of my thighs. It tickles, but I don't laugh. Pull at your mane, press you hard into me. Breathe in the crotch sweat from my pubic nest. Brace myself as you rake your hook along my skin knowing you can puncture me if you wanted to. You pull me closer, lifting me slightly off the king-sized brass bed. I can feel the tip of your dick at the crack of my ass.

"You got any rubbers?" I ask.

"Yeah, sure," you say in unbelief. "Let me in you," you keep repeating. It hurts like hell. You are so painful down there. You fight for the bottle of Lubriderm with the sticker still on it that sits on the bedside table next to an iPod. I can hear it being squeezed from its spout onto your dick. Can hear you slathering it on. Your dick feels so cold going up in me. The aloe burns, but I say nothing out of fear that you will rip me to shreds with that hook hand of yours. Brace myself, bare down as you plunge into me. My legs rest still on your freckled shoulders as you hold them steady to pillage my ass. Sweat burns my eyes, causing them to redden and tear up. I can't make out the plastered heaven above me, the circling ceiling fan, so I shut my eyes from the sweat and let you do what you want until you throw my legs over the bed after having your fill of me. You feel like a ton on top, biting at my chest, suckling my nipples. Your arm presses firmly against my throat.

I've lost count of how many times you have raped my mouth tonight. That piercing in your dick head clings against my roof. The shit and lotion forces me to puke on your dick, but you don't care and face-fuck me anyway. The vomit burns my throat like cheap tequila. I'm so embarrassed. You flip me over. I can't see what you're up to, but can hear that aloe-laced lotion being pinched from its bottle. My butt is still sore, still stinging. You pull my ass to your crotch, can feel that hard plastic under my belly. It doesn't hurt so much this time. I lay there, my torso dipping into the covers. I look to the stolen clothes that lay slumped across the arm of your desk chair as you fuck me from behind. With your dick still in me, you tug me up to you and kiss me; your tongue explores my dry mouth until you force me back down on the bed, slithering in and out of my butt. You pull out as you're about to come. Can't make out what you're doing, but can feel your ejaculation on the backs of my thighs. You fall on top of me, heavy. I lie there under you in a room that reeks of puke and ass. Your come holds us together until you fall asleep, snoring and breathing hot in my ear.

I slide from beneath you, make my way to the bathroom of electric toothbrushes, mouthwash, and body spray. The tile is freezing under my feet. My dick is hard, not because it's turned on, but because of the liquor that fills it. Been holding it in ever since we left the piano bar. Booze is wearing thin and the hangover is kicking in. I piss all over the rim of your toilet. Dick looks like it's been twisted and turned into a balloon animal. Sit and wipe myself. Surprisingly, there's no blood, but I'll be damned if I'm not sore. I tip-toe over the pirated merchandise where my clothes lay bunched at the foot of your bed. I leave you there naked and useless, sounding like a buzz saw, your arm, that hook lying limp over the edge of a bed that smells like throw-up. I examine one of the leather jackets. "$375," the tag reads. It's exactly my size. It's the least you can do. I stumble down the set of stairs. The break of dawn burns my eyes as I make my way home, alone down the sullen streets of the Village.

THE CAPTAIN'S PLEASURE

Bearmuffin

Captain Vergagrande was awakened from a sound sleep by a loud knocking on his cabin door. He squinted and reached toward his groin to scratch his hairy, plum-sized nuts.

"Who is it?"

"Jacob Blow, Cap'n."

"Enter," he barked.

Jacob Blow was a strapping member of the captain's hardy, muscle-bound crew. Jacob had been captured in a raid on an English ship on its way back to London where he was to be hanged for murder. He figured he might as well be hanged for plying the waters of the Caribbean, pillaging, plundering, and pilfering, so he quite reasonably decided to become a pirate.

A shit-eating grin spread across Blow's darkly stubbled face. He informed his captain that a fellow shipmate had been discovered ass fucking a prisoner down in the ship's dungeon.

"Who did it?"

"Juan Hidalgo!"

"Bring him to me," the captain snarled, and Jacob scampered away to perform his task with glee.

Captain Vergagrande yawned and slowly stretched his big body out on the bed. His green eyes narrowed as he pensively fingered the gold hoop earring piercing his left earlobe. Everyone aboard the *Satan's Shame* knew the rules. The horny captain had first pickings of any studs captured on his many brazen raids on English cargo ships, raids for which he was licensed by the Spanish authorities.

Whatever booty he captured Captain Vergagrande had to split fifty-fifty with the greedy Spanish, but any prisoners were his for the keeping. And all prisoners were off limits until Captain Vergagrande had his filthy way with them. Then he would pick out the humpiest of the studs to serve as his personal slaves. Afterward, he would toss the rest of them to his crew. His big, vein-etched 10-incher twitched at the thought of his crew satisfying their depraved, perverted lusts with young, virgin English studs.

Captain Vergagrande glanced over at the hulking figure lying next to him. Moanin' Jude snored loudly. The captain smiled. He had many hot studs among his English slaves but Jude was his favorite. The blond-maned, blue-eyed Jude had been captured on their last raid and he proved to be an expert fucker with a fat, uncut cock, a tight ass, and an eager cocksucking mouth.

The captain hesitated to wake him. Jude had already taken several hot loads up his hot, humpy butt during a hot all-night orgy in which they had polished off several bottles of fine Jamaican rum. No doubt Jude had one hell of a hangover, so the captain decided to let him sleep it off.

Even so Captain Vergagrande couldn't resist inserting his thick forefinger up the stud's smooth, muscular butt. A slow shudder quaked through his meaty ass. Jude yawned and farted. A big glob of come oozed from his butt hole and soaked the captain's finger. Captain Vergagrande slowly licked off the creamy goo. Fuck! The taste of his own come mingled with the hot, manly smell of Jude's butt made him dizzy with lust.

Moments later, Jacob appeared with Juan Hidalgo. Captain Vergagrande could barely conceal his sexual excitement and awe when he saw the swarthy, muscle-bound Hidalgo. The stud's long and sturdy legs were packed into tight, black-and-white-striped breeches. His upper torso was bare.

Juan Hidalgo had joined Captain Vergagrande's lusty crew but a month ago and already he'd made his reputation as being the hottest fucker on the ship. He couldn't keep his hands off anyone when he was horny and he loved to fuck any and all new prisoners who had been captured on a raid. He had never been caught in the act until now. And he had yet to tangle ass with the captain.

Captain Vergagrande took a good look at the tall, hulking Hidalgo, whose long raven hair brushed against his brawny shoulders. His intense, rugged handsomeness was softened by deep, dark, soulful eyes. A beard framed his full lips and powerful jowls. His mouth was full, and ever so kissable.

Hidalgo's thick bull neck was connected to mighty shoulders, his wide chest tapered down to a solid, muscular waist. Meaty pecs were capped by thick, brown nipples and a row of superb abs glistened with perspiration. Captain Vergagrande smacked his lips when he saw the ripe thickness at Hidalgo's crotch. His eyes were focused on the downward curvy shaft running alongside Hidalgo's inner thigh. Yes, no doubt about it. Hidalgo had a super-thick cock. Captain Vergagrande felt his asshole twitch with lust.

"What have you to say for yourself?" Captain Vergagrande said.

But the swarthy stud didn't answer. He hid his shame behind an impenetrable wall of reserve. The arousing odor of sweaty Spanish stud made the Captain lightheaded. His cock rose up and swelled. He opened a window and took in a lungful of bracing, salty air.

He turned to Hidalgo. "You know the rules and you know the punishment. To the cross!"

He was referring to the St. Andrew's Cross prominently displayed in his cabin. Captain Vergagrande loved to administer all corporal punishment himself. The sight of a sweating, swarthy stud at the receiving end of his trusty cat-o'-nine-tails never failed to arouse his lust to a fever pitch. Jacob Blow grinned. The most minor of infractions called for at least fifty lashes.

Hidalgo gulped but did as was ordered. He spread his arms and legs on the X-shaped cross. A snap of Captain Vergagrande's fingers and Jacob hurried to fasten the thick, wide leather straps over Hidalgo's sturdy wrists and ankles. Jacob chuckled merrily to himself as he kneeled behind

Hidalgo. His face was but an inch away from Hidalgo's superbly muscled ass. It was just too tempting not to attempt a bit of a lick here and there. His eager tongue shot out of his mouth as he applied the tip ever so gently along one of Hidalgo's smooth, satiny buttocks.

Captain Vergagrande picked up his cat-o'-nine-tails and flicked it at Jacob, who recoiled with a scream. "Sorry, Cap'n," he whimpered. "Sorry!"

"You'll be rimming the stud soon enough," Captain Vergagrande said.

Jacob's painful grimace of pain became a wicked leer of pure lust.

"Strip him!" Captain Vergagrande ordered.

Jacob did as he was told yanking off Hidalgo's breeches and exposing a heart stopping pair of buttocks that were the crowning glory of his virile, superbly muscular torso. The captain smacked his lips. He just couldn't keep his eyes of Hidalgo's magnificent body. That squarish face with the firm chin. And those hot green eyes! Fuck me! Hidalgo was one hot fucking pirate stud!

Captain Vergagrande grinned. He walked over and patted Hidalgo's humpy butt. "A shame to scar these cheeks." He ran his hand over one of Hidalgo's buttocks. He felt a shudder go through the swarthy flesh. The skin felt smooth, the flesh was taut. "And such beautiful cheeks, too! Even so..." Captain Vergagrande stepped back a bit and raised a muscular arm, the cat-o'-nine-tails firmly gripped in his hand. "An example must be made of you for the rest of the crew."

A quiver of sexual excitement coursed through Captain Vergagrande's wonderful muscles as he raised the cat-o'-nine-tails. But he found himself unable to proceed. No, Hidalgo was just too beautiful. He could not move himself to mar the beauty of that superb, muscular body.

He could hear Hidalgo's fast breathing. No doubt the stud was wondering when and how the blows would be administered. Captain Vergagrande could see Hidalgo's body tense and tauten with anticipation. And he wondered what effect it was having on Hidalgo's cock.

A harsh whoosh sliced the air in front of him and the cat-o'-nine-tails landed on Hidalgo's cheeks. But Captain Vergagrande made sure not to strike too hard. He aimed the dreaded tails carefully so they never landed twice in the same place. Each blow was more of a caress than a lash, eliciting a low, harsh, guttural gasp from Hidalgo. Another quiver of excitement ran through Captain Vergagrande's body, shot down to his loins, and spread over his cock as it rose and began to stiffen with lust.

Captain Vergagrande repeated the strokes with a steady rhythmic action, peppering the light blows along the lower back, moving up toward the broad shoulders, lightly dusting the neck with small, staccato taps, and then bringing the tails down again to those magnificent buttocks.

Jacob Blow was flabbergasted, disappointed that the Captain was not administering a good flogging to the unfortunate Hidalgo. Aye, a flurry of blood-letting blows was more to his taste. Even so, his own lust was inflamed at the sight of the beads of sweat forming on Hidalgo's broad, muscular back. He too wondered if Hidalgo's cock was being aroused by the whipping and would have given anything to see it now.

"Go ahead, rim him, Jacob," Captain Vergagrande commanded.

Jacob was only too eager to comply and he clamped a grimy paw on each one of Hidalgo's cheeks, exposing Hidalgo's tight brown sphincter. Jacob pressed his face against it, running his rough tongue all along the crack, digging it deep into the hole, burrowing farther and farther until he almost touched Hidalgo's prostate.

Captain Vergagrande's fingers tightened around the leather handle of the cat-o'-nine-tails as he continued to administer lashes along Hidalgo's beautiful broad back. And Jacob rimmed Hidalgo as if his life depended on it. This continued for a good quarter of an hour. Captain Vergagrande's cock was rock-hard, sputtering thick drops of precome that splashed on the cabin floor. He was certain that Hidalgo must have a hard-on by now and he could restrain himself no longer. His curiosity had to be satisfied. Jacob was busily rimming Hidalgo but Captain Vergagrande pushed him away and ordered him to untie Hidalgo.

"Turn around, Hidalgo!" Captain Vergagrande barked.

Hidalgo did as ordered. The captain's mouth stretched wide, his pearly whites exposed, in a supremely self-satisfied smile. Just as he had imagined. Hidalgo's proud cock was stiff and upright, slicing the air in front of him. His thick, dark brown foreskin was pulled back under the shiny knob. His full, pendulous balls swung low and heavy between his muscular, tree-trunk thighs. The captain knew Hidalgo had a huge gusher of come just aching to be released.

Captain Vergagrande began massaging his own erect cock, his lips smacking hard with lust and desire as he ran a hand over the plump, rosy-purple knob.

"Rim him some more!" he told Jacob who eagerly resumed his task. Captain Vergagrande went up to Hidalgo and plucked his nipples, pulling them out a bit and letting them snap back. He breathed in the fresh sweat streaking down Hidalgo's muscles. It was like a heady perfume making him delirious with lust.

Captain Vergagrande kneeled before Hidalgo who raised his arms up and began flexing his muscles in a gesture of triumph. Hidalgo grinned back at Captain Vergagrande, only too eager to satisfy his captain's lusts.

Hidalgo's thick uncut cock bulged obscenely. He stepped toward the captain. Then the swarthy stud began to laugh wildly. His deep booming voice bounced off the walls. He was smacking his big brown dick against the Captain's face. Slap, slap, slap! That big horsedick was bruising Captain Vergagrande's cheeks and mouth.

Hidalgo's evil grin exposed a perfect set of pearly whites that flashed brilliantly. The pirate shoved his fat precome-dripping cock into the captain's mouth. Hidalgo proceeded to fuck the captain's mouth with short, rapid strokes. Captain Vergagrande choked when Hidalgo thrust his cock to the hilt and hot, thick precome gobs gushed down the back of the captain's tongue.

Hidalgo loved his captain's expert attentions to his mighty cock. Aye, the captain was proving himself quite an able cocksucker, his warm, loving mouth worshiping every inch of Hidalgo's proud Spanish cock.

Without any warning, he wrenched his cock out and aimed it at Captain Vergagrande's face. The captain's eyes grew wide with amazement at the sight of Hidalgo's beautiful cock throbbing hard, the crown flushed with purple. Hidalgo grabbed the thick root of his cock and grunted hard as his cock exploded, sending gush after hot gush of potent jizz splattering over the captain's amazed face. Fuck! He was almost blinded by the hot, shooting streams of semen.

Hidalgo laughed and howled. A wild smile creased his handsome face. He whirled around and pushed his hot ass against the captain's face. "Eat my ass," he barked. Captain Vergagrande was transfixed by the beauty of Hidalgo's ass, which resembled two brown sweaty melons of hard, taut muscle. Short brown hairs bristled along the cleft. Captain Vergagrande poked a finger between Hidalgo's cheeks, rubbing it along the cleft, the asshairs brushing over his probing finger, which he pulled out and sniffed. The hot, pungent aroma of sweaty butt hole flooded his nostrils like a magic perfume that sent lusty tingles up and down his spine.

The captain pressed his come-dripping, trembling lips along the musky crack of Hidalgo's butt. Fuck! The hot smell of ass was intoxicating. The captain's dick throbbed hard. Jacob Blow was stunned at the incredible sight of his captain rimming Hidalgo. He couldn't restrain himself: He began masturbating as he watched the two pirates go at it.

Hidalgo zigzagged his butt over the captain's hot, flickering tongue. "Suck my butt," he hissed. Captain Vergagrande mashed his face into Hidalgo's ass, the butt hairs scratching his nose. The captain's heart began to pound faster as the powerful, manly smell of Hidalgo's ass blasted up his flared nostrils.

"Hah!" Hidalgo grunted. "Eat my ass! Eat it!" He squashed his butt down on the captain's face, smothering him with hot, pungent butt. The captain's tongue darted in and out of Hidalgo's ass cheeks. "Fuck!" Hidalgo exclaimed with barbaric pleasure as he felt Captain Vergagrande's tongue probe deeper and deeper inside him. The captain masturbated himself into an unparalleled frenzy as he sucked hard on Hidalgo's sweaty hole.

Captain Vergagrande rimmed Hidalgo for a good while until Hidalgo spun around suddenly, his cock dripping with freshly ejaculated semen. He scowled at Captain Vergagrande who was fisting his cock with one hand and pinching his nipples with the other. Hidalgo's glaring eyes burned into Captain Vergagrande. Hidalgo's huge cock was hard and throbbing, jutting out over his huge brown balls. The pirate grabbed his thick cock by the root and wrapped a hot fist around it. "Shall I fuck you, Captain?" Hidalgo said. Captain Vergagrande smacked his lips when he saw a long ribbon of precome trickle from the stud's peehole.

"Oh, please, Cap'n," Jacob begged. "Please. Please let him fuck me first!"

The sight of a kneeling Jacob Blow, his hands clasped together as if in fervent prayer, elicited a hearty round of laughter from Hidalgo and Captain Vergagrande.

"Go to it, men," Captain Vergagrande said.

"Bend over, mate! I'll ream you!" Hidalgo barked.

Jacob grabbed the St. Andrew's Cross for support and stuck out his butt, exposing it for Hidalgo's sweet pleasure. Hidalgo pulled down Jacob's breeches and the horny pirate thrust his butt out some more brushing it against Hidalgo's hard cock. Hidalgo grinned and rubbed his knobby cock head along Jacob's puckers. Jacob sighed with pleasure.

Hidalgo said, "Like that, do you?"

"Aye, mate."

"Love my cock on your ass?"

"Aye!"

"Such a beautiful body," Hidalgo said under his breath. His hands were running all over Jacob's muscles, his ass. "Such a beautiful ass." Hidalgo was impressed with the masculine beauty of Jacob's ass, the tanned globes of smooth, solid flesh, the upward curve of the buttocks as they merged with his powerful lower back.

Hidalgo loved to see the fine golden hairs whirling on Jacob's hot ass. He ran his hands over each cheek, the silk gliding under his rough hands. Then he explored the cleft of Jacob's superb ass. He pressed his thumb on Jacob's hole, rubbing it along his puckers, groaning with pleasure as he felt them spasm and throb against his fingertip.

Hidalgo whispered in Jacob's ear, his lips brushing against Jacob's peach-fuzzed earlobe.

"I want to fuck you, mate."

"Aye."

"You want me to, don't you?"

"Aye, mate!"

Hidalgo placed a hand over Jacob's abs. He felt the excitement surging through Jacob's sweating body. Hidalgo wrapped his hand around the horny Jacob's cock. It bobbed wildly as Hidalgo continued to whisper hypnotically into Jacob's ear, his hot breath mingling with his heavy sighs.

"I'll fuck you, mate. Fuck you hard!"

Jacob's butt hole itched and throbbed as he reached behind him and grabbed Hidalgo's spasming cock. He ran a hand over the immense shaft, feeling the veins, imagining how every bulge, every ripple would feel inside his tight asshole.

Hidalgo reached for Jacob's cock, his hand massaging the blunt, triangular knob as it throbbed with lust.

"I'm ramming my cock up your ass!"

"Aye, mate!" Jacob anxiously wiggled his butt back and forth. "Fuck my hole!"

Hidalgo teased Jacob's puckers with the spasming knob of his cock. He circled it along Jacob's twitching hole, coating it with precome. Jacob gasped with macho pleasure, hoping that Hidalgo would fuck him good and hard.

Hidalgo plunged his cock right inside Jacob's hole.

Jacob screamed, he wailed. Hidalgo was ramming into his butt.

"You're getting fucked, mate. Fucked but good!" Hidalgo cried.

Hidalgo laughed when Jacob tried to wrench himself free. Hidalgo continued to plunge his cock up Jacob's ass. He felt his cockveins swell with lust, searing Jacob's butt hole.

Hidalgo ass-fucked Jacob for as long as he could take it, until he was ready to come.

"Ungh, ungh, ungh," Jacob grunted. "Please, mate. Please come now." He desperately wanted Hidalgo to shoot his wad.

"Now?"

"Aye, give it here, mate. Shoot!"

Hidalgo's mega-muscles suddenly went taut. He clenched his eyes and his tongue waggled to and fro .

Hidalgo gave a deep macho groan as the first load of white-hot come streamed out of his cock right into Jacob's spasming asshole. Jacob cried out, pushing his ass back, as Hidalgo's cock banged into his prostate, making him spurt comeload after comeload of creamy, hot come.

Hidalgo pulled his cock from Jacob's sore asshole. He turned around and faced Captain Vergagrande. His cock rose into the air, still hard, still ready for action.

"Ready to be fucked, Captain?"

"Fuck me!" Captain Vergagrande cried out. "Fuck me!"

Captain Vergagrande got down on all fours, for he loved to be fucked like a dog in heat. Hidalgo ran a hot, swollen tongue over his thick, frenzied lips. With a grunt, the stud clapped his hands on Captain Vergagrande's haunches for support and slipped his hard, pulsing prick between the captain's sweat-soaked butt cheeks. The doorknob-sized tip of Hidalgo's cock was pulsing hot, ready for action. The stud rubbed it back and forth across Captain Vergagrande's hot puckers.

"Up my ass! Aye, up my hole!" Captain Vergagrande howled. Hidalgo thrust his fat, pulsing cock through the captain's spasming asshole.

Captain Vergagrande gritted his teeth and clenched his eyes. He tried to choke back his agonizing cries, but the pain was just too fucking intense. "F-u-u-u-c-c-k-k-k!" the captain howled, pounding his fists on the floor. He flailed wildly, hot spit frothing from his lips.

Hidalgo proceeded with his anal assault, causing Captain Vergagrande's slimy butt hole to open wider and wider. Then it quickly sucked around Hidalgo's ramming cock. Hidalgo grinned with satisfaction when he felt the captain's asshole suck around his cock. And the captain clutched hard with his butt muscles to keep the swarthy stud's cock inside his stinking, sweating hole. "Aye, fuck. That's the way!" the captain shouted, encouraging Hidalgo to fuck him even harder. And so Hidalgo continued to power-fuck his horny captain for a good quarter of an hour.

Captain Vergagrande decided to change positions, so he flipped over on his back and wrapped his thighs around Hidalgo's powerful waist. His hard cock jabbed into Hidalgo's washboard abs. Their mouths were mashed together in hot macho passion as Hidalgo sucked on Captain Vergagrande's quivering hot tongue. Hidalgo reinserted his mighty cock up the captain's asshole. He embraced the captain fiercely as he lunged forward and buried his cock to the hilt. The captain howled with glee as he felt Hidalgo's invading cock stretch and widen his throbbing anal canal. Hidalgo fucked the captain hard and fast, plunging again and again up the captain's tight butt hole. The captain squirmed and thrashed within Hidalgo's arms as he felt Hidalgo's thick, wiry pubes scratch his sensitive asshole.

Captain Vergagrande whipped his head back and forth. Hot drops of funky sweat flew off his head. His entire muscled body shook in one long, convulsive shudder. Hidalgo felt the sexual heat blazing within his burly balls as he pounded Captain Vergagrande's butt.

A wild expression twisted Hidalgo's handsome, brutish face. His snorts became harder and angrier. His nostrils flared wildly. He pawed at the captain's thick rubbery nipples. The stud twisted and pulled at them savagely as he shoved his hard cock deeper and deeper up the captain's tight, aching hole.

Another quarter of an hour flew by while Hidalgo powerfucked his captain, who was delirious and overcome with lust.

Captain Vergagrande raved like a madman, his hands digging into Hidalgo's brawny biceps. "Fuck!" he cried. "Shoot your load. Shoot it up my ass!"

A final shudder shook through Hidalgo's hot, sweat-drenched muscles, his powerful cock ready to explode. "F-u-u-u-c-c-c-k-k-k!!" he yelled. Hidalgo sunk his cock to the hilt as thick jets of sperm blasted from his cock and flooded the captain's ass. Captain Vergagrande shouted a torrent of obscenities when he felt the thick scalding jets of sperm burn his asshole, making him shoot one powerful load after another that drenched Hidalgo's abs.

Hidalgo and Captain Vergagrande's cries of lust finally woke up Moanin' Jude. He took a good look at the two sweating, stinking studs, his hungry eyes roaming over every inch of their muscular, come-drenched torsos. He picked up a bottle of rum and took a hearty swig from it. Then he wiped his lips with the back of his hand. A grin brightened his chiseled features as he ran a hand over the beginnings of a ripe hard-on. Jacob was horny as well and it wasn't long before the four pirates indulged their perverted lusts in a wild orgy of homosexual passion, fueled by many more a bottle of spicy Jamaican rum.

Exhausted from their all-nighter, the four pirates finally passed out in a drunken stupor. It wasn't until the next evening when Captain Vergagrande awoke. The captain blinked his eyes and looked over to see a loudly snoring Hidalgo snuggled against Jude. Jude's head was nuzzling contentedly in the captain's musky, come-drenched pubes. Captain Vergagrande's thickening cock twitched and throbbed, rubbing hotly against Jude's half-open lips. Jacob Blow was nowhere to be found. His lusts inflamed, he had gone to find satisfaction amongst his fellow shipmates.

Captain Vergagrande whacked Jude and Hidalgo on the butt. "Wake up, mates."

Hidalgo grunted with a toss of his head. He took one look at Jude's inviting butt, licked his lips and mounted him. Jude gasped and a hard shudder shook his body when Hidalgo rammed his thick cock up his ass. Jude howled at first but then relaxed as the stud plowed into his humpy butt. Jude let out a long, contented moan as he shoved his ass back to meet Hidalgo's long, pumping thrusts.

Captain Vergagrande said, "Hidalgo, you're the horniest man on board!"

Jude looked up with a wolfish grin. "Aye, Captain!" Spit and precome dribbled down his square-cut chin.

"Aye!" Hidalgo added as he slammed powerfully into Jude's bucking ass.

Captain Vergagrande put his hands behind his neck and spread his legs. Jude reached for the captain's jutting nipples. He squeezed and twisted them, noisily deep-throating the captain's thick, vein-ridged cock while the perpetually horny Hidalgo continued to brutally pump his muscular ass. And so they fucked like three dogs in heat, fucking their brains out until the next pirate raid.

A PIRATE'S LIFE FOR ME

Simon Sheppard

I wish I was born about a thousand years ago.

Nick would always be a lost boy. One of Peter's boys, on the run from Hook. He'd always be a cabin boy. In his dreams, he'd be a cabin boy, serving gruff men on the Spanish Main, freebooters looting treasure-laden ships. Surrounded by men, real men, men outside the laws of God and man.

In his dreams.

Plucked from his impoverished family half a dozen years before, taken aboard the pirate galleon to swab the decks, to tend to the vittles. Sailing up and down the coast of Hispaniola, the Jolly Roger blazoned overhead. A dream of pirates.

Broiling sun, freezing gales.

About a thousand years ago.

A lost boy.

The ship would anchor off a deserted isle. In rickety launches laden with treasure, they'd go ashore, the brutal crew and him. The captain, reeking of salt and violence and untamed masculinity, would supervise the burial of gold. It was, Nick knew, even in his dreams, a powerful metaphor—though in his dreams, he was never sure for what.

The captain's first mate, a blond man beautiful as Billy Budd, would, after the backbreaking labor was through, strip off all his clothing and plunge into the waves.

"You've become," the first mate, whose name was, er, Billy, once told Nick, "quite a fine young man." It was after he'd emerged from the waves, his lean, tautly muscled body dripping wet in the tropical sun, gleaming, his long, pale cock crowned by a flurry of gold. "A fine young man." But Billy's cock wasn't hard, though Nick's was, and so nothing came of it. Not then.

No, it was after a raging storm at sea, the sort that sent laden galleons to the briny deep, that the captain came to him.

"Nick, my lad," said he, grasping his swollen crotch through his filthy… what, doubloons? No. Doublet? Not that, either. "Nick, my lad," said the captain, grasping his swollen crotch, "'tis time you became a man in more than name and years."

Nick, who'd been plucked while an innocent book from the fetid slums of London, would have liked to believe he had no idea what the captain was speaking of. But he did, he knew. His body flushed, feeling as though he were standing waist-deep in water as warm as a bath while thousands of tiny fish schooled about him, nibbling gently at his flesh. He knew, yes, he knew, even before Billy entered the captain's squalid cabin.

He knew.

And then the captain was lowering his breeches—yes, that was the word, "breeches"—and his cock, huge and veiny, the head still sheathed in foreskin, sprang forth, standing stiffly from between his massive, hairy thighs. Billy dropped to his knees, his golden head beside the pirate captain's cock, and parted his beautiful lips.

And what was Nick doing meanwhile? He had his cock in his hand—not as massive as the captain's, no, nor as beautiful as Billy's—but it was hard and warm and trembled at his touch.

The captain, still thrusting brutally into Billy's mouth, down the young man's throat, all the way down his throat, growled out, "It's time now, William. It's time to give yourself to young Nicholas."

And then Billy was naked, totally naked, thoroughly beautiful, standing before them, captain and cabin boy. He said, gently, to Nick, "Aye. Go ahead," then turned his back to him and leaned up against a rough wooden bulkhead.

Nick looked down at Billy's ass, pale, perfectly formed, covered in just the wispiest of blond fur. And the fish nibbled harder.

From somewhere on the deck came the sounds of singing. An obscene sea shanty that Nick recognized, a favorite of the sailors. "I signed aboard for a bit of cash..." Billy stuck out his ass, reached back, parted the flesh. "Damn'd rum, sodomy, and the lash."

The lash. Memories of men flogged till they were half-dead, left buried on the shoreline as the sea lapped around their heads, nailed into barrels of raw meat and left where wild beasts roamed. Unthinkable cruelties. And he was part of it, part of it all now, receiving a gift of flesh from his leering, bearded captain. The gift of another man.

Nick shuffled over to Billy, hobbled by trousers that had fallen to his ankles, and grabbed the beautiful young man around the waist. A pungent smell arose from Billy's cleft.

"G'wan, then, lad. What are ye waiting on?" The captain quaffed deeply from a mug of grog.

And then Nick was filled with cruelty, too, cruelty and desire, plunging himself, without lubrication, into Billy, his lust implacable as the tides. He felt himself enveloped, plunging into darkness, into light. Shining silks from the Orient, gold from El Dorado, none of it could match this plunder. Nothing.

Nick had once met a guy on-line who'd said he was "into pirate scenes." His e-mailed pictures had shown a handsome guy, in a boyish way, but he turned out to be kind of a twerp, into the poufy-sleeves and theme-park-ride brand of piracy. Just another erotic joke: Buttpirates of the Caribbean, all phony eye-patches and stuffed parrots. Nothing as real as being left to be eaten by wolves under a broiling tropical sun. Nothing as cruel as the real thing. Nothing as cruel as life.

Now Nick was deep inside Billy's ass, thrusting deep as a sword into enemy flesh, a saber, a cutlass. And then the captain laughed, a deep, unkind laugh. "I swear, laddie. If you don't half have a mooncalf expression on your face. Go at it. Go at it. Fuck that hole. It won't bite back. And I've well prepared the way for ye, I have."

He might as well have said "Avast, matey!" but in Nick's dreams, pirates rarely were engaged in such overripe dialogue. Nick went back to the serious work of fucking First Mate Billy's ass, struggling to keep his balance as the ship plowed into increasing turbulence.

In Nick's dreams, he rarely reached orgasm. Though the feeling of this dreamed-of fuck was—well, oceanic—he didn't this time, either. Instead, he suddenly found himself up on deck, as tawny men, stripped to the waist, scrambled through the rigging. One sailor, a man he was sure he'd seen before somewhere, was offering him a ladle of grog. "Aye," he said, squinting, "all the ship knows what you were up to down there. And there's not a man of us who don't envy you."

He'd once gone on a cruise with his mother, of all people. He couldn't remember just now why she had taken him. He'd spent the whole time on board trying not to come out to his elderly shipmates. The food had been good, though. He'd actually gained a little weight. The lost boy could barely squeeze into his jeans.

It was night, now. He lay in his hammock belowdecks, still awake, looking up through an open hatch at the Southern Cross. All around were the sounds of snoring, the smells of sweat and puke and shit. The rocking of the ship was sending him to sleep, at last. The creaking and groaning of wood. He shut his eyes.

"Stay still, lad." It was Billy's voice. And then Billy's touch, caressing Nick's face, moving down over his naked chest, softly over his belly, pushing its way beneath the ragged blanket, down to Nick's throbbing, eager cock. The hand was moist, wet as the sea, but warm, so warm. Nick, his eyes still closed, arched his back.

The hand was replaced by Billy's mouth, even warmer, even wetter than his hand had been. The beautiful young man took Nick all the way down, tongue working the cock's tender underside until his throat muscles milked the head. It was amazing. In the darkness behind his eyelids, Nick could hear the waves lapping at the wooden ship, and, maybe improbably, the cries of gulls soaring overhead. He felt good, so very good.

The mouth came away from his dick. *No, keep it there,* he wanted to plead. *Keep it there forever.*

But no, Billy's mouth moved up Nick's torso, nibbling, licking, kissing. At last it reached his face, kissing him softly on the lips.

"Oh, laddie, me laddie. You're mine."

Nick opened his eyes.

It wasn't Billy, it was the captain, his leering face so close to Nick's that his foul breath made Nick nearly gag. The captain's rictus spread ever wider. It was the face of evil, the face of death. A skull without crossbones.

"Hoist the Jolly Roger, me hearties!" the captain cried out. "This one's mine!"

Nick tried to squirm away, to cry out, but only a miserable, nearly inaudible groan came from his tight throat.

And then Nick was running down a beach, an endless Caribbean beach where someday gigantic, luxurious cruise ships would dock, but for now the sands were littered with rotting bodies. *Dead men tell no tales.* Skulls, grinning skulls everywhere. These are pearls that were his eyes.

The crocodile had swallowed a clock. Tick tock. Tick tock. Peter Pan, forever young, forever callow. Hook, the mutilated pirate, pursued implacably by time. By time.

He was trying to run. The sand shifted under every step, leaving him where he started. Even further back. The captain was getting closer. The crocodile. Tick tock. Tick tock.

I wish I was born about a thousand years ago.

At last a scream escaped Nick's throat.

☸

"Nick?" Jordan was leaning over his bed, a look of intense concern on his face. "You okay? Want me to call a nurse?"

The monitor beeped softly, steadily. Oxygen was flowing through the tube in his nose. Tubes everywhere, really. He looked down at the gauze beneath which a Hickman catheter pierced his chest. A dead man's chest. Nick would have liked to smile wryly.

"No, honey. I'm fine. Just a dream." It wasn't a dream, of course, not really. That would have been too easy, like some grade-school story that ended, "And then I woke up." That old Zen puzzle, what was it? *Am I a man dreaming I am a butterfly, or a butterfly dreaming I am a man?*

"You want me to increase the morphine drip?"

"Hand it here," Nick said. "I'll do it." His lips were dry.

Jordan handed him the button, and Nick pushed it.

The sun, morning sun, was flooding through the window. Jordan caught his glance.

"Too bright? You want me to shut the blinds?" Lines of concern were etched on Jordan's fiftyish, still-handsome face. Nick loved him so much.

"No, that's fine. Nice. Leave it." Even to himself, it sounded like a croak. Off in the corner somewhere, the sound of a ticking clock.

Am I a dying man dreaming I'm a pirate?

His eyes, gratefully, began to close.

Or a pirate dreaming I'm a dying man?

☸

It was a beautiful day, a glorious morning, warm sun streaming down as the galleon rode the gentle waves, skimming above murky depths. The ship was piled to the gunwales with newly looted treasures, the gold and jewels the freebooters had confiscated from the clutches of the Crown. *How the soldiers had screamed when the sabers pierced their guts.* An albatross streaked across the sky. Not an evil omen, not an omen at all.

Nick, just finished swabbing the decks and changing the captain's stained bed linens, was seated on a coiled hawser, smoking a pipe of West Indian herb. After one last puff, he lay back, looking up. Silhouetted against the shining sky, Billy, stripped to the waist, was scrambling through the rigging, sunlight sweet as honey on his perfect skin.

Swinging arm over arm, the first mate approached Nick till he was suspended just overhead, then dropped to the deck.

"Hey, Nick."

"Billy…"

The beautiful blond man bent over to stroke Nick's face. The smell of Billy's fresh sweat went straight to Nick's cock.

"Billy…"

"Sssh, laddie." He brushed his moist lips against Nick's.

"But the captain…"

"The captain will always be with us, Nick." His lips were on Nick's again, his tongue briefly brushing Nick's own. Nick's cock was so hard that it hurt. "But the captain is nothing to fear."

He wanted to believe that. He did. He did believe that.

A thousand years ago…

"And the crew?"

"Look around you, lad."

Nick did, scanning the deck. There was Parmalee, chubby and smiling, his arm around gaunt Carver's shoulders. And Grosz, muscular Grosz, looking straight at Nick and Billy and slipping his hand down the front of his billowing trousers. The sun emerged from behind a passing cloud, and the piles of precious booty that were scattered about the deck glinted anew.

☸

"Nick?" A voice, a familiar voice, from somewhere beyond the horizon. It was a voice Nick loved, but one that he wanted to go away. For now. "No, I think he's asleep." Go away. Sail away. "Let's let him rest."

☸

Treasure. The decks were piled high with treasure.

Nick removed Billy's boots, the worn leather warm and soft in his hands. Billy's feet were sweaty and beautifully formed.

Billy undid his broad leather belt and let his breeches fall to the deck.

It was such a lovely day, a day that could go on forever.

Billy's cock was marvelous, hard now and rising up.

Seaman Lunt, gruff, tattooed from head to foot, had emerged from belowdecks, a brimming goblet in his hand. He walked over to Billy and proffered the crystal, and the beautiful young man gratefully took a drink. Then Billy bent over, put his lips to Nick, and let the wine flow from one mouth to the other, the Madeira port sweet as life itself.

Nick thirstily gulped it down, reaching up to Billy's crotch as he did. The engorged flesh was so stiff, so hot to the touch. So amazing. Beyond the laws of God or man.

The alcohol hit him, gently warm. He took his lips from Billy's. "Thank you," he said. And again: "Thank you." He opened his mouth and took Billy's cock inside. It was all he ever wanted. He nursed on the cock, coaxing out pearls of precome. Briny. As Venus was said to rise from the waves, so did penis. Bad pun.

Billy stepped out of his breeches and pulled off Nick's shirt. He ran his fingers over Nick's back, over the scars from the floggings the captain had loosed upon his innocent flesh. Gently, so gently. Then he withdrew his dick from Nick's mouth and pulled Nick to his feet, holding him in his warm, strong arms, stroking his scars. He firmly spun Nick around till they were front-to-back and trailed his fingers over the traces of the whip, then bent over and kissed them, the souvenirs of pain, his fingers trailing downward, down past Nick's waist, down the crack of his ass.

"Yes," said Nick. "Yes." He leaned forward, hands on a keg, as Billy's expert fingers continued to probe his hole.

Casting off from the moorings, weighing anchor, Nick gave himself fully to the pirate life. He felt the head of Billy's cock insistently demanding entrance. Nick relaxed, letting it in. He felt the hard flesh begin to penetrate, then slide further, further and deeper, filling him up with its glory and damnation. In the wake of the ship, dolphins danced.

The rest of the crew was gathering around. Grosz had his hard-on out now, surprisingly small for someone so huge, and was stroking away. Skinny Carver was on his knees, sucking off Parmalee. And Lunt was standing right beside them, frigging Nick's cock as Billy fucked away.

Only the captain was nowhere to be seen. In a drunken stupor? Enchained by a mutiny? Or something else? The questions vanished from Nick's mind as Billy's pace increased, plunging in again and again, taking Nick, taking all of him, robbing him of his loneliness, giving him the world.

I wish I was born about a thousand years ago.

The timeless world. Billy pulled him upright, till they were both standing, Nick impaled on Billy's flesh, and every movement of the ship drove the dick deeper inside him. Billy's hands roamed over his nipples and belly, and his scarred back was caressed by Billy's sweaty, smooth chest. Meanwhile, Lunt crouched before him and sucked his straining cock.

Billy turned Nick's head to face him, and they kissed, their tongues meeting, twisting, tides of affection, desire, need.

"Land ho!" came the cry from the crow's nest. "Land ho!"

And when the kiss had ended, Nick looked up and saw it—a sun-drenched island not far away, verdant palm trees, rocky cliffs. Billy was pounding harder now, and Lunt's mouth had brought him to the brink.

"Nick?" There was that voice again, now faint as a distant gull's cry. That voice. But there was no time for voices, for memory. Nick turned and kissed Billy again, and the pirate groaned and shot off inside him, filling him, flooding him, redeeming him, damning them both to outlaw ecstasy. Parmalee found release in Carver's mouth, Grosz's small, hard dick shot off messily, everywhere, and at that moment, Lunt pulled back and Nick shot off, again and again and again, salty streams into the soft sea breeze.

And there on the horizon, the beach grew ever nearer, more distinct. It was a place free of skulls and death and decay. It was, rather, a place to store up gleaming stolen treasure. Safe harbor.

Nick would always be a lost boy now. Now and forever.

Safe harbor.

A thousand years ago.

Forever.

Land ho.

SWIFT AND CHANGING TIDES

Michael Cain

It was my first voyage. I'd been in France for six months for business, but had been restless and yearning to go back home to England, to my beloved Mina: We were to be married in the fall. For a fortnight I'd woken in sweats, dreaming the most sinful, libidinous dreams about her. Envisioning her naked and touching me. That's when I'd wake up, the instant her hands touched me.

I needed to get back to her. I needed her, and I was already trying out reasons for us to move up the wedding. The church forbade husband-wife relations, until you were actually husband and wife. And Mina and I both were from good, strict Catholic families.

To do anything too soon would be unfathomable.

The ship was called the *Trade Wind*, and it was an enormous vessel. Settled securely at the docks, towering over us passengers as we milled around and formed a queue to enter. The masts spiked deep into the skies. But once on board, the creaking of the boards under my feet gave me pause. The wood seemed very old and stripped of all varnish.

My trepidation lasted only until we set off. Somehow the unleashing of the sails, the way they took the winds and pushed us off from the harbor, the knife-like way the *Trade Wind* sliced through the murky, roiling waters, put awe in my eyes. I'd never seen nature so pushed and sluiced by something man-made.

I moved closer to the front of the ship and watched our stunning progress with unfettered interest. At this rate I was sure the voyage would be over in no time, and I'd be with Mina—or at least in her sweet presence.

But that night, whilst sleeping in the cabin I shared with a large Swedish man who spoke only the most broken English and French, I awoke to dizziness, and sweating, and a churning in my gullet that made me think for a moment I'd come down with the plague or some other sea pestilence.

I opened my mouth to breath, and felt the ship rock, something I'd so far ignored, and then I popped, the meager contents of my stomach spilling vile and ugly over the coarse floorboards of the cabin.

I leaned over the edge of the bed and tried to stop, but another draught of slimy vomit poured forth and added to the puddle on the floor. The puddle itself sloshed about with the rocking of the boat.

"Up above, eh," said the Swede, his accent thick, voice sleepy yet annoyed. "Do that above!"

The cool night air above felt good against my heated flesh, but the rocking still persisted, and I barely made it to the balustrade before disgorging yet another wave of putrid liquid. I hadn't thought I'd eaten all that much, but now it seemed my very insides were trying to come out.

For the next few days it seemed I never left that spot, my head hanging over the railing, my hands wrapped tight about the wood. The sea was choppy, but fortunately there hadn't been any storms yet. My stomach rippled with nausea, churning and dry heaving, my eyes staring off into the foamy, brackish water.

Then on the third day of our voyage my insides finally settled. I suddenly found myself exhausted, and starving. I moved below and begged the cook for something, anything, since it would be a good half a day before there was another meal.

"Finally got your sea legs, I see," the cook chuckled in an amused baritone.

I nodded.

The cook was just about through with the morning meal clean-up, but he got me a large hunk of bread, and ladled some brown gravy into a bowl. The gravy had small chunks of the morning meal's meat still in it, and the two things tasted better than I could have imagined. I wolfed them down in no time and handed my tin plate back to the cook.

He nodded. "See you at supper."

I went back to my cabin, but the Swede was nowhere about. I fell onto my bunk, rolled over toward the wall and drifted off into nothingness.

☸

I awoke soaking wet, the ocean falling in on me, coursing through a large hole in the wall of the cabin. The water was cold, but not freezing, but still I found myself momentarily paralyzed with fear.

Where was I?

The ship! Yes. And now there was water pouring into my cabin. And as if to answer back my body jerked and hurtled itself through the glut of wet, toward where I knew the door to be. It was already pushed open, and the hallway was as full of ocean as my cabin had been. The hall was dark, the lanterns already extinguished by the raucous waves of water.

I made it to the stairs, and found it was already night outside. I stumbled out onto the deck and heard a cannon fire, saw a great spark flare out from far out on the pitch-black ocean, then felt the hit to the ship, a bucking and jerk, and heard the crack of wood letting go.

Panic filled me, and my breathing doubled in pace from the rapid beat it already had gained.

I turned to run to the other side of the ship, but the night hit me, hard, in the face, buckling me over, and then again in the back of the head, knocking me unconscious.

☸

I felt the sun on my shoulders before I opened my eyes. I had a vague memory of being dragged and thrown on the floor like a sack of flour. Now I was on my knees, my hands bound behind me, my head a riot of pain. I forced my eyes to open, and as if this turned on the world I heard the groans and cries of the other passengers and the crew. Through the blazing light of day I made out that I was kneeling in a line-up of sorts, and all those in line were bound just as I was. I heard the wind fluttering something, a flag, high above. I looked up and there blew a tattered black flag with a skull and two swords flanking behind it.

Pirates, I thought. I'm going to die.

Suddenly I heard a great booming voice. "Are they ready?"

"Yes, sir," answered an excited voice.

"Then we'll begin."

I heard some steps taken, and then the booming voice: "No."

I heard a sword drawn, and a man cried out, but was silenced mid-wail. I heard his head hit the deck of the ship with a sickening thump.

I closed my eyes as this happened over and over again, at least ten times. When I heard those steps stop in front of me, I opened my eyes and looked at the boots, black and dull, standing on the wooden boards of the deck.

There was a silence, and then I felt a hardened, roughened hand snatch me by the back of my hair, forcing my face up into the harsh light. I tried to see the man who was to kill me, but his face was outlined by the intense light of the sun, making him out to be more a demon than a man.

All I heard was, "Yes." And then all went black again.

❁

I awoke in total blackness, and in foul-smelling straw. I reached up and felt the stickiness of blood in my hair, where I'd been struck, then I reached out and found a wall of bars before me, and discovered that my wrists were in irons and attached to the floor. I tried to stand, but my head started to whirl, and then I slipped back into sleep.

For what seemed days I pulled out of and then fell back into this dark, fuzzy state. Sometimes I caught the sound of voices from above; sometimes there was sunlight spilling through cracks in the ceiling.

But when I truly came to I was shivering and I was starving. I called out and heard no reply. I looked about, my eyes finally adjusting to my darkened surroundings, only to find I was the only occupant of the cage. I felt a stab of panic and dread, but then I felt for one tiny moment lucky. After all, there were more than thirty other passengers and the entirety of the crew of the *Trade Wind*, and I seemed to be the only one left.

When the sun no longer slipped through the cracks of the ceiling, I heard feet clambering down to where I was captive. The feet belonged to two hulking men, and they pulled me out of my cage, releasing me from my bonds, but gripping me instead in their far stronger grips, their hands rough and cold and unyielding. They dragged me up the creaking staircase and onto the deck of the ship. My feet barely touched the ground as they transported me. I caught a glimpse of the ocean: still and glistening, and most beautiful.

They set me down finally at the open door of a cabin, warm golden light glowing from inside, and there in the door was a man just a touch shorter than I, with dark eyes, shoulder-length black hair pulled back in a tail, and the most beautiful face I'd ever seen on a man.

He smiled, and I felt a flush of embarrassment, for I'd never so much as contemplated the looks of another man, but this man had already caused my flesh to burn, and my manhood to stir.

"I am called Lorenzo," he said. "My masters want for you to be cleaned and fed."

"Your masters?" I asked. But then one of the hulking men behind me gave me a firm check in the shoulder and told me to do as I was told.

Lorenzo smiled again and gently took me by the elbow. "Come with me," he said.

The cabin was furnished plainly, but it was clean and very warm, and filled with a delicious aroma. There was a table with a chair, and there on an ornate pewter plate was a roast chicken and a large loaf of hot bread.

"Sit," Lorenzo said, pouring wine into a matching goblet. "Eat."

I needed no further encouragement, already pulling apart and eating the chicken even before my bum touched the seat. I ate and ate, and drank, yet unsettlingly I couldn't stop looking at Lorenzo. He was sleek, and though he was not a big man, he looked to be built solidly, and...I just couldn't stop wanting to see more of him. My eyes felt as hungry for his very flesh as my stomach was for the food.

When I could eat no more, Lorenzo led me into another room, where he closed the door and lit more lanterns. Their light flickered and rolled about the walls, moving gently with the calmness of the sea.

There was a steel tub filled with steaming water.

"Please undress," he asked.

I suddenly noticed he had an accent, only the slightest trace, but still. He was a Spaniard.

I suddenly felt my breath catch, and I found I couldn't move. I was shy in front of him, and I didn't want to him to see the sinful state of my manhood. Especially since he'd unwittingly caused it.

"Please," he repeated. "My masters instructed that you be bathed and fed before their return."

He had already started to unbutton my spoiled shirt, and the touch of his hands, their weight on me, made my pulse quicken and my flesh sweat. I did nothing...could do nothing to stop him...didn't want to stop him... as he pulled and unbuttoned and stripped me until I stood in front of him completely naked, my cock turgid and pointing straight out from my crotch at a ninety-degree angle.

He guided me into the tub of water, and I slowly sank into the blessedly hot, soapy water.

If he'd noted my erection, he gave no sign. What he did do was bathe me, rubbing soap and a soft sponge over my flesh, washing and detangling my filthy hair—even shaving the stubble of beard from my face.

Then he wrapped me in a blanket, heavy as wool yet soft as velvet. As I dried, his nimble fingers searched though my hair and found the gash in my scalp, and rubbed some sort of ointment into the cut flesh, causing it to tingle and then to cease to hurt.

Lorenzo then led me to a large bed, the linens a sensuous blood red.

I was naked and clean, my stomach was full and I was blissfully warm as I crawled into the bed. The mattress was luxuriously soft, and the bedding must have been born of silk. All these sensations mingled with an exotic, spicy scent, and as my weary head found refuge on a pillow, the dim candlelight faded and I fell fast asleep.

❁

I dreamed of Mina, a terrible, lusty dream. I dreamed she was with me, naked in the pirate's bed, and she was performing an unholy, prurient act.

I awoke not realizing at first that I'd left my dream and Mina behind. My manhood was engulfed in a warm smooth place, something so foreign and queer, yet I willed myself not to wake. It was the most glorious of sensations, and I felt myself lengthen and harden in its embrace.

My hands reached for my crotch, finding a head of soft, curly hair. Not long enough to belong to Mina. I opened my eyes and found myself looking down at a naked Lorenzo. His body was at a graceful angle to mine, his face buried in my lap, shoulders and arms astride my hips, and the rest of him sunny side up on the mattress below me. His own hips undulating, grinding his pelvis into the soft sheets of the bed.

My body involuntarily jerked, and my hands grasped his curls, trying not nearly hard enough to remove my molester from his lecherous act. Lorenzo's arms clasped around my hips, and his head remained stubbornly exactly where it was, his nose now pressed into my pubic hairs, and his chin grinding into my balls. But then my arms slackened, and I took one deep breath and relaxed back into the softness of the mattress. No sooner than I did, Lorenzo returned to his sucking and licking of my stone-hard cock, making faint suctioning sounds, and moaning in appreciation for my cooperation.

Lorenzo's hands were soft and warm, the softest, warmest hands I'd ever encountered on a man or a woman, and they lavished my flesh with their caresses and squeezes. My hips started to push into the downward movements of his head, involuntarily, yet seeming all too well to know exactly what they were doing. I felt my skin begin to warm, and then begin to sweat, and as my heart started to pound in my ears I felt my balls tingle, then churn in their fleshy sacks.

I felt myself start to let go, my climax so near. But then Lorenzo took a firm, hard grasp of me, stopped his wondrous sucking, and smiled as my balls spasmed, yet not a drop of my seed escaped from my piss slit.

It hurt, somewhat, and yet a moment later, as his eyes locked with mine, I realized what he'd done. It was as if I hadn't climaxed at all. My cock remained hard, my want and need was unabated, and my mind was so filled with heat that I couldn't stand it.

"More," I whispered.

Lorenzo smiled, yet his head shook a negative. "The masters will want you wanting," he said.

"The masters?"

He brought his legs up under him until he was kneeling between my thighs, and with a smooth motion his hands moved from my hips down under my bum, and down onto the back of my thighs. He pushed my legs up in the air, exposing my rump and throwing my stability completely off-kilter. But this I didn't have time to mind, for his face dipped down into the crack of my ass where I felt his breath hot and urgent, and then his face nestled into the crack, his mouth hot, his lips soft on my tender sphincter.

What on earth was he planning on doing?

But before I could verbalize this question his tongue slathered my hole, wet and warm and lapping at my until then utterly ignored orifice.

I moaned and cursed, and bit my arm not to call out in utter abandon. I felt my muscles tense, and my sphincter pulse and tighten, and then as Lorenzo's talented pallet wriggled even further into me, awakening something secret and wild inside me. I knew it was inside me, I could feel it churn and thump, and then my entire body tingled with it. My hands now found their way down to my own squirming bum, and pulled my buttocks apart, better to accommodate Lorenzo's slithering tongue.

Suddenly I wanted Lorenzo inside me. As if I was the woman, I wanted him to push his manhood into me. And at the same time I wanted to fuck him as well. I'd never felt like this, and I felt almost torn asunder by the duplicity in it. But no sooner did I have these thoughts than the great wooden doors to the cabin burst open, and the cool night wind of the ocean rushed in, causing the candles to flicker and my skin to break out in gooseflesh.

Lorenzo released me and clambered off the bed, leaving me exposed and indignant, my cock hard and embarrassingly visible to the two men who had entered. It was pouring rain outside, and Lorenzo first went and secured the door, then returned to the men, helping them wordlessly to strip off their rain-sodden clothing. Both were tall, broad shouldered, and savagely built. The two looked more like titans than human beings. And as Lorenzo pulled their shirts off, exposing their torsos, I marveled at how muscular they were, built like the carvings of ancient gods I'd encountered in tombs at the university.

The Masters, I thought.

But their stature and forms were where their similarities ended. One was fair, blond hair cascading down over his shoulders, so light that even wet it looked like spun gold, and his face was speckled with the thinnest of beards, trimmed short and neat. His chest bore tawny, blond hair that glistened, and the most alluring freckles accented his skin, over his shoulders and chest. Much like my beloved Mina.

But this flash of Mina lasted only the stretch of time that it took my gaze to flicker over to the other man. He was the color of night, skin darker than any I'd ever seen, stretching like marble or stone over his rippling muscles and making his smooth and angular face all the more beautiful... and sinister.

And his head was smooth as well, his skull shapely and tapering into his brawny neck.

"So this is the one?" the dark master said, his English perfect, yet the accent slow and practically a feral growl.

The other man had his hand down between Lorenzo's legs, stroking a prodigious length of hard flesh. But when queried he pulled himself away from Lorenzo and smiled in my direction, his teeth straight and white, his eyes sparkling emeralds.

"I knew you'd like him."

"Wouldn't go that far," the dark master said.

I felt his gaze travel over me, down the length of me, stopping, flickering on certain parts, brushing past others—then his look softened, and I saw heat in his eyes.

"At least not until we've tried him out."

"Um," I started, and all three men looked over to me, surprised. "I'm not sure I—"

Abruptly the dark master moved across the room and grabbed me by an ankle, dragging me down to the foot of the mattress, then gripped my face in one of his enormous hands and pulled me up to him until our faces were almost touching.

"Careful," I heard the pale master say. "Don't break the pretty toy before we've gotten our fun in."

The dark master grunted. "We're the masters of this ship," he said. "And you will not speak unless you are spoken to. Understand, slave?"

Slave? I gulped. I didn't know whether it was from the stranglehold he had on my throat, or the threat that the word "slave" implied.

"And you will do as you are told." His hand tightened even more, thumb pressing menacingly against my windpipe. "Do you understand?"

I shook my head, and tried to speak, tried to say, "Yes."

He let me go and I crumpled back on the bed, the air rushing into my lungs in gasps and sputters between hoarse coughs.

The pale master was now naked, and was drinking long draughts of wine from a silver goblet.

The dark master pulled open his britches, peeling them off, leaving them in a puddle on the floor as he climbed onto the bed with me, his rough hand finding, then squeezing and pulling at my still maddeningly tumescent cock.

I jerked again, my hands racing up to make him let go, but the look, the glowering of his eyes and the stern line of his mouth stopped me short. That and the fact that his other hand was now clenched in a fist, his arm drawing up to serve a blow.

I fell back, my body going limp and docile.

He almost smiled, a smirk really, and then he let go of my cock and licked his long red tongue across his palm, then returned his hand to my lap, pumping his spit-slicked fist up and down the length of my hard-on.

My legs wouldn't hold still, flexing and straining as I felt that alarming heat from before returning, mingling with ice-cold fear.

"There now, see?" he growled. "Being in our service has its pleasures." With his free hand he stroked his growing, haltingly large erection. It was covered in the same ebony flesh as the rest of him, and the veins were jet black, like roots wrapped around the trunk of a tree.

He licked this palm as well, then coated his length in the spit.

The pale master came up behind him, leaned in and kissed his shoulder, then smiled at me. "Time to try him out?"

The dark master grunted. With a quick, violent grabbing of my legs, and a hard twist, I suddenly found myself flipped over on my belly, my erection crushed and poking into the mattress, my face temporarily smothered in the same downy softness. I tried to pull myself up, but he was instantly atop of me, his entire body pinning and pushing down on mine. It was all I could do to turn my head enough to take breath.

And then I felt it, the pressure at my sphincter, and then the searing tearing apart of my insides as his massive manhood pierced my chute, pushing down, down, down into my guts without a moment of hesitation, and not stopping until I felt his groin, his scratchy pubes against my backside, his balls completely covering my own.

I cried out, my hands fists, my head smashing into the soft mattress, willing it to be stone or brick, something solid and fatal to beat my head on.

"That hole's tight," he moaned into my ear, his breath hot and vile against my skin. "I think we've got a virgin piece of tail here."

He started to push in and out of me, making the pain burn hotter, and the ripping of my insides more assuredly fatal. I was going to die, being stabbed like this. I'd probably bleed to death if I didn't smother in the softness of the mattress first.

Suddenly I felt the man's lips press against my earlobe, and then his lips parted and his tongue licked the tender flesh. And then just as abruptly his teeth sank in, biting like an animal, ripping my attention immediately from the searing pain of my impaled asshole, and honing in my attention fully on the electric shock of having him trying bite my ear off.

Oh God ! I thought. Are these cannibals as well as sodomites?

But then I felt it, faint at first, but then as blazing hot as the pain had been. It was pleasure, it was the deepest physical pleasure I'd ever felt. And with each churn of his magnificent cock into my guts, the more I craved it.

God forgive me.

I suddenly found myself with the pale master's rock-hard cock in my face, and without a moment's hesitation I opened my mouth to let him push it into me. It only seemed natural, only seemed...damn it to hell, I had to taste it, as much as I had to have the dark master's cock pushing in and out of my bung hole.

His cock tasted salty, and before I could think he'd plunged his length deep down into my throat, causing me to gag, and sputter, and to spit him out and cough miserably.

I'd unreasonably wanted to take him into my mouth as easily as Lorenzo had taken me. But now I felt the blood rise in my face, not with lust, but with the shame of failing so totally.

The pale master caressed my cheek, and then brought my chin up to look him in the eye—all the while the dark master kept plunging in and out of my now wide open hole with increasing speed and power. My bum was lifting up to meet his every downward movement.

"Very good," the pale master whispered. "You'll do just fine here." And then he pulled my head back into his lap and I took him into my mouth again, sucking and drawing on the smooth, thick flesh of his prick. Tears sprung from the corners of my eyes as I forced myself to take more and more of his cock into my mouth, inch by solid, hard inch, until literally I could cram no more of him into my mouth.

His hips began to gyrate and he drilled into my mouth, spiking my head as efficiently as the dark master was drilling my bottom.

I suddenly felt as if these two men owned me, and always had. And I liked that thought.

The masters filled me from both ends, fucking my mouth and ass with hard, soul-shattering blows, too many to ever be counted. Somewhere along the line my now mush-like hole had made its own lubrication, and now the dark master's cock slipped and slid with sloppy staccato suction noises.

The masters roared at the same moment, both pushing themselves into me as far as they could, holding themselves there. I tasted the salty spray of the pale master's seed, washing over the back of my tongue and pouring down the back of my throat. I also felt my sphincter slicked up even more, until the dark master's cock made lewd slurping and smacking sounds as he churned slowly in and out of me.

A moment later I found myself alone on the bed, the linens uprooted about me, my body limp and exhausted and sweaty, yet my prick was hard and red and shuddering, sticking up from my pubes like one of the masts of this mighty ship. I watched as the masters sauntered and staggered drunkenly over to the table where Lorenzo, still naked, had set out plates of food for them.

The pale master looked back at me and smiled. "Our guest needs assistance, Lorenzo."

My chest heaved and my heart raced as Lorenzo crawled smiling up onto the bed with me, and then climbed up onto me, straddling my hips and with perfect precision lowered himself down onto my cock, impaling himself all the way down my shaft to my balls, until his own nut sack and cock rubbed ardently against my belly.

He dragged himself up and down on my pole a few times, his soft, hot hands against my chest, holding himself upright, his insides hot and velvet smooth. But I could take no more, and as my hips swung up, plowing my manhood into him, my hands reached up and seized his handsome face and pulled him down to me—I kissed him. Long and deep, and sweet. He tasted like the ripest, freshest fruit, and our tongues grappled with each other as my seed shot up into him. His breath caught, then he panted as we kissed, and I felt his own load now spurt and slosh over and across my belly, warm and silky smooth.

For only the briefest of moments I thought of my eternal soul, how it would now be cast into hell. And Mina's smile flickered in my mind's eye. But then I saw the warmth in Lorenzo's eyes, peering down at me as his ass contracted and relaxed, stoking my hard-on and doing a very good job at resurrecting the want in me to a blazing inferno. And then I saw the two masters, bodies bulging, sinewy with perspiration, handsome and dangerous, their cocks still hard and bobbing in front of them as they strode back to the bed.

"I think we'll have another go," said the dark master, pulling Lorenzo up and off my cock, sprawling him onto his back and then mounting him with swift, cruel efficiency. The pale master pulled me by my ankles until my butt hung precariously from the edge of the bed, and with deadly aim speared me straight through to the hilt, knocking the wind from my lungs but filling me full of the very things I'd never possessed.

Lust and life.

BLOW THE MAN DOWN

Zavo

The *Queen Mary* lay at anchor in a cove formed by one of the nondescript, ubiquitous islands that dot the West Indies. The water was a light turquoise, juxtaposed against a stretch of sand so white it hurt one's eyes. Abutting the strip of beach was a copse of palm trees so thick they looked all but impenetrable. Behind them rose tree-covered mountains, their tops touching a blue, cloudless sky. A light breeze blew across the ship's main deck, filling my nostrils with the scents I loved. I looked down at the naked pirate on his knees in front of me, his back pressed against the gunwale. He was sucking my cock as if it would be his last one. To my right and left stretched a line of pirates, each with their trousers at their feet, each having his prick worked on by one of the captives from yesterday's raid.

It was the unwritten rule of the sea that all sailors captured during raids were made to service their captors or be tossed into the waters they traveled on. There were some stubborn ones who became food for the ravenous sharks that filled these waters, but they were few and far between. Truth be known, many a raiding ship had given up without a fight, knowing what their lot would be and preferring that over death. While sexual trysts routinely filled the dull hours in between the never-ending chores and ceaseless raids, the captain had mandated this morning routine for new captives and those who had not yet earned their place among the crew.

The handsome man kneeling at my feet certainly was hairy. His long, thick, dark-brown mane flowed over his ears and onto his shoulders. A scarlet sash kept most of it out of his eyes, which were a brown so deep they were almost black. His face was almost masked by the hair of his full beard and mustache, which for a pirate was unusually kempt. I didn't know his name, nor at this time did I care. Once he had earned his right to stay on the ship by proving he could service the sailors, he would be given a new name. All I knew of him was that he was the bosun of the English frigate that had surrendered to us yesterday morning. It had been a quick but bloody battle, our efforts heightened by the fact that we knew this ship was out to destroy us. Our exploits were becoming legendary on many of the seas we traveled, and we, along with numerous other brigands who plied these waters, were beginning to take a heavy toll on trade to the New World. Many frigates and man-o'-wars from England, Spain, and France had been dispatched with the sole intent of putting as many pirates to the sword as they could, thus destroying our stranglehold on their livelihood.

I grabbed two handfuls of the young pirate's hair and used them to guide his efforts on my stiffer. He slid his finger up the inside of my leg, searching for my secret spot. I spread my legs wider to give him access, and he quickly found his target. After some initial probing he wet his finger and pressed insistently against the tiny opening. Suddenly, his finger popped through and slid deeply into me. He began with short thrusts and alternated them with slow deep ones. The young pirate certainly was no novice at sucking cock, and much too quickly I felt the familiar sensation at the base of my pole, heralding my approaching explosion. I began pumping my hips faster, driving my dick deep down the throat of the lusty sailor. My balls slapped against his chin till he grasped them in his hand and began kneading them roughly. He also must have sensed my impending eruption, for he redoubled his efforts on my stiffer and with his finger in my ass. Saliva was fairly flying from his mouth as he bobbed up and down. He was soon rewarded as the first blast of my spunk hit the back of his throat. The sailor sawed up a final time, then let my saliva-soaked stiffer plop from his mouth. The second blast landed in his moustache, and his tongue quickly found it. I placed my hand on his head to steady him, and he stuck his tongue out for me. He began stroking my dick while aiming the slit in the head at his tongue. When I was done shooting he eagerly swallowed the substantial pile, licked my dick clean, withdrew his finger and sucked that clean as well.

I adjusted my trousers and stepped back to allow one of my shipmates to take his place in front of the kneeling man. Walking down the line watching the rest of the action, I met Captain Sterling coming from below deck; he was leading a naked man on a chain that looped around his neck and connected to his hands, which were chained in front of him. It was the captain from the raiding frigate. Another rule of the high seas was that if the captain of the captured vessel chose not to be thrown into the sea, the conquering captain got the use of him for a few hours before he was shared with the rest of the crew. Once the captain had put him through his paces, the rest of the men had their turn. The captain was leading the man around the length of the ship as if he were showing off a prized stallion. The man held his head high, the wind tousling his black locks.

The man was indeed a fine specimen, and just to the captain's liking. His legs and arms were corded with muscles, and covered in a pelt of black hair. His chest was massive and also covered in hair; his nipples were the size of small plums. However, it was his cock that drew all eyes to it. It was as thick as my wrist and, even soft, it hung halfway to his knee. It flopped as he walked, slapping audibly against his leg. It was a wonder the captain was able to walk at all, I thought to myself. The man seemed to intuit he was something to look at, and strutted to great effect. The procession stopped frequently to allow each of the pirates to admire and heft the manhood of the captive captain. When Captain Sterling had made a complete circuit of the ship, he returned to the ship's wheel. He ordered the first mate to spread several blankets on the deck; once that task was done, he forced the captain onto his hands and knees facing the wheel, and looped the chain through several wheel spokes. In further preparation, Captain Sterling spread the ass cheeks of the bound man and applied the cooking grease that was typically used for this occasion. The pirates lined up in order of rank, with the first mate at the head of the line. He dropped his colorful trousers and knelt behind the giant. His cock was enormous, and his penetration was slow but steady. The bound man arched his back to accommodate the position and the size of the cock entering him. The first mate paused, gripped the captain's ass cheeks, and began hammering him for all he was worth. While the rest of the pirates, including Captain Sterling, cheered the man on, the giant man gave as good as he received. He met each thrust of the sailor's with a back thrust of his own, the smacking of their coupling interspersed with the shouts of the pirates. When the first mate had deposited his seed, he stood up, donned his trousers, and stepped aside to make room for the next pirate. The captive captain took everything he had coming to him. Sweat was running down his back in rivulets, and the smell of spunk was heavy in the air. As I waited for my turn, I recalled yesterday morning when the attack had begun that had brought these recent captives to our ship.

☸

We were laden with stolen goods and headed to the nearest port in the West Indies to offload them and relax for a few days. We had been going at it hard for several months, and the men were starting to get frazzled. Even with the daily sexual activity on the ship and the rigorous chores, it was simply too close quarters for too long for this many men.

Although all the sleeping quarters were below deck, the captain's cabin was separate from the rest of the crew. Once you descended the slick stairs, rows of hammocks were nailed to the strong wooden beams that supported the main deck above. The captain's cabin was off to the right, accessible through a heavy oak door. No one entered without his permission, except for me. Since being kidnapped and brought aboard this vessel, I had been the captain's favorite, and others had me only upon his consent, which was seldom, typically when he was drunk and wouldn't admit his true feelings for me.

The cabin was small, as were the men's quarters, since as much of the ship's room as possible was needed to store raided goods. The furniture in the room consisted of two chests that housed the captain's assorted, colorful clothing. The rest of the room was consumed by the captain's large bed. The sheets and pillowcases were of the finest silk, and the blankets were of the softest wool. However, all the bedding was in a tangled heap on the floor, thrown there during our wild contortions. The captain was sprawled on his back on the bed, with me impaled on his substantial cock. He had a knack for timing his movements with the rocking of the ship, driving his member deep within me, meeting each of my downward plunges. He gripped me at the waist to steady me; I was holding two of the crossbeams over my head to keep from toppling sideways. The only sounds in the room were the slapping of my ass cheeks against the captain's thighs, and our combined grunts and groans. The odor of our coupling filled the small space, and added to the effluvia of sweat, spunk, and numerous past dalliances.

"I'm almost there, William," he moaned.

Suddenly, the ship was rocked from stem to stern. I had been on board long enough to know the difference between shudders from waves that heralded an approaching storm and those that signaled an attack; I knew we faced the latter. The captain knew it too and, uttering a string of curses, increased the tempo of his thrusts into me. I obliged his efforts by squeezing his hefty pole with my asshole on each upward lunge.

"I'm gonna shoot, William!"

He emptied his spunk into me, then kissed me on the lips before lifting me off his still-hard dick. He pulled up his silk breeches as I hurriedly got dressed, and we quickly climbed the wooden ladder to the deck. When we emerged on the main deck we were swamped by the sprawl from a cannonball that had fallen short. I could see the frigate a few hundred yards off our stern. She was small and sleek, her only intent to quickly sink or board us. Never one to run from a fight, Captain Sterling ordered us around so that all our side cannons would take her broadside. The wind caused the distance between us to be quickly closed. Our guns had a longer reach, and when we let off the first volley, pieces of the frigate's gunwales disintegrated and two of its masts were snapped in half. Our next volley swept her main deck clean of sailors and took out several of her cannons on the side facing us. Their second, and last, volley tore off portions of our gunwale and several pirates in the bargain. The captain of the frigate quickly realized his predicament, and soon the white flag of surrender was hoisted. Once we were close enough, we used our grappling hooks to board her. Only two of the crew chose to be thrown overboard. Nearly twenty men climbed onto our ship. When all were aboard and the frigate had been sunk, the captain ordered us to this cove to lay low for a few days.

❁

When I knelt behind the bound captain, the spunk of several men coated his ass and dripped down both legs. I knew this would be a quick one for me. I placed the head of my cock against his hole and easily slid home. Although well lubricated, his chute was still surprisingly tight. He grunted as I began pumping into him with deep long strokes. His slippery hole clenched my stiffer on each plunge, bringing gasps of pleasure from deep within me. Much too soon I felt my explosion building and I cried out as I dumped my load deep within him. As I slid out of him he shouted, "Next!" and I was replaced by the next sailor.

Once the crew was done with the captive captain, preparations were begun for our excursion to the island. The men needed to get off this ship and stretch cramped muscles and breathe air other than the salty sea air that engulfed us. We would go in two shifts to leave most of the crew on ship to ward off any attackers. Two rowboats were lowered to the water, each carrying a half dozen sailors, and we rowed to shore. All eyes scanned the beach and the growth beyond for any signs of life, be it friendly or otherwise. Within minutes the prow of the boat struck the sandy bottom and the lead oarsmen leaped into the water and tied it to a fallen tree half submerged in the lagoon. Once it was secure we exited en masse and went ashore. We waited while the second boat beached, then walked single file to the jungle's edge. As we drew near it became apparent that the foliage was not quite as impenetrable as we had first thought. In fact, we found an overgrown trail that was hard to discern beyond 20 feet.

We hit the trail with cutlasses in hand, our pistols thrust in the sashes at our waists; those with muskets had them slung over their shoulders. Captain Sterling was in the lead. We were immediately assailed by numerous insects; between fighting them off and hacking at the undergrowth, it was a slow and miserable trek. We heard numerous unfamiliar sounds in the jungle, but did not sight another living soul. I got the distinct impression we were being flanked on both sides, but could catch no glimpse of any pursuer. After what seemed like days on the trail, but was in reality only a matter of hours, we heard the sound of rushing water. As we continued the noise grew louder and within minutes we faced a good-sized, deep pool formed by water rushing from a fissure in a rocky ledge.

Fresh water was always welcome after days and sometimes months of not bathing while at sea. The captain ordered two of the pirates to stand guard, while the rest of us eagerly shed our clothing and dove into the pool. The water was cold and refreshing, and the pool was large enough to accommodate all of us. I swam several laps, then paused to watch the rest of the men. Captain Sterling swam circles in the pool, his strokes powerful and even, his muscular back and hairy ass surfacing on each stroke. After he had taken several more turns around the pool, he crawled onto a large rock to dry in the late afternoon sun.

"Come here, William."

I swam to the rock he was laying on and climbed to his side. His cock was fully hard and pointing straight up at the sky. As I looked down on him I could see that the rest of the pirates had stopped whatever they were doing, and now all eyes were on us, in anticipation of what was about to take place. I knew the captain often loved an audience during his pleasuring, and that he loved to put on a good show. This was not the first time we had performed for the rest of the crew. I knelt beside him and wrapped my hand around his manhood. It was thick, soft, and warm to my touch. The captain began pumping his hips slowly. I formed an "O" with my fingers, spit on his cock several times, then let the piece of flesh slide through. The captain pulled me to him roughly, and kissed me full on the mouth. After a few quick strokes I spread the captain's legs and slid in between them. I ran my tongue over the head of his cock, then slowly teased my way down the thick shaft, working the thick veins, till I got to the hairy root. His crotch hair was thick and dark-brown, and I buried my face in it, inhaling deeply of his smells. His balls were enormous, and I hefted them inside their sac of flesh. I then licked them thoroughly, as Captain Sterling moaned and implored me with soft words to continue my efforts.

I left his balls and licked my way back to the head of his cock. I quickly engulfed the fat knob and slowly sank down on him till his crotch hair was tickling my nose. I held it in my mouth, sucking gently on it, then began sawing up and down on it slowly, letting my tongue trail along the thick shaft. The captain moaned incessantly, and began thrusting his hips frantically, slamming his cock into my mouth. I knew he was close, and within moments the first glob landed on my tongue. I held his cock head in my mouth as he emptied into me. As always, his load was tremendous, and I swallowed as fast as I could. When he was spent I held his cock in my mouth till it was soft once more. Captain Sterling stood up and stretched, as did I, and then we dove back into the pool.

One of the pirates standing guard suddenly cried out and plunged into the water. When he bobbed to the surface a spear was protruding from his chest. No sooner had this fact sunk in on us than loud, sharp cries filled the air. Scores of naked, ebony men burst from the bushes, carrying blow guns and spears. The second man standing guard took a spear to the heart. As the rest of us scrambled to grab pistols or swords that were laying within reach, three more of our group went down. Realizing we were hopelessly outnumbered, we quickly raised our hands in a sign of surrender.

With the tips of their spears the dark-skinned men forced us out of the pool and into a line. They studied us for several moments before one—who, judging from the extent of his adornment, was the chief—stepped in front of Captain Sterling and ran his fingers through the thick brown hairs of his chest. Two spears pointed at the captain's chest kept him from objecting to the scrutiny. I noted that none of the warriors had a lick of hair on their bodies from what I could see. The leader turned to his companions and spoke several short words, in almost a singsong fashion. The men laughed, each showing small, white, even teeth. I was relieved to note that none of the teeth were filed to points, as was the custom of the flesh-eaters in this region. When he was done with his hair inspection, the chief stepped back and motioned for the rest of the warriors to come and have a look.

While our captors were busily examining Captain Sterling's chest hair, I in turn was studying them. They were quite an impressive bunch, even though I had never seen their like before. Not one of them was less than six feet tall. Each had skin as dark as night, and it appeared that some oil had been heavily applied to it, for they all glistened in the sun from head to toe. That skin lay over what seemed to be yards and yards of muscle; muscles were everywhere. Each man wore a scant cloth at the crotch that could not even be termed a loincloth, for it was open in the back with only a tiny piece of material embedded in the crack of the ass. The front pouches at the crotch were cut low, revealing the roots of their cocks, along with the first hair I had seen on them: a thick patch of black. The pouches did little to house the large bulge each man possessed.

When the chief's men had satisfied their curiosity with the captain, they trussed all our hands in front of us, formed a line with an ebony warrior between each of us, and moved us off through the jungle in the opposite direction from the beach. The pace quickly became grueling and the trail was uneven and intercrossed with treacherous roots. The sun was high overhead when we came to a large clearing in which stood a good-sized village. At least two dozen dark-skinned warriors emerged from the huts to greet us. The huts of the village formed two semicircles around a large fire pit. There were two dozen huts in all, with twelve in each row. In front of each hut were two stakes, each around 6 feet tall. While we were still tied, our clothing was unceremoniously cut from us and we were each led to a stake and tied to it. I immediately tested the strength of mine but found it to be firmly embedded in the ground. Shortly thereafter two additional black warriors entered the village with two boars suspended by their feet from bamboo poles. Two stakes were driven into the ground on either side of the large fire pit, and soon a large blaze was burning. The boars were skinned, gutted, and were soon roasting over the fire. The smell of their flesh quickly made my mouth water. It had been several hours since my last meal. Several men returned from the bushes carrying armloads of mysterious fruits of all shapes and sizes, while others butchered and cleaned gray-feathered birds the size of small chickens. They were wrapped in leaves the size of a man's head and laid in the hot coals to cook.

To the right of the fire pit stood three large drums, each around three feet high. Two men took positions on either side of the drums and began beating them, slowly at first, then quickly increasing the tempo to a feverish rate. The warriors began dancing around the fire pit, and as they worked themselves into a frenzy from the music, the small pouches that covered their crotches were untied and tossed aside. What greeted my eyes were cocks the size of which I had never seen. They didn't flop as the men danced, but literally swayed, they were so ponderous. Even soft, most of them hung halfway to ebony knees. My asshole twitched at the thought of those massive members entering it. As the men continued to circle the flames they grabbed their dicks and began a hypnotic dance with them. While my first inclination was to laugh, I found that I couldn't; I was mesmerized by their slow steps and the sensual, intimate way they were touching themselves. Soon all pricks were fully erect, to proportions I don't think I could truly comprehend unless I held one in my hands.

Encircling the fire pit a few feet from us I noticed a half dozen enormous tree stumps, about three feet high and five feet wide. The surface of each was well worn, as if from repeated use of some kind. As I was pondering the implications of this, three warriors appeared with armloads of palm fronds. They made several trips until they had a large pile of fronds, then arranged them on the stumps to form what appeared to be bedding. All the while the drums continued unabated in their fever pitch, and the dancers remained enchanted. The same men who had carried the fronds now returned each carrying several gourds. These were handed out to the dancers and the musicians who drank eagerly without missing a beat. Once each of the warriors had drunk from a gourd, the original bearers of the gourds came over to where we were tied.

Captain Sterling was the first in line. One warrior tilted his head while a second warrior poured a portion of the gourd's contents down his throat. As he sputtered and coughed, they moved on to the next pirate. I had seen these men put away copious amounts of hard liquor, so I knew the stuff had to be potent. When it was my turn I braced myself for what I was sure was coming. The liquid hit my tongue and the back of my throat and it burned its way down my gullet. I was also used to hard drink, but this was like nothing I had ever tasted before. And its effects were almost immediate. My body began to tingle all over, and my vision seemed to increase tenfold. At the same time an intense feeling pervaded my body that sharpened my other senses as well. Everything around me took on a new clarity, while the sounds of the instruments took on a quality of their own; I swear I could feel their notes pulsating within my body.

Captain Sterling was then blindfolded and led to the first stump, where he was laid on the bed of fronds. One man positioned himself at his feet while the other stood at his head. The warrior at his feet raised the captain's legs in the air, parted the cheeks of his ass, and spread something over his asshole. Without further ceremony he entered the captain in one swift lunge. Captain Sterling grunted audibly as the warrior began driving in and out of him, the sound of his balls slapping against the captain's ass cheeks. Meanwhile, the warrior at the captain's head had turned his back to his comrade and straddled the captain's chest. He pressed the head of his cock to Captain Sterling's lips, and the captain opened his mouth and swallowed as much of it as he could. As he serviced the two warriors, the next sailor was blindfolded and led to the next stump. This man was placed on his knees, and soon black dicks entered his ass and mouth. In succession each of the remaining sailors were blindfolded, brought to a stump, and placed on the fronds, the positions varying according to individual tastes.

When my turn came I was pushed down onto my hands and knees on a frond-covered stump. I felt the mysterious substance spread on my asshole and then what felt like a good-sized plum was pressed against it. I was so relaxed from the potent drink that the large head easily popped through the ring of muscle. My suitor was more considerate of me, and sank slowly inside me, making me feel every inch and definitely discovering unexplored territory. At the same time I felt another large cock head pressing insistently against my lips. I opened my mouth and relaxed my throat to take as much of the large dick as I could; I figured I made it about three quarters of the way. Both men grunted their appreciation of my attributes and began steadily pumping in and out of my orifices. As their thrusts quickened along with their grunts and groans, both shot inside me. At the same time, musket fire suddenly erupted from somewhere behind me.

The drums stopped abruptly and cries of pain and angry shouts filled the air. Both warriors immediately withdrew from me. Suddenly my blindfold was removed and I was staring up into the face of one of Captain Sterling's sailors. The fight was still going on around me but the weapons of the black-skinned warriors proved to be no match for our weapons, and soon the remaining tribesmen had turned and fled into the jungle. Captain Sterling rushed to my side and put his arms around me.

"Are you hurt, William?"

"Besides a sore asshole, I'm fine, Captain Sterling."

He inspected me from head to toe as if he did not believe my claim.

"Okay," he said. "Then let's get back to the *Queen Mary* as soon as we can before those that fled regroup and attack us again."

We retrieved our clothes, gathered our wounded, and followed the trail back to the beach without incident. After paddling the rowboats furiously to the galleon, we climbed the rope ladder to the main deck amid cheers from the skeleton crew on board. Captain Sterling began barking orders, the sails were hoisted, and we caught a lucky breeze that pushed us gently out of the cove toward the open sea. No sooner had the sails caught a full breeze than a cry from the crow's nest heralded a ship on the horizon, moving quickly away from us. All thoughts of our island escapades evaporated as Captain Sterling gave the command to intercept the ship. As the men scrambled into action, he took out his spyglass and studied the vessel.

"It's a Spanish galleon," he cried, "and we all know what they say about

Spanish men!" A cheer went up around the deck . The captain put his arm around me as we drew inexorably toward the fleeing ship.

LOST

Brian Centrone

"This is a really nice place you got," this "Pirate Pete" said when we entered my home.

"Thanks," I mumbled, looking behind me before I closed the door, making sure no one had seen us. "It's been in the family for years."

"You live alone then?"

I looked directly at him for the first time since we met as I had arranged. "Yes." I switched on the lights. "I'm the end of the line," I attempted to sound whimsical. "The end of a long line…"

We stood quietly for a few minutes. I wasn't sure what to do next. This wasn't anything I had ever done before and, to be honest, I was scared to death.

"Do you mind if I take a seat?" my pirate broke the silence.

"Oh, of course!" I was flustered. "Do you want a drink?"

"Some rum, if you have it? Just to set the mood," he winked.

His remark made me laugh, which helped me to calm down. Taking a deep breath, I went over to the bar and poured us both a generous glass.

Handing him the rum, I sat next to him. Our thighs grazed and a shot of electricity surged through me. I tingled in places I never thought another man could make me tingle.

"This is your first time, isn't it?" he remarked, sipping his drink.

Clearly he was picking up on my sheepishness. It couldn't be helped. I wasn't gay, after all, and here I was, bringing a man dressed in a costume back to my home just so I could know what it was like to be fucked hard by a pirate.

I nodded silently, looking at the dark liquid in my glass.

"We don't have to go through with this if you don't want to. I won't be offended. You just seem really uncomfortable."

I looked at him again. He had gone all out for the part. Tights, head wrap, ruffled shirt and vest, boots, gold hoop earrings, a sword (fake, I think), and even an eye-patch. I sighed heavily and opened my mouth to speak. Before I could get a word out, Pirate Pete leaned in quickly and covered my mouth with his. Our lips met and his stubble felt rough against my smooth skin. I dissolved into his kiss instantly and let myself be carried away. My pirate pulled away and smiled as I attempted to stay connected.

"I knew you would like it and get into it with a little help," he laughed.

He was right. All I needed was a little push. Perhaps I was more like my great-great-great-great-great-grandfather than I thought. After all, he was the reason I was doing this.

Pirate Pete leaned in for another kiss; this time I was ready for it, wanted it and took control of it. This second kiss was harder and more passionate. It lasted longer and while our lips got to know each other, so did our hands. Our bodies fit tightly as he ran his hands down me and I got to feel just how hard this pirate was. He pressed against me, straining, and I knew for sure that was exactly what I wanted and needed. Any doubt I had was gone. I was about to share the same experience my grandfather had all those years ago. This is what I was after, why I found my pirate. Before the night was over I would share more with my grandfather than just his name.

James Gloust was a famous explorer. He kept extensive journals of his travels that have been coveted by museums, historians, and scholars for centuries. And though his journals don't differ much from any other explorer's, what makes my grandfather stand out above the rest is what he doesn't say. The part of his time at sea that has never been recorded is the short period he spent lost. No one seems to know why he never wrote about this particular time, or, if he had, when and to where those missing entries disappeared.

The truth is, his questionable time did not go unrecorded. My grandfather did in fact write about his time lost at sea. But the nature of what happened to him was seen as so taboo that my family kept it hidden away, claiming never to be in possession of these highly sought-after documents.

For all of my life I, too, believed these journal entries did not exist or were lost. I only discovered the truth after inheriting the family archives, passed down from generation to generation. Losing both my parents, I became the last member of the Gloust line. I was left with no other choice but to bear this secret burden thrust upon me.

Needless to say, I was shocked. Not simply because these entries actually existed and were in my family's possession, but because of what was written. Reading them, I couldn't help but understand why they were made to disappear. What troubled me wasn't the tale my grandfather told, but the need I developed—more than a need, a desire, an obsession to fully understand his emotions and actions that all started that stormy night in the Pacific....

☸

I was feeling a bit queasy as the boat rocked to and fro. Housed in the bowels of the ship, my sleeping chamber was particularly ideal for discomfort and annoyance, and often, as on this night, the rowboat had not been brought on board from that morning's exploration and was left to trail from the ship—the crew and captain being the laziest of all seamen I've ever encountered—and was banging up against the walls around me. Taking it upon myself, I emerged from my chamber and fought my way on deck. The sea was troubled that night and I should have paid it some mind, but all I could consider was being well rested for the next day's adventures. Making my way to port side I attempted to raise the tiny boat myself. Of course, not being experienced in such things, I could not. Instead I decided

I would try to alter its position so that it would cease its attack on the side of my chamber. This time I was positive I could accomplish my task but as luck would have it—and I can only say that now—the sea grew angry, sending a swell of water that rocked the ship, causing me to stumble over.

Before I knew what was amiss, I was struggling to seek shelter in the rowboat. In achieving this I realized that the rope, due to my efforts, had come undone and I was being carried away in a direction no compass could determine. I held on to the seats for dear life as the sea carried me away through the night. I was sure I would never see my native England again and, even worse, that I would be leaving behind my fiancée, whom I was due to marry upon my return from my expedition of the islands in the Pacific. It was not until the break of light that I dared to look up and in doing so, released my precious hold, for land was dead ahead.

Even I could not express the joy that bubbled inside of me as my row-boat washed up on shore. I snaked my way onto the dry sand that clung to my wet attire. I cared nothing except for the fact that I was alive.

After regaining myself (I must sheepishly confess that took a great deal of time), I got up from my haven of sand and took a good look about the island. Fear began to set in. I knew not were I was, nor did the crew on my ship. Could they locate me? Would they locate me? Panic took over and I moved farther into the brush in search of survival aids. Would there be food for me to get by? If there was any form of animal on this island besides the birds that soared overhead, I could not find tracks. I thought for sure my life would end on that island. Nevertheless, it was not until I reached somewhere around the middle of the thicket that my path crossed with destiny.

A rumble and crush. A swoosh and snap. An "arrrgh" and a sword. He stood before me, chest puffed and exposed, eyes squinted, and thighs firmly set. His clothes were in tatters and he wore a stained strip of cloth around his head, his long, dark hair, dirty and matted, flowing beneath.

I thought my heart would stop! Paralyzed with fear, I surrendered. He pushed his sword toward me as far as it would go before piercing my body and scowled.

"The name's Radley. Cap'n Drake Radley. What business have you on me island?"

I stammered and he pushed the sword in harder.

"I'm lost," I spat out. He released some of the pressure. "I was thrown overboard in a violent storm." I stumbled over the rest, unsure of how much detail he actually desired. It must have sufficed, for he lowered his sword completely and began to laugh like a mad man.

"So yer shipwrecked, are ya?" he finally got out.

I didn't think disputing the difference between being shipwrecked and thrown overboard would particularly sit well with this swashbuckler, so I decided against calling it to his attention. Instead I merely nodded.

After his cackling ended he eyed me with a look that made my skin crawl. A sneer spread across his face.

"I'm not here for trouble," I said, trying to put on an air of confidence.

"What trouble ye be talking about then?"

I gulped hard. "I would like to get back to my ship. If you can be of any assistance, I'm sure I can arrange a monetary reward."

Drake looked at me hard as if I had offended him greatly. He growled again and sprang forward, grabbing hold of me and pulling my body, rigid with fear, close to him.

"Now listen here, matey, I don't need yer gold and I don't need to help ya get off me island, ya see? I'm in control here and whatever I says goes."

He shoved me to the ground and stood over me, one foot perched on my chest.

"Please," I began to mutter over and over again, sounding like a terrified child crying for his mother.

The pirate just laughed, digging the heel of his boot into my chest harder before releasing his pressure, giving me a little kick on the side.

"Get up," he ordered.

I struggled to my feet, trying to steady my legs. I was aware I was wobbling with fright and it would do me better if I put on an air of bravery, but for the life of me, and at this point I was positive there wasn't much of it left, I couldn't do anything but cower.

"Now that ye be on me island, there be some rules to follow."

I nodded vigorously, not wanting to upset him.

"First, yer mine for as long as ye last here. And second, there's been nobody on this here island for a long time." He looked me up and down. His gold earrings glistened in the sunlight as he did so. "A man can get very tense when his needs aren't met." He wet his coarse lips with his tongue.

I knew for sure that I was about to be devoured like mutton, but I hadn't quite realized how.

"Ye understand those two things there and ye be fine. Now get movin'." He pointed his sword at me again and I forced my legs to start walking.

I tripped over roots and brush as he forced me along an unclear path. I dared not ask where we were headed.

The sun poured down on us as we made our way. The palms did little to cool me as they should have, but my body was tense and my heart pounded feverishly. Sweat dripped down me, soaking my sea-logged clothes even more.

We seemed to be walking without any chance of stopping. There was either no end to this island or, as I began to expect when the morning sun shifted positions for afternoon and finally early evening, I was being led in a deliberate circle, sword tip pinned to my back.

When I thought I couldn't carry on anymore I was ordered to take a sharp turn and I fought my way through a heavy gate of trees, finally coming to a clearing. There in the distance, docked on shore, was one of the most amazing ships I had ever seen, and raised high above it was a Jolly Roger flowing in the breeze.

The sight sent more terror than what already surged through me. Seeing this flag brought me to my knees. What I would find once I was on that ship was a thought I couldn't bear.

"There's me ship. The *Molly*. Ain't she a beaut?" he whistled.

I nodded silently, eyes fixed on that black piece of cloth. "Do you always fly your flag when you're not on board?" I dared to query.

"Lets it be known where people are trespassing." He looked over at me and cocked his head. "Why ye be curious?"

"Are you really the only one on this island? Have you no one on your ship?" My terror was forcing me to speak against my better judgment. I knew my questioning would anger him, but I had to know whether or not I was being led to a gang of bloodthirsty pirates where I would undoubtedly meet my fate. In all my years at sea I had never come across these barbaric men, but knew fully their capabilities. The stories of their attacks were known and feared by any good-natured soul who sailed the seas.

Drake growled at me. Just as I suspected, my words had set him off.

"I'm the only one on this here island. And like I said, things can get pretty tense on yer own ..." Drake shoved his foot into my back and I fell on my chest. "I was goin' ter wait till we got aboard, but I thinks yer wantin' ter know what I mean when I says I'm in charge."

Drake turned me over with his foot and ran it down the length of my body until he reached my crotch. He toyed with it, putting just enough pressure to arouse it against my will.

I looked up at him for the briefest of moments, catching the lust that had filled his eyes before looking down to where I was growing steadfast at an alarming rate. Despite my terror, I couldn't help but feel a tinge of heat searing through me.

The pirate removed his foot and, pushing at my bottom slightly, said, "Get up and strip."

I lay there quite still for a moment before his foot jostled my bottom again, this time with more force.

I was on my feet in no time, but the removal of my clothes was slow going. This angered him, as he pulled at me again, ripping off what was left.

"That's more like it," he sneered, wetting his lips again.

He examined my naked body, turning me this way and that. Oh, how I thought I'd never live that moment down, if I lived at all.

"Excited, are ya?" Drake laughed, eyeing my rigid pole. "Good, good. That makes two of us."

With a swift motion he released what had to be the biggest cock I had ever seen through a slit in his worn trousers. Thick and veiny, his battering ram pulsated as he bobbed it up and down.

"Get down here and clean it," he ordered.

I obeyed without hesitation for fear of what might become of me if I did not follow his demands.

My bare knees scraped against the dry sand and foliage beneath me. I stared directly at the beast before my eyes, seeming even more monstrous up close. The concept of what was supposed to be done was the only thing I had to go on, never having been with a man in this way. Closing my eyes I opened my mouth and leaned forward. The pirate's giant timber slid in, his extra skin moving back as his bulbous head hit the back of my throat. The scent of his manliness hit me like a falling mast, my nose buried deep in his scruffy pubes. I gagged reflexively, but my captor only thrust further, snarling and moaning as he did.

Tears began to well in my eyes and I thought I would pass out from lack of breath, but to my surprise, I began to get used to his torpedoing. Eventually his cock was sliding in and out with no problems at all.

I was leaking heavily by this point and desperately wanted to relieve myself. I couldn't quite understand my body's reaction to my pillaging, nor did I have time to attempt to make sense of it.

Allowing me a breath, the pirate removed his mass fully.

Relaxing back on my heels, I took a gulp of air.

"We're not done," he informed me, whipping out his full, hairy balls. "These need tending to as well," he smirked, grabbing my head and pushing me back for a second round of tongue bathing.

Weighty as coconuts, I began work on his balls, licking and sucking as he instructed. He became more vocal with this venture, telling me what to do and if he liked it.

"There, matey, just like that," he groaned as I mouthed his hairy nuts. "Now get back to me log." He pulled away from me slightly so he could get a proper angle to shove his massive meat back down my throat. Again he moaned, closing his eyes and tilting his head back. "Yer better than any of my cabin boys...and crew for that matter," he chuckled. "I used to make them stand around me on deck and one by one me men would swab me cock with their spit till I was nice and slick. Just right to roger the young lad or two we had sailing with us."

Morally I was appalled by what he was telling me and what he was making me do, but sexually I was more excited than ever.

Drake seemed to go into some sort of trance, as if remembering these moments, but he wasn't in it for long before jerking his cock back out of my mouth and giving me the dirtiest look yet.

"I think I'm nice and slick now."

No matter how hard my own cock got, I knew I wasn't ready for what was about to happen.

He turned me around, making me support myself on all fours. Kneeling behind me, he positioned his mast at my never-opened hatch. I could hear him hacking up spit, then felt it wet my hole. He rubbed it in and around with his thumb and pointer finger before spitting again and going through the same routine. When he was done, he placed the head of his cock against my lubed entrance. The feeling sent a series of reactions through my body. My stomach sank with nerves and fear while my cock jerked with excitement and anticipation. He pushed in, the head prying open my tight ring. I took a deep breath and waited. Without any sense of care he rammed the rest home once the fat head had been swallowed. I let out a scream and he laughed, pounding away, his heavy balls slapping against my ass cheeks. Drake grabbed onto my hips for a harder, faster pound. "Oh fuck," he cried. "Nice and tight. Just the way I like it."

I whimpered along as he stretched me out, my cock leaking like a sinking ship.

"It's been so long," he muttered roughly as he bottomed out, stayed in me for a few seconds, then withdrew fully only to slam his wood back in at full force.

The pain was subsiding and I was getting used to the feeling of having my insides turned out. In fact, I was beginning to enjoy his barrage of my hole so much so that I began to back up against him, trying to match his thrust.

"Yeah, get into it," he moaned, "ride me pirate cock."

I did what he commanded and before long I was the one doing all the fucking, bouncing off his hard pelvis as I rode his pole.

Jerking my body up he pulled me with him while he lay on the ground, me on top. I bounced up and down, loving the feeling of his invasion. I cried out myself, causing Drake to take action again, matching my motions. He thrust up as I did down, and soon we were both ready to explode. He spun me around on his stick just in time for me to unleash a load of come all over his ripped abs. The act alone set him off his rocker and with a grunt resembling that of a wild beast he shot his own load, swearing and moaning as he did.

I collapsed onto him, our bodies sweaty from the hot sex. His chest rose and fell as he tried to regain a normal breathing pattern. My head rested on his developed pecs and I could hear and feel his heart beat. It was pounding in him as hard as he had pounded in me.

I was beginning to calm down when he violently threw me off without warning. My body hit the ground hard. I winced from the impact.

"Now get up and dressed," he ordered.

I did as he said, waiting for his next command.

"Come. I'll show ye me *Molly*." He slapped my back and moved ahead toward the shore.

I followed behind, careful not to trip over any of the brush that rustled beneath my feet. By the time I reached the ship, he was already on board. He gave me a hand up, beaming from ear to ear.

"How d'ya like her?" His demeanor had changed from the gruff pirate I had experienced on land. He became a little boy showing off a new toy.

"She's something," I said, meaning it. The ship was impressive. From the angle of the bough, the entire horizon spanned across. The starry night appeared endless while the moon delicately dipped itself into the Pacific.

"I'll show ya me cabin," he said, coming up behind me. He placed a hand on each of my shoulders, letting them rest there.

A tingle ran up my spine and I tried to keep from quivering. I liked the touch. It was soft. Very different from the way he had grabbed me and made me do his bidding. But all of it was confusing me. I didn't know why he made such a switch once we were on his ship and I didn't know why I was beginning to like the contact. I wanted to shake off the feeling I was having.

Turning away from him, I walked in the direction of the cabin. He strode ahead of me, leading the way. I was in complete awe of what I saw. The spoils of piracy had done him wonders. The cabin was decked with luxuries only found on the best ships of Europe. Silks and satins, jewels and crystals, gold and silver, paintings and statues, they all filled the space. It was as if I had just walked into the Queen's bedchamber.

He had to notice the expression on my face, for he remarked, "What can I say. I like to live like royalty," then laughed heartily.

I merely nodded.

He came up behind me again, this time pressing his body into mine. I could feel his hard mast straining against my well-worn hatch and a surge of excitement and fear filled me.

"Get on the bed," he whispered in my ear.

As before, I obeyed.

He fucked me softly that second time, both of us falling asleep after it was over. I awoke in the middle of that night to find myself curled up in his strong arms. I moved slightly and he stirred. He turned his head toward me, opening his eyes. Leaning in, he kissed me. I was taken aback. His lips were rough like him, but the kiss was as gentle as a lamb. I loved the way it felt but immediately broke away, moving back.

"Why are you on this island?" I asked, trying to slow things down, even more confused than ever by his behavior and my emotions. I couldn't help but wonder how this man came to be on his own.

"Arrr. Now that's a story itself." He turned away. "I was one of the greatest pirate cap'ns ever to sail the seven seas. There was no port where I wasn't feared. Me crew was known to be the most ruthless cutthroats you'd ever shiver to come across. For years we went wherever and took whatever we pleased. I was always hungry for more. It took its toll on me mates. I began to share less, order them around more. It was me greed that did me in. A mutiny was in order, that was for sure. I knew it would come, and soon. So I did what any great pirate would do: I got rid of them."

"You mean you killed them?" I shot up. I was startled and dismayed at the thought.

"Nar. I just left them at port. They all went ashore after a long haul and while they were pillaging the village I sailed away. But ye see, all I did after that was come here. I couldn't continue without a crew, no matter how crafty a pirate I be. So I docked on this island waiting for the right time to sail again."

"When will that be?"

"Don't know. Been here for years, I reckon, and still haven't gotten the urge to return. I quite like it."

"But surely you must get lonely?" I couldn't fathom the idea of living an isolated life on an uncharted island. It was preposterous to me.

"A man needs no one but himself for company. You'd do best to learn that. The only thing I have been missing is something nice and tight, and ya fixed that," he winked at me.

I laid back down thinking of all he said. He seemed content with his life on the island, happy to be alone, but I still couldn't grasp it.

Over the next couple of days things began to change. He became softer and the sex became passionate and personal. When we weren't in his bed we were exploring the island. He showed me what fruits to eat and which animals lived on the island. He even put me to work on the ship, explaining how I could sail and tend to a vessel if need be. We talked more and more and soon I began to feel for Drake. When he wasn't being a pirate he was like any other man you would find on the street and wish a good day. And, I dare say, at times I even thought he was better. But no matter how fond of him I grew and no matter how much I had come to enjoy having him plunge my depths, every time I spied that flag I couldn't help be reminded that he was a villain, plain and simple. He had to remain exactly what he was, a pirate.

Before I had time to rationalize the situation I had found myself in, fate took another twist. One morning I was on deck for a breath of fresh air. The pleasure I felt from the night's splendors faded quickly. Looking out to sea, my heart sunk. There in the distance, right in front of the rising sun, were the white sails and the bright flapping flags of my ship. Somehow they had found where the stormy sea had carried me. All my senses told me I should feel elated to be discovered and rescued, but I was feeling quite forlorn. In the short time I had been on this island, in the capture of this pirate, I began to see what he saw. Or least understand why he was content with being on his own.

I had lain awake all those nights while he slept beside me and thought how peaceful I felt. The island was calm. There was not a thing to worry about. Everything that was needed was there. It was an escape from the world, one where you didn't have to worry what other people thought or expected of you. You were your own person and capable of enjoying the company of a fellow man in the most intimate of ways without being an outcast of society. It wasn't exactly heaven, but it was some kind of rapture.

I heard footsteps approaching from behind and I turned to see Drake sauntering over in the nude. I gave him a half-hearted smile.

"They found me," I said softly. I turned back to look at the looming vessel.

Drake neared and looked out over the waters as I was doing.

"Are you going to put up a fight or let them take me back?" I queried. I needed to know the answer. Deep within me, how he replied weighed heavily.

"Yer not a captive. You can come and go as ye please." He walked back into the cabin.

I felt like a shattered man. Dressing fully I prepared to leave the ship. Drake remained quiet and out of sight until I was ready to disembark.

"Here," he handed me a lit torch. "It will be easier for them to find you with this."

"Thank you." I looked into his eyes. They had turned stony.

"Now go." With that he was gone.

I trudged my way through the thick and brush until I reached the shoreline. I waved the torch adamantly, the black smoke sending signals of my existence on the island.

The ship got as close as it could, then out came a few men in a rowboat to fetch me and the boat on which I had vanished.

"We weren't sure we would find you, Mr. Gloust," the captain said, "but you are definitely worth a try." He smiled brightly.

I put on airs, thanking him repeatedly for his generosity and belief in me.

As the ship rounded the island to get back on course, I thought for sure we would see the *Molly*, its Jolly Roger flying defensively, but it wasn't there, at least, not on shore. I looked around furiously, for where it had gone I was most determined to discover. And then I saw it, or thought I did. I called to the first mate to lend me his spyglass. Through that long wooden tube, my sighting proved correct. The *Molly* had set sail once again. Far off in the distance, she glided along the ocean. How she got so far so fast I could not fathom. I felt a mix of joy and loss. For I was sure I would never come across my pirate again, and I knew that once I returned to society I would never experience what I did on the island. Yet for Drake, I knew something had changed and it was I that had changed it. Whatever I came to represent to him, my desertion, if you will, set him on a course back to the living world. Whether that was good or bad, I couldn't quite determine. He had left his paradise, but perhaps from a need to find another one. A paradise where others existed and where a man did need something more than himself. I knew not what our destinies held. My only hope was that he found what I'd lost....

☸

Pete reached between my legs and I spread them, giving my pirate full access. His frilly shirt came off and so did mine. I stroked his bare chest. Hard and defined with just a hint of hair. I ran my hands down his strong back until I reached the waist of his tights. Yanking on them, Pirate Pete helped me to take them off, then assisted me with my own pants . While he wore nothing underneath, I had boxers on. He soon shucked those and climbed back up on me. Our rigid cocks rubbed against each other and I swelled with desire. I had to know what it was like to have him inside me. I spread my legs and lifted them so I could wrap them around his waist.

He breathed into my ear, "Oh yeah, baby. You want my pirate cock deep in your hole."

I was so overcome that all I could do was nod.

Pirate Pete bit my ear softly before suckling it. "You ready for my meat?" he asked, positioning himself after slipping on protection and lubing me up.

This time I replied. "Shove your mast in my hatch."

I winced and clenched my teeth to try to handle the pain of being rammed hard for the first time. But as he docked in and out of my port, the pain subsided and the pleasure my grandfather must have felt when Drake rogered him soared through me.

James Gloust never mentioned Drake in any other of his journals, nor did he ever mention being with another man ever again. It could have been a one-off. It could have been that what he and Drake shared on that island was so precious to him, he knew he could never replicate it with any other man. Or it could have been that when he returned home from his journeys he settled into married life and wanted to remain faithful and true to his new wife and children. I can't say for sure, but I can say, knowing what it's like to be fucked hard and passionately by a pirate, going back to anything ordinary seems unfathomable.

MR. GUV'NOR'S ASSISTANT SECRETARY

Morris Michaels, Jr.

I felt sick. The waves tossed themselves against the wooden hull, breaking into clouds of spray that drenched the men standing above me on the deck. But I was locked in a narrow cell down below and I was tossed from side to side, banging my shoulders and head against the sloping sides of the ship as it lurched through the choppy seas.

Not only was I sick from the motion of the ship, I was sick with fear and despair. What would happen to me? I was the assistant secretary of the royal governor of Antigua and I had been kidnapped by pirates during a raid on the coastal plantations we were sent to establish as a means of solidifying our control of the island. None of us had thought that pirates were still much of a threat; after all, it was 1710 and the British Royal Navy had begun to demonstrate its superiority over the buccaneers.

Yet, here I was, prisoner on a ship of vengeful pirates—no doubt desperate renegades, if they had embraced a life of such lawlessness. They espoused strange and rebellious notions of "democracy." The captain of such a ship was elected by the crew and could be replaced by the sea dogs they commanded. Captains were expected to fight in battle, right next to the men, not like proper captains from behind a safe line of loyal men that enabled them to direct the battle before them. The spoils captured by these crews was also known to be shared evenly among them and not parceled out in shares based on rank or ability.

Given the strange and dangerous notions these pirates held, and the probability that they would soon all be swinging from the end of the hangman's rope, it was impossible to predict what they would do with me. I was sure they would demand ransom. But would they wait for it to be delivered before killing me? Or worse, they might sell me to a Spanish or French plantation owner to serve as a field hand and thus collect gold coins twice for me—the ransom money plus the price I brought in the slave markets of the other Caribbean islands. These men did not have the luxury of waiting long to earn their ill-gotten rewards.

But I was afraid that the rescue ships, which the pirates no doubt feared were closing in on them even now, would in fact never arrive. The plantations had been stoutly defended by our soldiers and the pirates quickly rebuffed. I was sure they had seized much gold and other valuable objects from the royal governor's house and the homes of the plantation owners and businessmen clustered around the governor's residence and I could see some of it here in the hold with me, just outside my cell. But I was the only prisoner and I feared that my position was not as important as the pirates hoped. It was, in fact, unlikely that the governor would expend valuable resources chasing down these vermin simply to rescue me. I feared that I was doomed, here in this ship's hold that tossed me from side to side of my prison as if I were laundry that one of the serving girls at home washed by slapping it first against one rock and then another.

Not that the governor's secretary hadn't been fond of me. He had spent several evenings enjoying my body, as his wife was waiting for him back in London and it would be quite some time before he was free to return to enjoy the pleasures of her flesh. I, almost but not quite young enough to be his son, had enjoyed his use of me. I had no fiancée and no prospects of one in the near future. My family was of little wealth and even less account among the gentry of Kent and I had embraced government service as the one way to improve my meager lot. There were girls in the Kentish countryside that might have been happy to marry me but I was hoping for more. A better match than any available at home. But it would take time to establish myself here in the Caribbean and in the meantime—well, the colonial secretary was a handsome man and important as well. Powerful. Rich. Everything that I would have wanted in a wife. It had been a good omen for my future when I first noticed him casting an eye along my backside when he thought I wasn't looking. When he took me to his bed, I thought that perhaps my dreams of success were on the verge of fulfillment.

Besides, there was some deep yearning in me to serve—to be owned and possessed by a man such as I wished my father had been. Any way in which I had been able to give the governor's secretary pleasure gave me pleasure as well. If there were times when he did not allow me a full release of my own manhood after releasing his with my mouth or receiving it up into my backside—well, that was part of the joy of service. To be the instrument of the powerful. One day, I hoped to be one of those counted "powerful." In the meantime, I was happy to serve. I knew my place in society. (Unlike these buccaneers who thought they were all equals, none better than the other. Notions such as that that might someday overthrow decent, well-ordered, godly society.)

But the secretary had to carefully guard his affection for me from becoming public. If the governor had known, we could both have suffered for it: The secretary would have been dismissed and I would have been thrown into jail—into a cell not unlike the brig I was held in now—to languish until a ship was available to carry me home in disgrace. A disgrace that would have made any hope for improvement of my position in society impossible. A fate only slightly more preferable to the one that now awaited me. The boat lurched forward again through the waves and I hit my shoulder against the hull of the boat again.

I heard footsteps climbing down the ladder into the hold. Big, heavy boots. More than one pair. Was there a ship on the horizon they thought I could be sold or traded to? We couldn't be near enough land yet to take me ashore for sale or trade. Wait… I could hear the jingle of metal as well—they were bringing something down into the boat for storage. More bags of coins? Platters and candlesticks from the fine dining rooms they had plundered? Flagons and goblets meant for fine wine? I twisted around and pressed my face against the cold bars of my cell to see what was going on.

Two crewmen were bringing down great sacks of booty in their hands, which accounted for both the thud of boots and the metallic jangle that I heard. Their backs were to me as they descended the rickety stairs into the hold but in the bright shaft of daylight that descended the steps with them, I could see their tall, sagging leather boots and baggy black pants held up by wide leather belts, as well as their powerful, muscular sun-darkened backs, as they wore no shirts. A serpent tattoo writhed along the upper back of one. The muscles along their shoulders and arms rippled as they strained to hold their plunder. At the bottom of the steps they turned to toss the bags they held onto the piles already scattered around the bilge and then faced me.

Their hair was unkempt and descended to their shoulders in tangled locks. The one with the tattoo on his back was black-haired, the other a redhead. Both seemed to be older than I would expect most pirates to be—not nearly as mature as the governor's secretary but certainly older than I. The dark-haired one had a powerful torso, the muscles sculpted by long hours of hard work (no doubt on the deck above, given the suntanned look he sported). The redhead's chest was just as powerfully sculpted but covered in a thick, orange carpet of hair that ran down his forearms as well, ending only at his wrists. He had a series of animal tattoos—a charging bull, a galloping horse, a goat—running down his left arm. He seemed only slightly less dark from the sun than his mate, and the blond streaks in his hair also hinted at the hours he had spent above in the light. I had been here in the hold only a few hours and already I felt myself growing pale in the half-light below deck. Their chests glistened, slick with sweat, as they stepped out of the direct sunlight and into the gentle dusk below deck. They reached into their back pockets and each pulled out a bandanna to wipe their sweaty brows and as they raised their arms I could detect thick nests of matted sweaty hair there (even on the smooth-chested dark sailor). Their sweaty fragrance filled the narrow confines of the pen in which I was held; it was both nauseating and intoxicating. I couldn't help myself. These sea dogs who held me were clearly the ones with all the power now.

My fear of them struggled with my desire to serve them as I crouched there against the wooden hull. If I could win their goodwill, at least there was a chance I might survive.

They stood before my cell now, eyeing me I as I watched them. Wary. We were all three suspicious of what the other would do next. I took a deep breath and stood. I shook my head to clear my senses and my own auburn hair, tied in a ponytail behind my head, curled around my shoulders. What had been my fine linen shirt was now stained and torn, revealing one of my own dark nipples set in the midst of an almost alabaster hued chest. The dark-haired buccaneer licked his lips.

"What d'ya think, John?" the dark one growled to his companion.

"I think he'll do just fine, Obadiah," redheaded John replied in what was almost a guttural purr. John rubbed his hands together and hooked his thumbs into his belt, standing directly before the door to my cage. His nipples stood erect through the bright pelt that spread across his chest.

"I'll do just fine for what?" I asked, unable to control the tremor that crept into my voice. They paused and continued to run their eyes up and down my figure. I could see the calculating going on in their heads. I took a guess. "I know you sea dogs share all your loot equally, with no one aboard taking more or less than another—not even the captain. All the gold down here will be divided among you. No doubt there are even more valuables above deck still being inspected before it is deposited down here. But me? How can a prisoner be shared by the crew? Will I be sold and the money distributed to all? Or will I be killed and the small ransom—when it arrives—shared between you all so that you each get another farthing or two added to your share of booty? How can the prize of governor's assistant secretary be shared among you most equitably?"

"We wasn't thinkin' of killin' ya, boy," growled dark Obadiah.

"Or sellin' ya."

"But we was thinkin' of sharing you, Mr. Governor's Assistant Secretary," added Red John. His wide smile revealed an astonishingly white set of teeth. In other circumstances, he would probably have been considered handsome by many. A large bulge beneath his oversize silver belt buckle, growing larger by the moment, could not be ignored either. "We was jus' gonna take our turns now, before bringing y'up to the quarterdeck like the captain asked." He produced a key from a pocket somewhere in his pants and unlocked the cell door. The door swung open with a rusty squeal and John stepped into the opening, filling it with his muscular torso. Dark Obadiah was right behind him, close enough that his nipples must have been pushing into John's shoulder blades. "Don't try'n run nowheres, boy," Obadiah warned me, a mouth blossoming into a smile as well.

Sparks of excitement danced along the hair on the back of my neck. Don't try to run nowhere? As if there were a chance of getting around the two of them. Or the desire to throw my life away in a futile attempt to escape. Clearly, the key to survival here was to make them happy. All of them, if need be. First these two, and then the rest of the crew on the main and quarterdecks above. I could figure out the next step sometime later. Service would save me until then, and if I knew how to do anything, I knew how to serve.

I slowly reached up and began to open the top button of my shirt. I looked down at my hands and then glanced nervously back at my captors. The blatant desire burning in their eyes was undeniable. I lowered my eyes again and slowly opened the next button.

"Aye, we'll be here forever at this rate!" grumbled the dark one, pushing past John and bending his mouth to my exposed nipple. He took the edge of the torn cloth in his teeth and ripped it further, so that the front left of the shirt fell away completely, exposing my torso on that side. He dropped the fabric from his teeth. "We haven't got all day, Mr. Fine Guv'nor's Secretary. The resta' the crew will be waitin' above decks for their share an'll be wonderin' what's takin' us so long to bring y'up to them." He grasped my waist firmly with both his strong hands and pulled the other side of my shirt away with his teeth as well. The cloth hung limply down across my ass, still tucked into the back of my pants. He let go of my midriff with one hand and grabbed the shirt, tossing it into a corner of the brig.

"A finer prize we ain't seen in a long time. Right, John?" Obadiah asked his fellow buccaneer over his shoulders as he allowed his eyes to slowly trace the outline of the muscles under my skin along my ribs.

"Aye, not in a long time," fair John agreed. He stepped forward and, reaching around Obadiah, gently ran his palms across my chest. Then he suddenly grabbed one pec forcefully, knocked Obadiah slightly to one side and planted his mouth on my nipple. His tongue raced around the dark island there as his teeth sunk into the mound of flesh. Obadiah, not to be outdone, grabbed my head and twisting my face toward him, drove his tongue deep down my throat as if searching for my tonsils. His tongue lashed mine and caressed the roof my mouth. With one hand, I cradled his head near mine and with the other I held the back of John's head, keeping his face firmly against my chest. My tongue responded to Obadiah's and searched for his tonsils as eagerly as his tongue searched for mine. A deep growl rumbled between the three of us.

A few moments later I pulled my face back from Obadiah's, to catch my breath. In that pause, Obadiah undid his belt buckle and the buttons closing the fly of his trousers, which promptly dropped to the top of his boots. A swarthy log was there, growing taller before my eyes, like a ship's mast appearing over the horizon. The large sac beneath was deeply folded in on itself like a sail waiting for the wind to fill it.

John pulled his face away from my chest, which I could feel would be black and blue tomorrow but for right now felt like an cannon charge of pleasure had just been discharged there. He stood up and I reached forward, running my hand along his chest as he had done to mine a moment ago. With the other I reached forward and undid his belt buckle. His trousers, apparently held up only by the belt, fell and bunched around his knees.

I leaned forward and planted my mouth on his nipple as I reached down to caress the precious cargo between his legs. His prow, already large and pointing the way before him, was as wide as it was long. The cargo underneath the prow was wrapped in as furry a blanket for safekeeping as his chest and arms were and I could tell that the blanket extended underneath and between his legs and up his ass and backside as well. With my other hand I reached over to fondle Obadiah's goods so as to not let him feel ignored. He stepped closer. I fondled him more assertively, even aggressively, and his eyes closed. He bent his knees and let the weight of his manhood rest in my hand that pulled, twisted, and caressed it. John relaxed as well, pushing both his nipple into my mouth and the prow of his own private ship into my palm. I was also becoming dimly aware that my own cannon was growing larger between my legs and straining against the fabric of my livery.

I ran my tongue along what seemed the mountain of his nipple and chewed on it as well. The sweaty hair tasted salty and the aroma tickled my nose. I wanted more, much more, of this. I slid my tongue around under his arm and he raised his hand and reached over to hold the bars of my prison to support himself. I buried my face in the deep, aromatic nest of red hair which reminded me of some of the giant kelp beds the ships of the Royal Navy would sometimes encounter on the open sea. I buried my nose and tongue there, breathing slowly and deeply so as to properly appreciate the gift I was being offered, tasting the banquet he had so thoughtfully prepared for me.

Obadiah would not let me forget that he was there as well, however. Without a word, he demanded that I bestow similar attention beneath his arm as he reached around John's shoulders. I licked them both, gulping the salty feast. I buried my face between the two smooth muscular islands of Obadiah's chest and licked the rivulets of sweat that trickled there as well. They heaved and sighed as they leaned into each other and into me as well. Rumblings of pleasure rose from somewhere deep within each of them. I sighed, happy to be able to make them happy.

I pulled back and shook my head, to clear my vision and regain my sense of balance. As I glanced downward, I could see a distinctly damp patch that marked the spot where my cannon met my pants. I dropped to my knees before the two mighty evidences of virility before me, however, knowingly keeping my hands away from the mounting ache of my own down below even as I adjusted my hips so that the fabric stretched more tightly across my groin. I pressed my shirtless torso against their legs, reaching around each of their buttocks and felt those firm mounds of flesh as well. As firm as the mounds that were their chests. My mouth opened and engulfed both the cocks before me, filling my cheeks and reaching the back of my throat. Thanks to my long practice with the governor's secretary, I was able to suppress my gag reflex and wrapped my tongue around one, then the other, then both of them. Salty, but with the slightly sweet taste of their precome present as well, I tasted this next course of the banquet. I could think of nothing but the treasures I was receiving.

John and Obadiah seemed to be unable to think of much else either. Holding onto each other and the bars of the cage on either side, they closed their eyes. John tilted his head back while Obadiah swung his from side to side. Inarticulate groans filled the brig. (I wondered whether the groans of the tortured or the groans of the served were more common down here among the sacks of stolen goods waiting to be distributed.)

As I sucked and licked, the two men began to thrust themselves into my face in a common rhythm. I glanced up at them and saw that they had found each other's faces. Eyes still closed, John's tongue was deep inside Obadiah's mouth and Obadiah seemed as anxious to eat John's lips as a starving man would eat a well-cooked steak. Their slick torsos slid against each other there in the dusky gloom of the ship's hold and the common thrusts were more and more forceful. I wondered if I would be able to keep suppressing my gag reflex. I finally just held my head still as I grasped those powerful buttocks that flexed, tightening and relaxing, beneath my firm grasp. I worked my fingers between their cheeks and my fingers found the tender openings of the assholes; coated with the sweat of my two privateers, my fingers were able to slide into those berths and begin to massage the centers of pleasure within them. Each man pressed his pelvis into my face even as he almost sat back on my hands to force my fingers further up the docking. My wrists felt they might crack and my lower arms felt they might snap from the weight of the two powerful renegades I held, but I was happy. As happy as I had ever thought I might be. Somehow, even happier than when I was serving the governor's secretary. I felt something shift in my soul. With the secretary, I knew that I was hoping to win his favor by my serving him and be given a post later; here, I simply served because—even though I hoped to win my life—it was really all there was to do. Even if they threw me overboard later, I would have been at peace having had this opportunity to simply kneel before them and give them what they craved. Give them what I craved. We each were given the chance to make our dreams come true in the brig that afternoon.

Suddenly the two began to roar and I could feel their asses grind forward and clutch my hands in the grip of their buttocks. Thick, hot barrels of come shot into my mouth and down my throat. I swallowed and swallowed. And swallowed again. And again. Either one of them alone would have been more than a mouthful; the two together were like trying to drink a pint of ale without taking a breath. White sea foam spilled out of my mouth and dripped down my chin.

I gasped. They each gasped and almost doubled over, clutching each other and grabbing onto my head to support themselves in their sudden exhaustion. They looked into each other's faces, smiled, and kissed again. One of them tousled my hair as the other pushed himself upright away from me. The ache of my own ironworks was almost unbearable but I knew better than to touch myself without permission.

"Good job, Mr. Assistant Secretary," Obadiah muttered as he pulled up his pants.

"Allow me, sir," I told him as I reached over and adjusted his trousers, buttoning the fly and closing the great belt buckle. "Anything else right now, sir?"

He looked at me a moment and then shook his head. I turned to John and reached toward his trousers, still bunched around his knees. As I knelt, I pulled his pants up and centered his belt buckle just below his navel; the metallic buckle glittered in the midst of that furry sea that was his stomach. Gazing in admiration of such masculine beauty, I was suddenly moved to bend forward and kiss each toe of his boots.

"Thank you, sir," I said. "Thank you both, sirs, for allowing me to serve you." I kept my eyes on the ground.

After a moment, I allowed myself to look up at them. John was smiling, amused and happy. I could tell he understood my need to serve just as he—no doubt—needed to be served in turn, despite the claims of fraternal equality among the pirates. Obadiah chuckled, but seemed to think I was simply crazy. Or trying an elaborate charade to gain his trust and good will. I bent my head again and looked at the floor.

"Am I still to have the honor of being shared among the crew above?" I asked after a moment of listening to the heavy breathing around me. "May I be allowed to serve them or am I to be kept here only for your pleasure, sirs?"

John pulled me to my feet. "We'll take you up to them and allow you to serve each of our crewmates, boy," he whispered in my ear. "But you'll always be our special cabin boy, un'erstan? You can serve them all they want. But you'll always come back to me an' Obadiah in the end."

"Yessir. I understand completely, sir." I nodded. Obadiah headed toward the ladder and started to climb up. John shoved me, indicating I should climb the ladder after Obadiah but before him. I would appear on deck between the two of them. As I climbed the ladder, the tight but threadbare livery stretched around my hips finally tore and my would-be masculinity spilled out into the increasingly fresh air. The back of my pants slid down, and I could feel the crack of my ass exposed to the air as well. I hoped John, climbing the ladder behind me, appreciated the view and that my dishevelment would meet with the rest of the crew's approval without revealing that John and Obadiah had already enjoyed their share of the latest prize brought aboard.

We climbed from the bilge up past the other two levels of the hold until we reached the main deck. I climbed up onto the deck near the mainmast and then Obadiah and John held me by my arms to lead me to the captain on the quarterdeck. We pushed our way through more pirates than I could have ever imagined fitting onto a ship this size. I lifted my face to the sun and closed my eyes, feeling the warmth of the late afternoon caress my face as the hair on John's body and the mighty pecs of Obadiah had caressed my face in my cage below. Although I hadn't realized it when I had been brought onboard, I had been brought home. My true home. Here to serve with no real hope of any reward other than the service itself. I didn't need to be rescued by the Royal Navy or restored to the office of the governor's secretary. For the first time in my short life thus far, I was truly happy.

BLUE RING'S BOY AND THE CURSE OF THE SIN SAPPHIRE

T. Hitman

He was magnificent to behold.

Painfully handsome, Lee thought, uncomfortably aware of the swell in his own pants as he carefully maneuvered the blade down the man's cheek. The sound of the blade's scrape as it slowly shaved off dark facial hair sent Lee's heart into a gallop. He willed his shaking hand to steady and continued. This terrible lesser god's unnaturally blue eyes, trained unblinkingly upon him, didn't help.

"Watch yerself, laddie," the man growled, his deep voice both dangerous and hypnotic. His Irishman's brogue fortified Lee's lust for him, and aided by the raw, masculine stink in the air—the smell of the man's sweat—his cock stiffened fully.

"Aye, sir," Lee said.

A hand clamped the wrist holding the blade, its length of visible hairy arm even more exquisite to Lee than the sapphire-encrusted silver dagger. Icy-hot electric pinpricks coursed over Lee's flesh, conjuring goosebumps across his naked torso and sending his exposed nipples into hard, painful points, the only landmarks on a pale, smooth canvas.

"See that ye do," the man growled.

Lee had skirted around the man's eyes without facing him directly. Now, he forced his gaze up to meet the privateer's haunting twin sapphires. The image of Jack Joseph O'Farrell's rugged good looks drained the last of the moisture from Lee's mouth. O'Farrell, with his tousle of dark hair, silvering just above both ears, and square, now-shaved jaw, uttered a lusty, feral growl. He passed his tongue from one corner of his mouth to the other, then left its tip hanging at the center. In their brief, bottled glance, Lee recognized the hunger in the man's expression and wondered what it would be like to kiss those lips, to feel the scrape of their roughness over his body from mouth to aching nipples to greedy arsehole.

Lee sucked down a sip of air, unaware that he'd been holding the last one until its dregs began to burn inside his lungs. The stink of O'Farrell's natural musk filled him, making Lee crave the pirate's touch even more.

"Put down the blade," O'Farrell ordered.

Lee felt the jeweled dagger drop from his hand and heard its tip jab into the floor, but was powerless to shift his focus. Eventually, he found the strength and blinked, his eyes tumbling down O'Farrell's mouth to the dark prickle covering his neck, and from there, into the thatch of hair protruding from the open neck of his ragged shirt.

He wandered lower, until long last reaching the obvious tent in O'Farrell's trousers. They were belted at the waist with a buckle encrusted in sapphires, much like the dagger. The flash of bare skin at both leg cuffs revealed toned musculature beneath a pelt of dark hair. A nagging itch teased Lee's dick; he gnashed his teeth and willed his cock to hold back.

The wet, loud clack of O'Farrell's lips brought his eyes quickly up from the pirate's crotch.

"Yer a fine lad, if I does say."

Lee's insides ignited in concentric ripples of pleasure. "Humble thanks, kind sir,"

O'Farrell's lusty grin leveled flat into a menacing scowl. "Ain't nothing kind about me, pup. Ye may wish ye'd never laid eyes upon the likes of Blue Ring O'Farrell by the time he's through with ye."

The man reached toward Lee and savagely tweaked a straining nipple. Before the explosion of pleasure wracked his body from ears to toes, Lee noticed the ring on the pirate's pointer finger, a band of silver clutched around an eyeball-sized star sapphire. The gem's vibrant star points glittered out of the pattern of dark hair lining the top of O'Farrell's hand, briefly hypnotizing him with a rich blue light as intense and magnificent as the pirate's eyes.

Then the time-delayed ripple of pleasure overwhelmed Lee.

His head snapped back as O'Farrell's mercilessness ripped a loud moan from his throat.

"Ye like that, laddie?" the pirate growled. "I promise ye, there's plenty more to come."

O'Farrell's fingers traveled to Lee's other nipple and gave it a hard twist. The rush of intense pleasure snapped the star sapphire's pull. Lee gazed up to see his captor's brutal handsomeness. O'Farrell's predatory eyes were narrowed with want.

"That's right, my beautiful one," O'Farrell growled. He passed his hand over Lee's naked torso, sweeping it lower, toward his groin. "Once I've claimed ye, yer mine. And when yer mine, yer mine forever."

Blue Ring O'Farrell, one of the most notorious pirates of the early 1800s, cupped the crotch of Lee's britches. Lee howled in shock, unable to hold back his climax any longer.

Two hundred years later, twenty-one-year-old Lee Desjardins bolted awake in the Salem Street apartment house, just as the first spurt of come blasted into the mattress.

"*What the fuck—?*"

Lee ducked a hand into the swampland contained in the front of his boxer-briefs and milked out several more squirts. He bit back the howl and shuddered as pins and needles rocked his sweat-drenched flesh. Even more confusing than the knowledge he'd experienced his first wet dream in years was the eerie feeling that he wasn't really dreaming. For several tense seconds, the afterimage of O'Farrell's sapphire-colored eyes hovered out of focus in the shadows, seeming to watch his climax.

"You okay?" asked a sleepy man's voice from the other side of the mattress.

Colin. Colin instantly anchored him back to the reality of his location: a triple-decker five blocks from the beach and the Friday Harbor Maritime Museum, not a twin-mast schooner prowling the eastern coastline of America.

Lee rolled his legs out of bed. His feet met the cold hardwood floor, and to his relief, that floor wasn't rocking. "Fine, babe. Go back to sleep."

His cock was still tingling, still hard and, as he learned on the short walk through the darkness to the bathroom, still unloading. Lee felt his way to the bathroom door, switched on the light, then sealed himself inside. The reflection in the mirror spoke volumes—fresh beads of perspiration streaked his face and chest, and the front of his gray cotton boxer-briefs was soaked clear through. Lee didn't think it possible that there was that much load left in his balls, especially following the previous night's fuck-fest with Colin. He tugged at the corner of his leg cuff and worked his sac free of its prison. His nuts hung heavy and loose and glistened with an oil slick of sweat and slime.

"Fuck," he moaned, absently scratching his balls with one hand while passing the other through the black spikes of his bed-head.

Outside, a baleful October wind whistled through Friday Harbor, strong enough to rattle the window in its casement. Lee sat on the toilet and looked out. Raindrops struck the pane; other than that, it was still too dark to see more than a distant flicker of light caused by a tree branch snapping back and forth in front of a streetlamp.

He ogled his cock. The trigger of nerves lining the underside of his dickhead responded. It wouldn't take much to make him bust his second load of that early, dark morning, and Lee considered it—his dream about Blue Ring O'Farrell providing the perfect fantasy to jerk off to. He wouldn't even need to retrieve the bottle of lube at the side of the bed or so much as need to hawk a wad of spit into his palm to begin the fun; the tepid load trickling down his balls and inner thigh would be more than sufficient.

A soft knock on the door slaughtered the urge. "Hey, pal, you okay?"

"Yeah, just had a bad dream, that's all," Lee lied.

He peeled off his nastified boxer-briefs and ran a hot shower. By the time he emerged, the lingering imaginary smell and taste of Blue Ring O'Farrell was gone from his thoughts, replaced by the daunting demands of the day.

❁

Lee re-holstered the hip bag and hurried across the mezzanine. The Friday Harbor Maritime Museum's permanent collection spread out below him, the cases of artifacts testifying to the town's rich seafaring history. Visitors on this blustery October morning were sparse, especially for a time of year that was prime for fieldtrips and caravans of school buses. All that would change, he knew, once the museum's big pirate exhibit opened in less than a week.

At the end of the mezzanine, Lee passed through the open French doors leading to the figurehead gallery. The antique honey oak floor groaned under the weight of his shoes with every footstep, something the gallery's designer had long ago conceived to create the illusion of a schooner rocking back and forth on its long voyage across the Atlantic. The gallery's tall windows even added to the illusion, each looking out upon the harbor's choppy whitecaps.

Twenty ship's figureheads jutted out from the brick walls. Their unblinking eyes tracked his course across the floor, unleashing the start of a shudder in the short hairs at the base of his neck. He'd spent so much time steeped in the lore of New England's pirates—especially Blue Ring O'Farrell—first for his senior thesis, and now using that same thesis in his job as a museum tour guide; was it any wonder he'd been hallucinating?

The next set of French doors opened on the organized chaos of the big pirate exhibit being readied for public viewing. "Swashbucklers of New England," the big, colorful placard advertised. The image of a saber-wielding privateer dressed in a white open-necked pirate shirt standing beside the Jolly Roger frozen in a suggestion of gusty wind owed more to Hollywood than the true star of the exhibit, the notoriously insatiable Irish-born lothario who'd recently begun invading Lee's dreams.

Lee stepped over the crisp purple velvet rope meant to keep out the public and continued across the special collections gallery. A giant diagram of a typical pirate schooner dominated the room. Several of the curator's most trusted helpers worked to uncrate artifacts, watched over by two of the museum's security guards. Colin was not among the pair of uniforms.

White-gloved hands were presently transferring various weapons into position behind the glass of the largest case. Among them, a boarding axe, the pirate's first choice to bring down his victim's sails, an elegant, jewel-handled gentleman's sword, and a short-barreled musketoon.

Lee caught a flash of wool sweater with elbow pads reflected in the glass. "Mr. Batchelder," he said.

Batchelder offered a standard tip of his chin. The topography of his face maintained its usual lack of emotion. In the past month, Lee had only seen the man smile once. "Lee."

"I got your message. What's up?"

Batchelder grumbled an order to the pair of white gloves now uncrating a larger, more ominous weapon—a blunderbuss, Lee noted, a rifle-like weapon nervous sailors once used to drive off boarding pirates.

"Yes, it's about your presentation." Batchelder waved him over.

Lee's stomach twisted into knots. "Is something wrong with it?"

"You know that I think it's very well scripted," Batchelder droned.

Of course it was; Lee's professor—one of Batchelder's oldest buddies—had given his thesis high marks along with plenty of praise. "But?"

"I'm afraid we'll need you to tone down some of the language."

"The language?" Lee gaped. "I hope you don't mean the part about Blue Ring O'Farrell and his sexual hunger toward some of his conquests—like Ethan-Daniel Butler, the man who betrayed him?"

Batchelder held out a time-ravaged, pink hand, indicating the doors. "Let's go to my office. I've got an edited version of your tour speech on my desk."

A jolt of rage surged through Lee's insides. "You want me to censor the truth?"

"The truth about O'Farrell and his damned Sin Sapphire ring is a bit too tawdry to be fully explored during a twenty-minute tour aimed at the general public." Batchelder's face barely registered movement while he said this.

"Tawdry?" Lee snorted. "I would have thought it was just the kind of

Hollywood scandal the museum wanted to sell tickets to this thing."

"The notations are fairly straightforward," Batchelder continued, Lee's snarky comment making little if any impact. "Walk with me."

Lee huffed out an angry breath and started to follow, but Batchelder slammed on the breaks without warning. For a second, Lee worried that his obvious aggravation at the curator's demand had put his job in jeopardy. But as Batchelder turned toward one of the stand-alone artifact cases and the exquisite oil painting hanging beside it, Lee understood that he'd done little to pierce the older man's impenetrable mask.

"By the way, we uncrated these this morning," Batchelder said, indicating the case, the painting, with a sweep of his heavy pink hand. "Your good friend, Blue Ring O'Farrell himself, and that damn ring that caused him so much trouble."

Lee barely heard the curator's words, and was only partially aware he'd started a slow shuffle toward the case until it loomed up in front of him, preventing him from going farther.

The portrait was of a distinguished man, *painfully handsome*, Lee thought, with dark hair just going silver above the ears. His cheek and neck were mostly smooth except for a suggestion of fine dark shadow, as though, Lee imagined, the man had shaved—or had *been* shaved—before sitting for the artist. The open front of his shirt showed lush dark hair, and the silent smirk his lips were frozen into seemed to hint of secret lusts. The most telling facet to identify the subject was the rich sapphire color of the man's eyes.

"Apparently, this was painted by one of Blue Ring's young male conquests," Batchelder announced. "A college student from Boston, headed to Paris."

Lee pulled his gaze away from the pirate's twin sapphires, only to fall into the pull of one giant blue Cyclops's eye. The Sin Sapphire glowed under the gallery's recessed lights, its magnificent star points leaping out of the gemstone to reflect prisms around the display case.

"Luckily for us, the sapphire never made it back to the Crown of England," Batchelder rambled. "Not so lucky for Ethan-Daniel Butler, however.

The sheriff of Friday Harbor pried it off his left hand after the lad hanged himself for betraying Blue Ring."

❁

Lee tossed the dog-eared pages over his shoulder and heard them drop to the floor, raining down like autumn leaves.

"Fuck it," Colin said. He knocked back a swig of beer and kicked his bare feet onto Lee's lap.

Lee shrugged and began to rub Colin's size twelves, running his fingertips beyond the cuffs of his security guard uniform pants and into the thatch of leg hair just above both ankles. "I'm pissed. If O'Farrell had pumped his wad into a bunch of big-titted English aristocrats, they'd make me focus my whole presentation on it. But because he liked to pillage young men—of legal age, mind you—I have to gloss over it. It sucks."

"Suck me," Colin growled.

Lee glanced up to see Colin stretched across the couch, his guard uniform shirt unbuttoned and open, the tails sticking out of his pants, the white T-shirt underneath also yanked out to expose a length of muscled, hairy abdomen. Colin's lusty smile was visible under the bill of his guard's baseball cap bearing the museum's name and logo.

Lee wandered a hand up from Colin's toes to his crotch and playfully squeezed the thickness. "Finally, my day's looking up."

He pushed Colin's feet off his lap and waved him over to the bedroom with a playful tip of his chin. Colin pursued, humming the lyrics of an unrecognizable song in grunts for the several steps it took to catch up.

Lee flipped on the light, but Colin quickly turned it off, leaving them in the muddy early evening darkness. Colin was a year older than Lee, one of four sons in a big Irish Catholic family, and out to none of them. He was only now starting to grow comfortable enough with his sexuality, the reason they'd fucked in the shadows since crossing that line from roommates to bedmates the previous August.

The ghostly howl of the storm raging outside the bedroom's two windows teased Lee's ears between breathy, heavy kisses. He imagined Colin's incredible body, muscled and hairy in all the right places, as they rabidly undressed one another, tearing at clothes. The warm smell of Colin's skin filled Lee's inhalations, a heady mix of clean sweat from a full day's work and the dregs of deodorant slapped on that morning. And, when he liberated Colin from his uniform pants and tight-white underwear, Lee feasted on the musky aroma of his crotch.

"Yeah, pal, that's right," Colin grunted, placing both hands on Lee's shoulders and piloting him down to his knees. Colin dropped his bare ass onto the bed, allowing Lee access into the warm space between his spread legs and giant's feet. "Suck my dick."

Lee took Colin's fullness between his lips and swallowed it almost to the root on the first downward plunge. He toyed with Colin's balls, rolling them in their loose sac, tugging playfully on them. Colin responded with a blue streak of expletives that only served to urge Lee onward.

"Best fuckin' cocksucker I ever met, pal. Hum on my meat!"

Lee spit out of the length of Colin's shaft so that only the head and an inch or so remained between his lips, then plunged down again. Colin howled his approval. This continued for several minutes, with Lee teasing him closer toward orgasm, one hand ogling Colin's balls, the other dividing time between rubbing Colin's right leg and Lee's own straining erection.

"Fuck, here it comes," Colin moaned, his voice fighting in the shadows with the roar of the Atlantic gale pounding against the house.

Lee pulled back, wrapped his left hand around Colin's root, and squeezed down as hard as he could—another of those sexual talents that had captured the security guard's lust, if not his love. Colin howled. By clamping down on his cock just as it readied to shoot, Lee prolonged the sensation, intensified it, holding the flood of come in check while also edging out the actual climax.

Lee released his grip. Salty-sour jets of sperm flooded his mouth, and Colin's shouts rang in Lee's ears with deafening fury, conjuring the image of crashing whitecaps against the harbor's rocky shore in his mind.

Rough, strong hands pulled Lee onto the bed and tossed him onto his stomach. Colin spread Lee's legs with his knees and the cheeks of his ass with probing fingers. Tense seconds later, a hot gust of breath teased Lee's asshole, along with a lone, whispered word.

"*Sweet.*"

Lee felt and heard the other boy sniffing around back there like a dog, then the moist clack of a tongue between lips. Wet velvet dragged across Lee's pucker; the darkness in the bedroom erupted in a supernova of exploding stars.

Time fell out of focus, so Lee had no idea how long Colin remained back there, licking at his asshole, only that the scrape of his five o'clock shadow steadily teased him closer to busting his load into the unmade bed's crumpled sheet. At one point, after the Big Bang burned down, Colin silenced Lee's moans by flipping him onto his back, scurrying on top of him, and crushing their lips together. The taste of his own asshole on Colin's tongue filled Lee's mouth as the other man's cock readied to do the same to his core.

The pressure of Colin's invasion surged through Lee's insides, but the pain quickly turned to pleasure. Lee clutched at the Colin's muscled ass cheeks, pulling them closer and sending his dick deeper. The sweet tang of the tongue that had probed his asshole muffled Lee's moans.

"Yes," he managed between hard, sloppy kisses. "Breed my fuckin' hole!"

Colin slammed in, the weight of his balls gonging against Lee's buttocks. His own dick, pinned beneath Colin's six-pack, was unintentionally masturbated without the intervention of hands or fingers. On the next thrust in, the darkness erupted in a Fourth of July display that only Lee could see. He yelped as Colin's abdomen again squeezed hold of his dick, and the other boy's cock head tickled his prostate to the verge of unloading.

"Fuck me!"

Colin tossed back his head and howled, "*Aye, that I will, my beautiful lad…*"

That voice!

Lee gasped in surprise. Colin again faced him, his head a shadow moving in the darkness, punctuated by two glowing sapphire eyes.

Lee started to scream. The pair of ghostly blue eyes locked unblinkingly upon him, and Colin thrust in harder, faster. His cock owned Lee's asshole.

"*Once I've marked ye, yer mine, laddie, forever.*"

Colin—or the thing presently buried balls-deep in Lee's core—grunted and growled as pleasure rocked its body. The next slam sent Lee over the edge, and milked a blast of scalding wetness out of his dick. The ribbon of come was stopped short against the muscles of a ripped torso; three more followed. Lee turned his face into the pillow, his shouts equal parts terror and pleasure.

Colin collapsed on top of him, grumbling in his familiar voice. When Lee dared look again, those glowing sapphire eyes had winked out.

"Dude, that was so intense," Colin sighed. "You probably woke up half of Friday Harbor with those screams."

Lee didn't answer. Tears welled in his eyes.

"What's wrong?" Colin asked.

Lee pushed the taller boy off him and ran out of the bedroom.

☸

Colin set the mug of steaming tea in front of him. Lee cupped the mug in both hands and nervously fingered the lip.

"You're just feeling stressed about being in charge of the pirate tour, that's all," Colin offered. "And it's not exactly like you've been getting much sleep since you and me…"

Lee glanced up in time to see Colin squeeze down on the meaty lump in the crotch of his tight-whites and shake it for emphasis. Most nights, that kind of suggestive display would have led them back into the bedroom, but it only conjured a weak smile.

"I know you're pissed because they won't let you present the truth about this ring dude—O'Flanigan?"

"O'Farrell," Lee corrected.

"Yeah, him." Colin cracked the cap off another bottle of beer and straddled a kitchen chair. One of his balls hung visibly out of the leg band of his tight-whites. "What's so special about him?"

Lee had practiced his presentation so often in recent weeks, he could recite it like a mantra. "The end of the Spanish War of Succession put hordes of legitimate sailors out of work. Most of those men were forced into a life of piracy in order to survive—and hence, the Golden Age of Pirates was born," Lee sighed. He sipped his tea and secretly drank in the image of Colin's naked legs, bare feet, and that one hairy, fat ball oozing down his inner thigh and halfway to his knee. "O'Farrell's story starts more than a hundred years later. He was born in Ireland, entered the military, and at the young age of twenty-two had earned the undying devotion of his crew. And by that, I mean he'd fucked most of them into following him into the cannon's mouth."

"No shit." Colin swallowed another mouthful of suds, then belched. "A whole ship full of tight assholes to bone—sounds sweet."

"Yeah, you think so, and I bet so did he. But the Crown of England frowned upon that kind of behavior with its officers. The tight-asses sent two warships to take out O'Farrell, but they didn't anticipate the fierce loyalty of his crew. They sank one of the warships and sailed away from England never to return—and spent the next five years preying on English cargo ships. That is, when O'Farrell wasn't sticking his uncircumcised dick down the throats and up the butts of his crew or any cute piece of tail unfortunate enough to be on one of the plundered ships."

"Or lucky, depending upon how you look at it," Colin chuckled. "Why did they call him 'Blue Ring'?"

"Because of the most famous score of his career. The Sin Sapphire."

☸

"...originated from the sapphire mines of Burma, considered the finest in the world for producing the velvety blue, pure aluminum oxide gemstones that are second in hardness only to diamonds," Lee announced to his rapt audience. "At the time, this star sapphire was among the known ten largest in the world. But it soon gained a somewhat dubious reputation—especially to those who possessed it. A traveling nobleman, Duke Reginald the First, had planned to bestow it upon his bride, Lady Mirith of Devonshire—that is, until the Duke's young bride uncovered his lusty pursuits with several of her household staff, including her lady's maid."

This conjured rounds of laughter from the tour, Lee's third of the afternoon. He wondered if they'd still be laughing if Batchelder hadn't drawn a black line through the bit about Lady Mirith cutting off Duke Reginald's overstimulated penis on their wedding night.

"And then it traveled to South America on the finger of the pious, well-to-do missionary Sir Finley of Eaton, who had the Sin Sapphire made into a ring. Sir Finley felt the call to minister to the savages of the mighty Amazon, and minister, he did," Lee continued. "Oh yes, he ministered them one, two, and sometimes four, five, and six at a time—to the dismay of the village elders, who eventually sent him down the river, never to be seen again. Not in one piece, that is. His magnificent star sapphire ring was found several days later in his tent—still attached to Sir Finley's severed hand."

A chorus of disgusted grunts sounded around the gallery. So far, the outbursts of laughter and horror were working perfectly in synch to Lee's vision.

"The Sin Sapphire, as it came to be known, was sealed in a chest and sent back to England along with various other spoils from the New World. And that's how it came into this man's possession." Lee turned toward the painting, locking eyes with the pirate. "Blue Ring O'Farrell, one of the most notorious pirates who ever sailed New England's waters."

He briefly relayed O'Farrell's history—minus the lurid sexual details Batchelder had stricken from his presentation.

"Having been born with hauntingly intense blue eyes, as this portrait painted by one of his concubines suggests, O'Farrell looked upon the Sin Sapphire as not only the greatest of his treasures, but also as his birthright, and it remained upon his hand until that fateful meeting with a young English officer named Ethan-Daniel Butler, an agent of the Crown secretly planted on board a cargo ship traveling between London and Plymouth. Private Butler's assignment was to seduce Blue Ring, and to execute him when the opportunity presented itself. Butler did both with masterful precision."

Another round of gasps and grunts filtered around the room. Lee tipped his gaze again toward the painting and fell into the pull of O'Farrell's unblinking sapphire eyes.

"Private Butler made it ashore to Cape Cod after committing the deadly deed, but there are those who believe he truly had lost his heart to O'Farrell, whose ring he took from the dead pirate's hand. Butler was wearing it on his left ring finger when, a day after coming ashore in this very harbor, he hanged himself, presumably out of guilt for what he had done. Friday Harbor seized the ring for its own coffers, and eventually, it was donated to this museum."

"Unbelievable," sighed one of the visitors, leaning his face to within an inch of the display case where the Sin Sapphire twinkled.

"Yes, it is quite the tale, isn't it?" Lee said, his voice dropping to a whisper.

He blinked himself out of the trance and noticed a tall, indistinct figure of a man standing in front of the giant schooner diagram, between the hold and the mizzenmast. Lee pinched the corners of his tired eyes in an attempt to focus clearly upon the dark-haired silhouette, but when he looked again, the man had vanished.

Sucking in a deep breath, Lee continued, "Moving on, the age of piracy in American waters pretty much ended after Blue Ring's reign of terror, thanks to the creation of the Coast Guard ..."

❁

"I think it went well," Batchelder said, putting only crumbs of actual emotion into the compliment. "I'll see you tomorrow." He extended his large pink hand. Lee accepted the gesture and shook, but wiped his fingers on the thigh of his khaki pants on the way out of the exhibit, once he was out of sight.

He exited through the open French doors and started across the figurehead gallery. The creak and groan of his footfalls echoed through the vastness, sounding twice as loud, accompanied by the eerie moan of the gale swirling outside the room's tall windows. A chill teased the short hairs of Lee's neck; halfway across the gallery, it rolled down his spine fully. Lee gasped. He knew that feeling—it was the sensation of being watched. His squeaking footsteps came to an abrupt stop. Lee turned, but he was the only person in the figurehead gallery, apart from the figureheads themselves.

Slowly, he looked up.

They were the same exquisitely carved avatars rescued from the bows of vessels long vanished from the harbor: a busty barmaid, a mermaid, and a woman in a Hellenic frock with a coil of snakes for hair among them.

Lee felt their cold, unblinking eyes upon him, and swore, for a second, that it wasn't the wind he heard, but a whisper of voices, stirring up in the rafters. He willed his legs into motion and hurried away from the gallery.

☸

He tossed the hip bag onto the table. It landed awkwardly and slid to the floor. Lee didn't bother to retrieve it.

Colin lay sprawled across the couch, one hand tucked into his underwear. "How'd it go?"

"It went well, I think. I don't think Batchelder's going to bump up my salary to top-dollar, but I think he liked what I did. The visitors sure did," Lee yawned. "Hey, did you stop by the tour late in the afternoon? I thought I saw you."

"Naw, they had me out all day doing parking lot duty. Must have been some other horny stud."

Lee smiled weakly. "I'm calling it an early night, okay?"

"Want me to come in and hard-fuck you later?"

Lee chuckled at the thought. "I'd probably sleep right through it. Later."

He unbuckled his pants and kicked off his shoes while staggering toward the door and left a trail of clothes in his wake on the final stretch to the bed. Lee dropped facedown on the covers, which stunk of the previous night's sex, and was asleep soon after that.

❁

The wet, slow brush of a tongue across his asshole roused him awake untimed minutes later. Accompanying the invasion was a lusty sigh, and the scrape of unshaved cheeks against the sensitive flesh of his crack. Lee groaned a breathy moan into the pillow. "Dude, you're insatiable."

The tongue buried deep in his asshole pulled back. For a brief and wondrous instant, its owner's mouth replaced it, scattering wet, and hungry kisses, even sucking upon its pucker. Lee's cock burned beneath him, its fullness pinned at an awkward angle against the mattress.

A rabid, masculine growl sounded behind him in the darkness and launched a cool gust of air across Lee's naked back. Colin's weight pressed down upon him. Lee smiled, closed his eyes, and waited for the familiar sensation of being plundered.

Colin's cock head invaded Lee's spit-lubed asshole. Lee seized in place and moaned his approval.

"*Yes!*"

As Colin inched more of his shaft forward, Lee arched his body backward, willing his hole to open to accept its thickness. Coarse pubic hair tickled the flesh of his ass, and another gust of breath rained down on Lee's face.

But that breath was icy cold, and filled his next shallow breath with the briny smell of salt water.

Lee's eyes shot fully open. "What the—?"

The powerful weight on top of him shoved his face into the pillow and stifled the rest of the question before it could emerge. The cock already buried to the balls inside him pulled back, only to thrust forward, and then not even the pillow could completely silence Lee's shouts.

Get out of here, now! shouted a voice in his thoughts.

But the next time the thickness lodged in his asshole slammed home, Lee's terror melted in a rush of pleasure. His cock, rubbed to wetness against the sheet, ignited with the itchy tingle of a rapidly approaching orgasm, and his core, filled to capacity, had never experienced such stimulation.

"*Fuck me*," he mouthed into the pillow.

"Fuck ye?" asked a deep, disembodied voice, a noticeable trace of Irish brogue infusing the words. "Laddie, *I own ye.*"

Lee's erection unloaded and he began to scream at the limit of his voice, partly out of fear, but also equally due to the incredible release that wracked his body. He was still crying out when, with his bare ass arched in the air and his torso lying in a puddle of tepid semen, the bedroom light snapped on.

"What the fuck's going on in here?"

Lee turned to see Colin standing at the door, and realized that he was alone in the bed.

❁

Lee reached a shaking hand toward the hip bag's strap.

"Maybe you should call out sick," Colin offered. "Stay home, spend the day in bed. I could get you some hot chowder from the deli."

"Chowder" came out sounding like "chowdah"; Lee usually found Colin's Massachusetts accent not only sexy but also comforting. Not today, however. Wordlessly, he tossed the strap over his shoulder and headed out the door.

It was still storming out, but the rain had diminished to a light, misty drizzle. Lee walked the several blocks from the apartment to the museum with his head down, reliving the previous night's confusion.

"Blue Ring," he whispered. "Fuck …"

The raw wind whipped the words past his ears, but the bite in the air did nothing to remove the swell in his pants. The memory of being fucked like he had been conjured his dick back to life. By the time he reached the special collections gallery, it was painfully stiff.

Lee moved in front of the portrait. His eyes locked unblinkingly on O'Farrell's face. "What do you want from me?"

But wasn't that much obvious? According to the legend, once Blue Ring O'Farrell laid claim to you, Lee thought, you were his.

Forever.

He wasn't sure how long he stood staring into the pirate's portrait, only that his eyes began to sting from not blinking, and his cock, choking in the cotton noose of his boxer-briefs, had edged all morning and was presently leaking a wet stain into the front of his khaki pants.

Lee only noticed this detail after turning away from Blue Ring's portrait and toward the display case containing the Sin Sapphire, catching his reflection in the glass. Even more shocking than the wet spot on his tented crotch was the sudden eruption of vibrant blue light from the gemstone contained within. A week earlier, he would have dismissed the effulgence as a trick of the light, but not now.

The glittering star pattern within the sapphire's magnificent facets hypnotized him; Lee's feet shuffled over to the case.

Blue Ring O'Farrell's face stared back at him from within the gemstone's glare. Lee only saw the image briefly; a shadow swept over the Sin Sapphire's hypnotic light, cutting it off the way an eyelid does a man's vision. A second later, the imaginary eyelid blinked itself open, and instead of O'Farrell, Lee now saw his own reflection had been captured inside the gemstone's iris. Lee licked his lips and began to work the lump in his pants, milking out a load through the layers of clothing.

He surrendered as the wave of pleasure rolled over him. The sensation, he imagined, was like that of sinking through endless fathoms of ocean water; deep, sapphire blue water so cold and numbing, it robbed his body of all feeling save the powerful orgasm. That climax, a voice in his thoughts proclaimed, would ricochet through his consciousness throughout the rest of eternity.

As he fell deeper into the sapphire-colored depths, Lee glanced up, and beyond the watery distortion, saw his own face towering over him, staring down. A lusty smirk sat upon his lips.

"*I've placed my mark upon yer hand, my beautiful laddie,*" this giant version of himself said in a voice heavy with an Irishman's brogue. "*Mine, for all eternity.*"

Glittering sapphire light engulfed him. Lee closed his eyes and shuddered as another wave of pleasure ripped through his being.

THE *SERPENT*

John Simpson

It was a crystal blue day in the year 1665 as the pirate ship called the *Serpent* slid into the pirate stronghold of Tortuga. With Captain Wills Stanford, an Englishman, at her helm, the ship's company dropped anchor and the long boats were lowered into the water as the sweat shone brightly off the bare backs of the men. The *Serpent* had been at sea for thirty-seven days, and the young crew and her captain were eager to sell off the spoils of the sea as well as drink and whore.

"All right, crew, listen here!" Captain Stanford bellowed. "We'll be in port here for three days and no more. The ship's quartermaster will see to the re-provisioning of the ship. We sail on the morning tide Tuesday, and anyone not on board will be left here to rot! First mate, set the watch; quartermaster, dismiss the crew!"

With those commands all hell broke loose on the deck of the *Serpent* as men scurried from one place to another getting ready to head to shore for leave. The eyes of the crew reflected the lust felt in their hearts as they dreamed of the young men they would soon bed. As was common on most pirate ships in the era, either men had a male companion called a "matelot" or male partner who served on the ship with them, or found their release in the arms of the men on shore. For Tortuga, like most pirate havens, was short of one thing: women. As a result, lust and love fell between men and no one said the worst!

On the *SERPENT*, only about their percent of the crew had their lovers with them, while others "rented" a pretty boy to accompany them for one cruise.

The crew rushed through the streets to the Black Pearl, where they were sure to find plenty of ale and willing sex partners. As the crew burst through the doors, the entire place went silent as pirates stared at land lovers, and land lovers stared at the horny pirates. One of the pirates yelled, "Gimme an ale!" and the atmosphere broke into hearty laughs and saucy taunts.

Rex grabbed an ale as it went by on a tray and then grabbed the nearest unattended male and placed a lustful kiss on the lips of the very willing male whore. With a little groping the two were off to mount the stairs that led to private rooms on the second floor, where a small fee was paid to an ancient washwoman who showed them which filthy room was theirs to be used. After the price was paid, Rex stripped off the tattered clothes worn by the young male of about nineteen, and without any subtlety, flipped his prize over and began to finger the hole of the man before him.

"Ahh, you feel nice and tight, lad, which is good, as I am gonna fill you up!"

"Be gentle, sir, as I am new to this sort of work," Jeremy pleaded.

With a loud laugh, Rex replied, "Oh, I'll be gentle, boy—you'll earn your silver here with me!"

Rex reached over and dipped his fingers into a can of animal fat that sat on a wooded chair next to the bed. He greased up his now rigid cock, and slammed his fingers into Jeremy's hole in order to plunge his cock into the boy.

"Now hang on you sweet young thing, 'cause I'm breaching your borders!"

Rex lined up his cock with the target and, without any ease whatsoever, slammed his cock into Jeremy's waiting hole. Jeremy let out a bloodcurdling scream as Rex's cock struck true to its aim, and buried itself deep into the ass of the now crying Jeremy.

"Ahh, nice and tight like I had hoped for, lad."

"Please sir, go easy on me and make it last that way," pleaded Jeremy once again.

"You've a fine ass lad, and I will take my time fucking you well."

As Rex was enjoying the flesh of a newly minted male whore, Captain Wills entered a more sedate drinking establishment known as the Crooked Rooster. Wills was recognized the minute he entered the Rooster and was given the finest table. Here, those available for bed service were lined up and a much more civilized selection process took place. While there were several handsome young men, none quite matched the beauty of a waiter who served drinks to the gentlemen of refined taste.

"Excuse me, Captain, but do you not find anyone to your liking for company?" inquired the owner of the tavern.

"Actually, I do. Who is that lad serving the tables, over there... with the blond hair?"

"Oh Captain, he doesn't give that kind of service, he only waits on tables."

"Nonsense! Send the man over here, at once!"

"Yes, Captain, right away, Captain!"

As the owner whispered to the waiter, the waiter shook his head and the owner clearly ordered the young man to sit with Wills. As the man approached, his eyes were cast down upon the floor and only looked up when Wills told the beauteous boy to sit.

"Do you know who I am?"

"No, sir, I don't. I am afraid there has been a mistake made. I am not a bed chamber servant, only a table waiter."

"I'm Captain Wills Stanford, of the *Serpent*. You've heard of me?"

A look of shock washed over the face of the waiter. He managed to stammer, "Why yes, sir, who hasn't heard of Captain Stanford?"

"Look, I'll not waste my time here. You are a good-looking lad whose companionship I would enjoy for the evening. What say you?"

"But Captain, I have never been with a man like that. I wouldn't know what to do!"

"Do? Why, you do what I tell you to do, that's what you do! How does ten pieces of silver sound for you to share my bed this very night?"

"Ten pieces of silver? That's more than I make in six months!"

"Well, do we have a deal? Come on, I'm tired and want release."

"All right, Captain, but again, I have no experience at pleasing a man. I will have to ask Mr. Durgess if I can leave my job to go with you."

"I'll take care of Durgess, you take care of me. By the way, how old are you?"

"Eighteen, sir."

"Durgess!" Wills bellowed to the other side of the tavern where the owner stood watching.

Durgess ran over to the table and said, "Yes, Captain?"

"This boy is coming with me upstairs for the evening. He is to receive his full wages from you as if he worked the entire night, is that clear?"

"Yes, Captain Stanford, anything you want, Captain Stanford."

As Durgess started to leave Wills's table, he looked at his waiter and muttered the word, "Whore!"

Stanford flew out of his seat, grabbed the tavern owner by the neck, and slammed his face into the table.

"Now you will apologize to this man, or I will slit your throat here and now, by Neptune!"

Through a bloody mouth and nose, Durgess apologized to the boy, Nate, and the captain took Nate by the arm. They went upstairs to the usual suite reserved for the captain.

Once inside the room, Wills barred the doors securely so as to not be surprised by any personal attack. He opened a bottle of wine that was in the room and offered Nate a glass.

"Here, Nate, this is from my personal stock and it's damn good."

"Thank you, Captain, I am very nervous and the wine might help calm me down."

A fire burned brightly in the corner to keep out any sudden chill brought on by the Caribbean night. As the captain stared into the fire, he said, "Take off your shirt and pants, Nate, and come over here."

Nate did as he was told, remembering what the captain had said downstairs. He moved to the right side of Wills in front of the fireplace with nothing on. He wore no underwear—that was a luxury he could not afford. Wills turned his head and almost gasped out loud at the sight of this young man, completely naked, with a body that was nothing short of beauty itself. Nate had a finely chiseled chest, a flat stomach that showed muscle, and a large penis with two nicely hanging balls.

"Turn around."

This command revealed a thoroughly masculine, muscular ass that had been built as a result of waiting on tables night after night. In fact, Nate's entire body showed the effort it took to work unending hours for little money.

Wills moved over to Nate and put his arms around Nate's chest and pulled him tight to his own body. He softly stroked the chest and stomach of this beautiful male specimen.

He whispered into Nate's ear, "You are truly gorgeous for a young man and you greatly please me. I will make love to you and promise not to hurt you."

Wills took the silent and trembling young man over to the bed and eased him down onto the bed. He then stood up and removed his clothes, revealing a body even harder than Nate's, with an impressive set of manly implements. It had been almost two months since he had made love to another and he had drawn a prize fit for a king for his reunion with lovemaking.

Wills covered the trembling youth with kisses from his neck to his knees, stroking the man's body as he moved over it. Wills was pleased to see a physical reaction to his lovemaking craft, as Nate grew hard before his eyes.

"Now you do the same to me, slowly, and stroke my body as you go."

Nate responded to the urging and did as he was told. The touch of the man's lips on his body sent shots of fire throughout his body and soul. It was if he had suddenly caught on fire as Nate, with surprising skill, tended to his charge. Nate took some initiative and took Wills's penis in his hand and gently stroked it as he kissed above the knees.

"You're doing very well, Nate, now come back up and run your tongue over my cock while playing lightly with my balls. Don't worry, it won't bite!"

With great hesitation, Nate took Wills's penis and held it straight up as it was now hard, and measured a full eight inches. He brought his mouth close to Wills's penis, but then hesitated and stopped.

"Sir, I am afraid that I will get sick if I do this," Nate said with great fear.

"Lay back and close your eyes."

As Nate did as he was told, Wills moved his mouth down toward Nate's beautiful virgin penis, which was not as hard as before. Wills took Nate's penis and began to lick the underside of it, as well as Nate's balls. Nate moaned out loud, and was heard to say, "Oh my soul!" Wills continued with the use of his tongue as he ran up and down both sides of the penis before finally taking it into his mouth and suckling on it.

Nate moaned in great pleasure, raising his hips off the mattress to meet the downward sucking of Wills's mouth. Wills sucked his cock like that for another minute or so before seeing the tell-tale signs of the balls rising to meet the base of the penis.

Wills laid back and said, "Now I want you to try the same thing. You felt how very pleasurable that was, didn't you?"

"Yes, sir, I liked that very much. I will do my best."

With that, Nate was able to lick and suck on Wills's penis, which finally put the captain in a state of ecstasy. Nate sucked Wills's dick long and hard before he was finally commanded to cease. Wills noticed that the man was still hard, which pleased him greatly.

"Did you like sucking my cock, Nate?"

"Actually, sir, yes I did. I also liked it when you did the same to me."

"Now, I'm going to show you how men really make love to other men. And while at first you will think it hurts, you will find that it brings a great joy to both of us. Now turn over onto your stomach, Nate."

Wills reached down to the table that sat next to the bed, and retrieved a fine French hand lotion from which he applied a liberal gob onto his cock.

When his cock was fully lathered, Wills applied some to the waiting rectum of Nate. He gently massaged it into the opening while inserting first one finger and then two. A soft moan was heard to escape from the lips of Nate as he lay in anticipation of what he knew was to follow.

As Wills covered Nate's back with his body, he said, "Now just try and relax. I am going to fuck your hole as it should be."

With that Wills started the slow process of opening up a very tight virgin asshole with the head of his cock. Nate resisted involuntarily by clamping his hole shut even tighter. When Wills felt that, he reached up and twisted Nate's ear hard, which led to the total relaxing of his asshole. As the boy screamed out, Wills pushed his cock into Nate by a couple of inches. He released his hold on Nate's ear and slowly pushed forward.

"Sir, it hurts, it hurts bad, sir!"

"Just relax, boy, and enjoy your becoming a man this night."

Finally, Wills had his entire dick inside of Nate, and he let it rest a bit so that Nate's ass could become accustomed to the feeling of the intrusion. When Wills felt that Nate had adjusted, he began to slowly fuck the virgin ass under him. Finally, he heard what could only be described as moans of pleasure emanating from the mouth of his fuckboy. With that encouragement, Wills picked up his pace of fucking and was now enjoying himself as in no other place on earth aside from the quarterdeck of his own ship.

"That's it, boy, you're taking it well. Your ass is like a piece of heaven on earth."

Not wanting to stop in fear of having to work too hard to restart, Wills decided not to use any other position besides the one he was in now. Finally, a climax slowly built up within the loins of the captain, and finally he was overcome by the plethora of feelings coursing through his body.

"Ahhh, I'm coming boy, I'm coming!"

With that pronouncement, the captain exploded deep within the confines of Nate's ass and filled the boy up with hot boiling come. After what seemed like a dozen or more shots up the bow, he began to soften, and let his dick pull naturally out of the boy's ass.

As he rolled over, Wills proclaimed, "That was the best piece of ass

I've had in ages! Good job, my boy, and an extra two pieces of silver are yours!"

"Thank you, Captain, it wasn't as bad as I feared. In fact, I kinda liked it, sir."

"Good lad, now let's get some sleep."

❁

It was nearly dawn on the third day and it was time for the crew to gather at the docks to fill the *Serpent*'s longboats for the trip back to the ship. Into the boats went the crew, their lovers, and newly rented pretty boys to accompany the men on this next voyage. One member of the crew by the name of Lyles, who refused to make love with men, brought a rather unkempt, haggard-looking woman with him for companionship. No one gave the crewman any grief for his choice and all were happy and recovering from three days of drinking and whoring.

Captain Stanford paid a visit to Nate's room on the way to the docks and found the young man still asleep. After banging on the door and finally getting Nate to answer, the captain stood in the doorway smiling at Nate.

"Nate, I want you to come with me onto the *Serpent*. I've never had a finer lad with more beauty and natural talent at bedding down for the night than you. You will be my cabin boy, and no one on the ship will show you the slightest disrespect. In fact, it will be the opposite. What do you say?"

"Captain, I don't know, sir. I've never been on board a pirate ship before, and I'm not sure that I would be any good!"

"You let me worry about that, my boy, now gather your things, and report down to the docks. We leave in fifteen minutes. Oh, and here. Put these clothes on so you don't look like I picked you up in a gutter. You're the captain's cabin boy, after all!"

With that the captain was gone, leaving Nate standing alone with a small smile creeping upon his face. Nate shut the door, turned, and ran to gather his few belongings into a pillowcase. He dressed and looked around at his very meager room one last time, laughed out loud, and bolted from the room.

At the docks, Nate found all sorts of men yelling and cramming into longboats that were headed to the *Serpent* under the watchful eye of the first mate. As Nate started to climb into one of the boats, the first mate yelled out, "Hey, you there! And where do you think you're going like you're some kind of little toff ?"

"Belay that, Rogers, he's my new cabin boy!" yelled the captain. "See to it that he gets on board safely and shown to my cabin."

"Aye aye, Captain sir!"

As the crew settled into their quarters along with their companions, Nate was shown where he would do the majority of his living. It was a spacious cabin as cabins go on board a ship. It had a double bed built into one side, with a large table in the center and a desk off to the side. Along the other side of the cabin were built-in cabinets for clothing and a lockable trunk.

"Nate, we will be setting sail shortly. Your job is to keep me clothes in order, the cabin neat, the bed made, and you in it when I am of need. When I have no need of your services at night, there is a mattress under the bed in that drawer. You pull it out, and you sleep on that. You will also see to it that my meals are ready and hot at the appointed hour. Any questions?"

"No, Captain sir."

"Very well, tend to things here as we leave port."

As the *Serpent* sailed out of Tortuga, the men all seemed excited to be back on the high seas, hoping for a profitable voyage that would allow for more drinking and whoring when back in another port. The wind came up and the ship sliced through the waters briskly, with the only sound being the wash of the sea and the movement of men on deck.

As the captain stood on the quarterdeck, his mind drifted off to the young man waiting in his cabin. If he were honest with himself, he would admit that he was quite taken by this strapping specimen of the male sex.

The *Serpent* performed flawlessly as she now sailed through the night with watchmen at the helm and in the crow's nest looking for targets to plunder and sink. Captain Stanford had retired for the evening to his cabin and found Nate standing by with his dinner.

"Good evening, Captain," said Nate upon his entrance.

"Hello, Nate. Is dinner on the table?"

"Yes, Captain."

"When it is just us two, you may join me at dinner and eat as you will."

"Thank you, Captain, I will," Nate replied with a seductive smile.

As Wills sat at the table, he couldn't help but admire the fine figure of his cabin boy and felt the usual rising heat in his loins. There was something to this having a cabin mate on board after all. After dinner had finished, and the table cleared away, it was time for bed.

The bed covers had already been pulled down and the mattress pulled out by the time Wills ventured away from his desk in the far corner of the cabin. Wills looked down at the mattress and again at Nate. This wouldn't do at all.

"Nate, put away the mattress and prepare to join me in bed."

Nate waited until the captain had taken off his clothes and gotten into bed before blowing out all the candles but the one at bedside. He checked the cabin door to make sure it was locked, and moved toward the bed. Once there, he began to remove his clothes as Wills looked at him with a growing hardness between his legs. Wills noticed that the French lotion that he so loved for sex was next to the bed.

Nate was now standing there naked with a semi-hard cock. Once again, Wills was struck with the beauty of this young man. It was now obvious that the look in Nate's eyes was one of desire and Wills knew that he had conquered this man for his own.

Wills drew back the covers on the other side of himself, and Nate climbed over the captain, taking his time to allow Wills to get a good look at the assets that Nate possessed. Wills turned on his side and planted a long deep kiss upon Nate's lips and found no resistance whatsoever to this intrusion into the mouth of his paramour.

This time, Wills had to give no instructions. Nate pulled back the covers and found Wills's now rock-hard cock, and immediately began to lick and suck. Nate worked his way down to Wills's balls and sucked one into his mouth and exchanged it for the other. As this oral attention was being given to the captain's cock and balls, Wills softly stroked the back of his bedmate. Nate moved up and began to lick and nibble on each nipple sending Wills into another world as now Wills began to moan. While attending to the captain's nipples, Nate continued to stroke the captain's now ever hard cock.

Nate stopped his lovemaking long enough to reach over for the lotion. As he began to apply the lotion to Wills's cock and his own ass, the Captain realized that Nate was fully accepting of his role as the captain's cabin boy.

"Are you ready, sir?" Nate asked.

Wills smiled and nodded his head. Instead of moving over next to the captain, Nate rose up and came down on top of the captain's hard-on, slowly taking it up the ass. Wills's toes curled at the exquisite sensations that were once again coursing through his body. After Nate had adjusted to the intrusion of Wills's penis, he began to slowly ride the captain's cock. Wills could see the pleasure on Nate's face as he rode Wills's cock. Wills reached up and grasped Nate's fully erect dick and began to jerk him off. Wills intended for them both to come at the same time. Nate picked up the speed of the upward and downward thrusts of his ass while squeezing his ass muscles at the same time. As Nate picked up speed, so did the captain.

Finally Wills could wait no longer and once again exploded into the firm round young ass of his cabin boy just as Nate blew his load all over the captain's chest, and both melted into one as the release became total.

Nate pulled off Wills's cock and grabbed a towel in which he cleaned up the captain's chest and cock, while also cleaning himself with the water that was always available in the captain's cabin.

Nate returned to the bed of the captain of the *Serpent* and was smiling from ear to ear.

"And what are you all smiles about, boy?"

"I think I could love you, Wills."

The captain overlooked the familiar use of his first name by the cabin boy. But, as Wills thought about it, this cabin boy might just be more than a one-voyage fuck. No one he had ever bedded down before had such beauty and innate talent for making love.

As these many thoughts crashed the captain's brain, he and Nate heard a loud commotion coming from below their cabin from the crew's quarters. Wills jumped up, put on his pants and grabbed a pistol.

"Stay here and lock the door behind me," commanded the captain.

As Wills quickly but silently went out of the cabin and went down the stairs to the crew's quarters, he found quite a row going on in the far corner. Wills could hear that it involved Lyles, the crewmember who brought a woman on board. As Wills entered the crew area, one of the men noticed the captain and yelled, "Captain's on deck!"

As the entire company of men present came to attention and became silent, Wills asked,

"What the devil is going on here?"

Rogers responded, "Captain, it seems that the lady that Lyles brought on board, well sir, she really is no lady!"

"Well, this is a pirate ship after all, Rogers, what did you expect—the Duchess of Windsor?"

"No, sir, I mean she isn't a she, but a he!"

With that the entire crew broke out laughing with Lyles sitting there fuming at the mistake he made. It seems when he went to do his own fore and aft, he found equipment that he didn't expect.

"Well, Lyles, what do you want to do with him? Throw him overboard?" the captain asked.

"Well sir, I guess you ought to dance with the one ye brought to the party, so, I imagine I'll just keep her!"

Once again, the crew broke out laughing and Wills turned away laughing himself and headed back to the beauty of the man who had just told him that he might be able to love him. In fact, Wills found that he himself could possibly fall in love with this beauty of a young man. Ahh, life at sea, none other like it! This was going to be a very good voyage.

ABOUT THE CONTRIBUTORS

SHANE ALLISON has published four chapbooks of poetry. His fifth book, *I Want to Fuck a Redneck*, is forthcoming from Scintillating Publications. His stories and poems have graced the pages of the *Mississippi Review, Windy City Times, Outsider Ink, Suspect Thoughts, Velvet Mafia, Van Gogh's Ear, Zafusy, McSweeney's, Cowboys: Gay Erotic Tales, Hustlers, Best Black Gay Erotica, Sexiest Soles, Ultimate Gay Erotica 2006*, and *Best Gay Erotica 2007*. He is the editor of *Hot Cops: Gay Erotic Tales*.

ARMAND works full-time and spends much of his free time writing erotic stories, poetry, and fiction. He is currently working hard to publish his first novel and lives alone in Ohio.

A native Californian, BEARMUFFIN lives in San Diego with two leatherbears in a stimulating ménage à trois. He has been writing erotic fiction since 1985. His erotic short stories have appeared in many gay publications, including *Hot Shots, In Touch, Manscape, First Hand, Jock, Mandate, Torso*, and *Honcho*. His stories can be found in the Alyson anthologies *Friction 5, 6* and *7*; in *Ultimate Gay Erotica 2005* and *2006*; and are featured in the anthologies *Dorm Porn* and *Hustlers* from Alyson and *Truckers* and *Cowboys* from Cleis Press.

P.A. BROWN has been writing erotica for nearly two years and is also the author of the murder mystery novel *L.A. Heat*. Pat originated in Canada and currently resides in Bermuda. She can be reached through *www.pabrown.ca*.

LEW BULL lives in Johannesburg, South Africa. Current publications which include published writing are *Ultimate Undies*, *Secret Slaves*, and *Travelrotica*. Upcoming publications include *Ultimate Gay Erotica 2007* (Alyson) and *Superheroes* (STARbooks).

MICHAEL CAIN is thirty-three. He lives where he grew up in Northeast Ohio, at the foothills near the panhandle of West Virginia. He counts money until his fingers bleed at a gaming resort, and lives with his dog Jack. Michael has stories currently published on the webzines *Wild Violet Magazine, After Burns SF, Demon Minds, Lunatic Chameleon,* and *Forbidden Fruit Magazine*. His stories have been included in the erotic anthologies *Just the Sex* and *My First Time, Vol. 3,* both through Alyson Books, and will soon be included in the e-zine *Logical Lust* and *Ruthie's Club,* and in print in *Sofa Ink Quarterly, First Hand LTD,* and in *Writer's Post Journal.*

BRIAN CENTRONE has an M.A. in novel writing from the University of Manchester. Before moving to the United Kingdom, he attended SUNY/Westchester Community College and Fordham University in New York City, where he started a gay sex column for the campus newspaper, upsetting many people. Brian is currently hard at work completing his novel.

CURTIS C. COMER is a frequent contributor to Alyson's anthologies, and lives in St. Louis with his partner Tim, their cat Magda, and lovebird Raoul.

ERASTES lives in the United Kingdom, and his goal in life is to get historical homoerotica pushed more into the mainstream. He's a member of the Historical Novels Society and the Erotica Writers Association, and his first novel—a Regency homoerotic romp, *Standish*—was published summer/fall 2006. Visit *www.erastes.com.*

RYAN FIELD is a thirty-five-year-old freelance writer who lives in New Hope, Pennsylvania . His short stories and essays have appeared in many collections and anthologies over the years and he's interviewed and reviewed almost every gay bloggerin the universe for Best Gay Blogs. He is currently working on a novel.

T. HITMAN is the nom-de-porn for a full-time professional writer who has published numerous short stories and novels. Always writing his first drafts using trusty Sheaffer fountain pens (some of them twenty-four years old), he lives with his awesome partner, Bruce, and their two cats in a very small bungalow on a very large plot of land among the pines of New Hampshire.

WILLIAM HOLDEN lives in Atlanta with his partner of nine years. He works full time as a librarian specializing in LGBT research and preservation. He has been writing gay erotica for more than five years. He welcomes any comments and can be contacted at wholden2@mac.com.

NEIL PLAKCY is the author of *M_h_* and *M_h_ Surfer,* mystery novels which star Honolulu police detective Kimo Kanapa'aka. He is an assistant professor of English at Broward Community College and a free-lance writer and web developer. He has published a wide range of fiction and nonfiction in mainstream and gay and lesbian publications, both in print and on-line. His work has been anthologized in *My First Time 2, Men Seeking Men, Cowboys: Gay Erotic Tales, Tales of Travelrotica for Gay Men,* and *Ultimate Undies.*

MORRIS MICHAELS, JR., has traveled extensively through Western, Central, and Eastern Europe. Based in Manhattan, he is a historian who writes and lectures on a variety of subjects throughout the United States and Europe. Ivy-educated, he is not above wallowing in the gutter on occasion and enjoys both cerebral and more intensely earthy pleasures.

SIMON SHEPPARD is the editor of *Homosex: 60 Years of Gay Erotica* and the author of *In Deep: Erotic Stories, Kinkorama, Sex Parties 101*, and the award-winning *Hotter Than Hell.* His work also appears in more than two hundred anthologies, including many editions of *Best Gay Erotica* and *The Best American Erotica.* He writes the syndicated column "Sex Talk," lives queerly in San Francisco, and hangs out at *www.simonsheppard.com.* His favorite movie as a kid was *Peter Pan.* Really.

JOHN SIMPSON is the author of *Murder Most Gay*, a full-length e-book carried by Renaissance E-books, and currently looking for a print publisher for his book *The Virgin Marine,* published in the *My First Time* series, volume four, by Alyson Books. John just finished writing another short story called "The Smell of Leathern," which will be shown to publishers shortly. Additionally, he has written numerous articles for various gay and straight magazines, and a full-length non-fiction novel.

From Vancouver, British Columbia, JAY STARRE has written for gay men's magazines including *Men, Honcho, Torso,* and *American Bear.* Jay has also written for over thirty gay anthologies including the *Friction* series for Alyson, *Hard Drive, Bad Boys, Just the Sex, Ultimate Gay Erotic, Bear Lust*, and *Full Body Contact.*

ZAVO was born and raised in the wooded hills of New England. He is now ensconced in the rugged hills of the Northwest, where the solitude feeds his imagination to pen tales of lust, adventure, and unrequited love. Check out his first novel, the wildly erotic cowboy tale *Hot on His Trail* from Alyson.